Drone: Awakening

Bill Siracusa

Drone: Awakening

Book 1 of the Drone Collection

Production copyright FurPlanet Productions © 2024

Text Copyright © *Bill Siracusa* 2024

Cover Artwork and Interior Illustration © *Snarky Sardine (aka Salty)* 2024

Published by FurPlanet Productions
Dallas, Texas
www.FurPlanet.com

Print ISBN 978-1-61450-648-5
eBook ISBN 978-1-61450-650-8

Table of Contents

To my BFF
(*Best Fish Friend*)

N.W.T.

Utqiagvik

Prudhoe Bay

Inuvik

See inset

B R O O K S   R A N G E

Anaktuvuk
Pass

Coldfoot

Kotzebue

ARCTIC CIRCLE

River

Circle

YUKON

Nome

Fairbanks

Dawson
City

A L A S K A

Yukon

DENALI

Anchorage

Valdez

Whittier

Bethel

Dillingham

Homer

Yakutat

Kodiak

To PRUDHOE BAY

Itkillik R.

5 miles

DALTON HWY

TRANS-ALASKA PIPELINE

The Facility

Old mine

Atigun
R.

ALEX McPHEE
PRONGHORN MAPS

To FAIRBANKS

DETOUR

Number 04 was the first of the dogs to notice the bear, but he was positive that Master had already seen him.

There wasn't much else to see, just a long, uninterrupted stretch of the Alaskan wilderness, pierced ineffectually for 400 miles by the Dalton Highway.

Hardly a highway, the so-called *North* Slope Haul Road ran from Prudhoe Bay, which was all the way up on the north coast of Alaska, down to Fairbanks, close to the center of the state. More than anything, the unpaved Dalton Highway was a massive service road, connecting the oil fields in the Arctic Ocean to civilization. For a passenger vehicle, it was a half-day drive under the best of conditions, picking along the gravel surface and pulling over for dozens of 18-wheelers to roar past, flinging oil and gravel as they roared past around dangerous turns. If the weather was bad… well, they didn't go if the weather was bad. They made three supply runs to ride out the winter, carefully timed for flexibility, because losing a third of their supplies was significantly less risky than a carload of dogs freezing to death on the shoulder of the highway or being crushed under a tanker truck.

But for now, it was late September, and it was just starting to drop below freezing at night. It was gray all day this time of year, which is why Number 04 had stopped even looking out the windows. They had driven six hours in a late-model Chevy Suburban with a winch, a raised suspension, and two spare rear-mounted gas canisters, towing a 6-foot box trailer, up to Prudhoe Bay, because Master had ordered a shipment of supplies and that's where the ship had docked. He'd taken three of the dogs with him, and as usual the small otter had gotten some very strange looks from the dock workers and tract houses full of oil workers, in his North Face jacket with three silent, identical-looking Siberian huskies in tow, but as usual, they picked up their fuel and supplies and piled back into the Suburban for the long drive back to their facility.

Idly, Number 04 wondered what was in the mysterious-looking parcels they had picked up. One of them had been huge and heavy and marked FRAGILE. It had a battery sticker on it. 04 wondered if it was the fucking machine — the "Husky Punisher," as he'd called it — that Master had lately been musing about. He swallowed, his heart beating a little faster.

As usual, 04 felt charged and electric just sharing a space with Master. It was conditioning, and he knew it, but he was excited, almost *delighted*, just to be sharing an SUV with the otter. The man's scent was burned into the dog's brain, and he felt himself wagging and his heart beat faster whenever he could smell the otter close. 04 had beaten 06 and 11 to the seat directly behind Master for the trip back. 11 had shot him a look, and 04 knew he would be getting facefucked in the middle of the night, but it was worth it to have the Master's thick tail between his legs, occasionally idly thwapping 04's ankles. 04 was on the driver's side, directly behind Master's seat, and as a result, he was the first of the dogs to notice the bear.

They were six hours south of Prudhoe Bay, north of Anaktuvuk Pass and the rest of the Brooks Range, and half an hour ago they had turned off the gravel highway onto a dirt road. It had been slow going, since the road was in poor maintenance and Master didn't like to speed with the trailer, but they were inching steadily toward "The Facility," which was really a network of six research trailers and a log cabin that Master had established to house his "employees." 04 had a feeling they would soon be adding some space. Master wanted more space, and Master always got what he wanted.

Always.

The bear saw them coming a long way off. He was a polar bear, judging by his white exposed head. He was dressed like a guard, with black uniform pants and an unadorned black hooded sweatshirt. He was almost wearing what 04 and the others wore on guard duty, or when Master was in the mood for that sort of thing (which was often). He was standing in the road, blocking it.

They were on a gravel road in the middle of nowhere. What else was on this road? Nothing but a long-disused gold mining operation. There was a little shack around here. Was that populated? He'd never seen anyone around it.

04 swallowed. Who the hell was this? He leaned forward, his mouth drying. Silently, he took off his seatbelt in case he needed to leap out of the car to defend Master.

Master turned down the podcast they'd been listening to for the last two hours and at the same time began to gently slow down the truck. 04 felt 06 and 11 tense up. Silently, he exchanged a glance with them. They both looked alarmed, alert, ready to act. He felt better. They would move as a pack. Three against one was pretty good odds.

As they rolled up on the bear, the Suburban slowly crunching to a stop, 04 was horrified to see the bear was at least two feet taller than him, probably three. He towered over the SUV and he was probably almost twice Master's height. 04 felt the blood drain out of his face. The bear was at least nine feet tall, and built like a tank. He felt worse about their odds with each passing moment.

Master was, as usual, undeterred.

The otter hit the button and his window smoothly rolled down.

"Hiya!" he said, dripping midwestern friendliness. "How's it going, friend?"

The bear leaned down to his window, *way* down, frowning. "Road's closed," he said, simply. His voice was deep and booming. It made 04's blood run cold. He glanced at 06, next to him, and saw the other husky's ears were pinned back against his head.

Master actually laughed. "Closed? This road doesn't close. There's barely a road to close!" He was being friendly, but 04 knew there was a limit to his patience.

The bear frowned. "It's closed today. Mine is starting back up."

"Oh wow!" said Master. "That old operation? I didn't know there was anything in those old mines. You're with the mining company?"

The bear nodded. "Yup. Now turn around, please."

Master let out a sigh. "Aw. Are you sure? The bypass is a couple miles back. It's an extra hour to go around." He offered a webbed paw. "I'm Masters. We're with the research facility at the end of your road."

The bear looked at the otter's paw, but didn't move. He leaned his head slightly into the truck to look at the huskies, and nodded. He was *huge*. The car darkened on 04's side just from the bear's massive presence.

The bear looked at them disapprovingly, and then back to the otter. "Ah. They told me about you all." He continued frowning. "I'm sorry," he rumbled. "Mining company traffic only. This has always been a private road."

Master was undaunted. "Aw, I know. But nobody was using it for the last ten years. Do you think you could let us through, just this once? Next time I'll go around but I was really looking forward to getting out of this truck." He chuckled amiably.

The bear frowned. He looked like he was getting annoyed. "No," he said, firmly, a little louder.

You've done it now, 04 thought.

Master cocked his head. He was thinking. Silently, 04 watched.

"You know," Master said, slowly. Deliberately. "You're *real* big."

The bear sighed. "So I've heard." Now he just looked annoyed.

If Master noticed, he didn't react. "Do you like being big?" he asked. He sounded amused. Relaxed.

The bear looked puzzled. "I...suppose," he said, noncommittally.

Master smiled. 04 could see his eyes in the rearview mirror. It made the fur on the back of his neck stand up. "*I* like you being big."

They stared at each other. The bear looked confused by that.

Master leaned gently toward him. "I like you being big *a lot*. What do you think of that, Mr. Bear?"

Now the bear furrowed his brow. "I...I..." he stammered.

Master didn't let him think of a response. "Why don't you...lean in here," he said, slowly and sultry.

Still frowning, the bear did. He dipped his long neck and stuck his big head into the car. He *filled* the space in front of Master.

Master took a deep, pleased breath. "Wow, you're even bigger up close. Boys, look at this fine specimen."

The bear just stared, perplexed, watching the small otter from twelve inches away. He looked a little confused, like even *he* had absolutely no idea why he was complying.

If 04's hazy memories were correct, the bear *didn't* know why he was complying. But he was going to comply regardless.

Master beamed at the bear, watching him with wonder. "Look at *you*," he said. "Look. At. You." He took a satisfied breath. "I'm gonna touch your face now."

The bear swallowed, nodding shallowly. "Okay." He put his paws on the windowsill and his hands were so huge they barely both fit.

Master reached up with both his webbed hands and rubbed the bear's face. The bear had thick, trim cheek fluff and Master rubbed it with his thumbs. He held the bear's muzzle as best he could get his fingers around.

"*Very* nice," Master purred. "How does this feel?"

"Good," whispered the bear.

Master smiled. "Call me 'sir.' How does it feel?"

The bear shifted, uncomfortably. "Good, sir," he grunted.

"And look at these *teeth*!" Master cooed. "Open up."

Expression blank, the bear opened his huge muzzle. Master slid his thumbs in, rubbing them along the polar bear's huge teeth. He wasn't gentle about it, pulling on the bear's lower jaw. The bear just let him do it.

"God, I love this. Very nice. Very, very nice." He pried the bear's mouth open further and forcibly turned his head back and forth. "Oh my word, look at this *tongue*! Stick it out for me."

The bear did. His tongue was a pale shade of blue. He dangled his tongue out like he was being examined by a doctor.

"Very good, bear. You're being *so* good for me." He beamed at him, releasing his teeth to stroke the bear's face, and then his neck.

The bear just watched him, compliant, relaxed, obedient, and still a little confused. Slowly, he closed his mouth, watching the otter from inches away, staring into his eyes as the small mustelid manhandled him.

04 could see the moment that the bear realized he wanted to kiss the otter. It was a moment of confusion, and arousal, and panic and excitement. A moment later the bear realized he was *going* to kiss the otter, and that was a moment of wide-eyed shock, and then Master leaned forward and pressed their lips together and the bear closed his eyes and melted into it.

They kissed with lips only for a few moments, lips smacking, pushing gently against each other. Then Master moaned, and the bear pushed forward.

Master arched his back, making his seat creak, and 04 heard a faint gagging noise. Master grabbed the bear's cheek ruffs and held on tight.

Master's seat groaned, and the bear surged into the car, rumbling loudly.

04 leaned forward, tensed, and as if sensing this, Master raised a hand to show him it was all right.

The husky squirmed in his seat. He could hear the smacking noises, see them writhing against one another, smell the bear now. He smelled like pipe smoke and snow. 04 was trying to mind his own business, but this was making him a little concerned and a lot aroused.

Finally, their kiss broke. The bear stared at him, breathing hard, eyebrows furrowed, confused, aroused.

Master held him lovingly, from inches away. "Did you like that, bear?"

"Yes, sir."

Master beamed. "Good! Can anyone see us where we are?"

The bear shook his huge head. "No, sir."

Master nodded. "Perfect. Why don't you take off your shirt?" he asked, congenially.

The bear stared at him for a moment, processing that, and then nodded. "Yes, sir." He took a few steps back, reached down for the hem of his hooded sweatshirt, and pulled it and his undershirt off in one smooth motion.

04 watched *intently*. The bear was impressively-built, with thick shoulders and long arms, and was surprisingly trim for a polar bear. He almost had a six-pack, could easily have it with a little additional work.

Master will get right on that, 04 thought, silently.

The otter nodded appreciatively. "*Very* good. Open your pants."

Silently, watching him, the bear unbuckled his uniform pants and unzipped his fly.

04 shivered in his seat. Master was going to make this bear show him his cock. Right here in the road. 04's heart started pounding and he felt himself grow hard in his jockstrap.

Master nodded silently. "Show me," he said.

The polar bear tugged his pants down slightly around his thick tree-trunk quads. He was wearing briefs, which was not particularly surprising, but the absolute heft of the mass stuffed into his bulge absolutely was.

"*Very* nice!" Master announced.

04 turned to make eye contact with 06. The other husky's eyes were wide in horror. They silently exchanged a terrified thought: *that thing is going inside us.*

Behind them, 11 swallowed hard. 04 turned and was mildly irritated to find the other husky barely able to keep his tongue in his mouth. Figured. Master liked to keep all types.

"Okay, that's enough," Master said, making 04 snap his head back around. "Get dressed. Thank you."

Wordlessly, the bear zipped up his pants and started to put his shirt back on.

"Bear, do you like your job?"

"Pardon, sir?" the bear asked. He frowned, quizzically. Now that he was compliant and not scary, 04 was having a hard time taking his eyes off the bear's handsome face. He wondered what the kiss had been like. Maybe later he would ask Master.

"Do you like your job? At the mining company?"

The bear frowned, confused by the question, and finally just shrugged his massive shoulders. "I guess, sir? The pay is okay. The quarters are small. I'm bored most of the time."

Master beamed. "Would you like to come work for me?"

The bear stared at him. "What do you do?"

Master grinned. "Just hang out. Just…hang out with my dogs."

The polar bear still looked somewhere between mad and confused. "Your dogs, sir?"

"My dogs. My good, good dogs."

The bear's original mask of annoyance was starting to come back. "I don't understand, sir."

Master reached for something on the door, and to 04's horror, the husky's side window started rolling down. He gasped.

The bear turned to look at him, *really* look at him, his brown eyes poring over him.

"My dogs!" Master said.

The bear nodded. His eyes were gray, 04 noticed, not brown. They were boring holes in the husky. It was terrifying but exciting. 04 felt incredibly exposed.

Master glanced back at him. "Kiss him!" Master suggested. "Give him a shot!"

The bear's eyebrows raised but he didn't take his eyes off of 04. After a moment, he furrowed his brow, and took a step toward the backseat.

Oh God, oh God, oh God, 04 thought. He was so, so hard in his jockstrap. But the bear was massive. He started shivering. He couldn't help it.

The bear frowned. He was right outside the window now. *He was so big.*

"He's scared," the bear said.

Master glanced back at him again. "He wants you!" he said. "Don't you, 04?"

04 swallowed. "Y-yes," he whispered.

"04 *loves* them big. I got a big jaguar at my Facility and - well, I'll let you see for yourself. For now, give that good boy a shot."

Trying to help, 04 nodded.

rowning, the bear slowly leaned down and pushed his head through the window. He was *so massive* up close. 04 let out a little moan as their muzzles connected.

The bear was shockingly gentle, his big muzzle soft and hot. 04 loved the feel of the kiss, so he leaned forward, and the bear pushed back. Their mouths opened, and it was heavenly, and *then* the bear's massive fucking tongue snaked out of his muzzle like a boa constrictor sliding out a transom window. It filled 04's entire muzzle in half a second, and jammed into the back of his throat, and the bear was holding the back of his head like an iron clamp so he couldn't even escape, and it felt horrible but so, so good.

04 moaned loudly, an involuntary whimper escaping him, and after a few moments the bear retracted his tongue and he could breathe again.

Shockingly, the bear reached into the car with his huge fucking paw and clamped it over 04's throbbing erection.

04 yelped, reflexively jumping, and the bear squeezed his nuts and cock with his big hand, and as much as it hurt he was hard and if it went on for a few minutes he probably could have cum.

The bear retracted his muzzle and paw, stared at 04 for a second, and then extricated himself from the vehicle.

"What did you think?" Master asked.

The bear wiped husky drool from his muzzle. He was rock-hard in his pants, 04 noticed. "Good," he said, simply.

Master chuckled. He scrounged in the glove box for a minute, retrieved something, and then extended one hand toward the bear with a business card. "Email me. I'll have one of the dogs pick you up. We'll bring you to the facility for a tour."

The bear took the card. He nodded. "Okay, sir."

Master watched him. "I'll probably enslave you right at that point, so wear something nice and be ready to get fucked. Then I'll let you dangle for about a week, until you're so obsessed with the thought of serving me that you'll play cumdump to a whole pack of dogs just to please me." He beamed.

04 felt the fur on his arms stand up.

The bear nodded. "Okay, sir. Thank you."

The otter grinned. "Call me 'Master' now."

The bear nodded. "Of course, Master. Thank you, Master."

The otter sighed happily. "Nice to meet you, Bear. 11, what will Bear's number be?"

"16, sir!" barked the husky in the back.

The otter grinned. "16. Can't wait to see you again."

The bear nodded, blushing. "Likewise, Master."

Master looked out the window, and then the windshield. He turned back to the bear, who 04 was already starting to think of as the number. "Will somebody see if we just use this road anyway?"

The bear had to think about it, and then grimaced. "Yes, Master. Sorry. It goes right past the new administration trailer."

Undeterred, Master smiled. "Oh well. Thought I would ask. We'll go around from now on. Thanks for your help, 16!"

The bear beamed, his pleasant smile full of teeth. "My pleasure, Master!" He was so hot. 04 squirmed in his seat.

Master waved. "I have to turn around with the trailer, so be careful now."

"Sure! Thank you! Bye, Master!" the bear waved.

Master rolled up his window. "See you soon!"

The bear left to go to the safety of his shack. Grinning, Master squirmed around in his seat. He was so small but 04's heart started pounding at the sight of his face.

"Whaddaya think?" Master asked.

04 swallowed. "I liked him, Master!" he said, hurriedly. 06 and 11 murmured their agreement. 04 could tell they were jealous. He tried not to puff his chest out reflexively.

"Okay. Wow, what a fun little detour," Master said, turning back around. He checked his mirrors, put the truck in gear, and very carefully drove in a big circle through the grass to get back on the road going the other way. He waved as they drove off.

04 looked out the back. 16 was standing in front of his shelter, waving his big long arm.

"God, this fuckin' rules," Master chuckled, happily. "Do you think they'll get another polar bear to replace him after we take him? Maybe we'll come get that one too." He laughed. "Maybe we'll start a polar bear collection to go with our huskies and sheps. What do you think, boys?"

04 made worried eye contact with 06 again. They were both sweating. The bear was big. Several of them would be terrifying.

Master was looking in the rearview and saw it. He laughed. "Don't worry, boys," he said. "I've already decided the bear is a bottom."

Quietly, at the same moment, 04 and 06 let out long, relieved, sighs.

Master smiled. "For now," he added.

The next week was when everything started to unravel.

Returning to the base on the day they met the bear had actually taken an extra hour and fifteen minutes to detour around the mine; they'd had to go all the way back to the highway, which meant they had to stop to refuel the Suburban, which 04 volunteered to do in order to build some good grace with the other two. When they returned, Master pulled the trailer up to the mess hall trailer, which was a doublewide and the only structure with any storage space to speak of. In addition to picking up Master's "special fun items" this had been the first of three supply runs before things got really cold in November and December. After that, in January through March, they would see days in the -25° to -30° range when they generally didn't leave the facility because it was actually dangerous to do so. A breakdown with rescue four hours away, when it was 40° below zero, could easily mean death.

But for now it was in the high 30s and stable. The other three huskies had been waiting for them at the Mess Hall when they pulled up, and even a few of the shepherds, probably more out of nosiness than helpfulness. The huskies were always first-tier for gruntwork, and the shepherds generally only helped when there was something exciting to see. In this case, it was food.

Like 04, all of the huskies and shepherds ranged in age from 25 to 46 (as far as they could tell), all male, and all of them exceptionally well-built. Of the six trailers, three were devoted to quarters, one was mess, one was research, and the entire last trailer was filled with weights and treadmills and four big workout machines, where six of them could comfortably work out at once. They were all in peak physical condition, and it showed. This was not a perk: this was one of Master's requirements.

"You got them!" gasped 05, holding a box of beef jerky sticks. 04 looked at the box. *Gochujang Flavor*. It looked like a case pack full of gas-station display packs, which would have been about 900 beef sticks. The shepherd's golden eyes lit up and he held the package like it was the Arc of the Covenant. "Master!!" he gasped. "I thought they were discontinued!"

Master stepped up, beaming proudly at the fit dog, and 04 swallowed his twinge of jealousy. "They are!" the otter said. "That's the last case pack in existence. Though I think Chef 10 could probably whip you up a reasonable facsimile. I'm pretty sure the name is also the recipe."

He chuckled at his own joke. 04 didn't get it.

05 nodded, and he seemed to actually be blinking back tears. "Thank you so much, Master! I'll work double shifts for these!"

The otter frowned. "That is…absolutely not necessary." His smile reappeared. "But you're welcome!"

After hauling boxes into the larder and freezer for 20 minutes, 04 reentered the trailer, waiting for his eyes to adjust to the darkness, and found himself staring at the huge pile of equipment. There were three items. The largest was in a plywood crate, and marked FRAGILE. It also said FOR MEDICAL USE ONLY. 04 swallowed.

"Why don't you leave that to me and 01," the Master said, behind him.

04 jumped, startled. He snapped his head around and looked down at the shorter otter. Why was his fur standing on end? "O-of course, sir," he stammered. His heart was pounding.

The otter noticed immediately. He frowned. "04, what's the matter?" he asked, softly.

The husky swallowed. "N-nothing, sir!" he stuttered. "I'm fine. Everything's fine."

The otter stepped forward and 04 felt his heart start pounding. He was panicking. Why was he panicking? This was Master. Master loved him. Master would never hurt him.

The otter reached for his face and 04 felt his panic crescendo in such a peak that he almost screamed. He would have, except it caught in his throat.

Then Master's webbed hands touched his muzzle, and 04 felt himself crash into a sudden, inescapable calm.

The otter's hands were soft and hot on his muzzle, and 04 felt himself immediately shut down. His breath caught in his throat, and his eyes wouldn't stay open, and he struggled to stay on his feet. His mind shut down, his racing thoughts quelled, and he stared, eyes half-closed, into the otter's calm, concerned red eyes. His head was spinning, and then swimming, and then nothing.

"Wh-...what…" he whispered.

"Shhh, it's okay," the otter whispered back. "Are you feeling okay, 04?"

The husky stared at him. His eyes wouldn't quite focus. "I…I…" he stammered.

"You're feeling fine," the otter told him. "You're feeling calm and relaxed and safe."

The husky stared into Master's eyes. He felt warm in his chest, and it started to radiate out, flowing through him. He took a slow, deep breath. "I…" He swayed on his feet, trying to focus on Master. "Yes," he whispered. His mouth didn't want to stay closed, and he was dumbly aware of his muzzle dropping slowly open and his tongue lolling out.

"Calm and relaxed and subdued and obedient," the otter told him.

"S-subdued and obedient," 04 repeated. The words sounded so right. It was like a church refrain. It felt so good to say. He felt so good. Master's voice was so calming. He shivered. Yes. Everything was fine.

Master smiled. "*There's* my good boy," he whispered. He rubbed the dog's cheek ruffs roughly.

04 shivered again, feeling himself wag. His body was burning. Master was so pleased with him. He didn't have anything to worry about. He was so calm and

relaxed and obedient. All was as it should be. His tongue dangled, drool spotting his shirt.

Master leaned up and kissed his nose, and 04 whimpered in pleasure.

Master took a step back, squeezing his shoulders, and grinned at him. "Okay, 04! Leave it to us!"

The husky felt the fog suddenly clear in his head. *Us?* Abruptly, he was aware that 01 was standing in the trailer, also, in a huge thick coat with a faux fur collar, and his feeling of calm left him like mist blowing away in the wind.

The black jaguar stared down at him. He was a full yard taller than Master and two feet taller than 04, massive and imposing and strong. Only 02 and the malamutes were nearly his size, and all of them were still a little scared of the big cat.

"Yes," the jaguar said, icily. "Leave it to us."

Trying to keep his tail from dipping between his legs, 04 nodded. "Yes, sirs," he said. He swallowed and shuffled out of the trailer.

"Good work today, 04!" Master called after him. "Tell 11 and 06 for me too, please!" he said.

Tail wagging, 04 nodded. "Thank you, Master!" he called back.

Walking back into the mess hall, he could smell traces of Master's touch on his cheek fur, and he shivered.

"Oh yeah? Did WE do good work today?" 06 growled, pushing 04 to his knees.

They were back in the Husky Trailer, where the 6 of them relaxed and slept. They each had a tiny six-by-six room. At the head of the trailer, with the connecting passageway, there was a little common area with a kitchenette, and a couch, and a few folding chairs. It was here that 06 chose to violently wrestle the other husky to the ground, probably to send a message to the other dogs. 11 was here too, and 13, and even 14, one of the big malamutes. None of them seemed to be particularly averse to the message.

"It wasn't on purpose!" 04 wailed. "I just happened to be in the trailer!"

"Oh yeah?!" 06 snapped. "And did you *just happen* to land behind Master on the way there *and* the way back?!" He grabbed 04's jaw and forced his thumbs in between the husky's teeth. 04 fought him, but he couldn't bite down too hard or he would hurt the other dog's thumbs, and he didn't want to do that.

"HI HIHN'T KNOW HERE HAS HOING HOO BEE A HO-AR HEAAR!" he wailed.

06 removed his thumbs, eyes a little wide. "What?" he asked.

04 frowned, swallowing. "I didn't know there was going to be a polar bear!" he repeated.

06's blue eyes narrowed. 04 tried *not* to think about how handsome he was when he was mad. "That's not what I'm talking about. We all know the best scents are closest to Master. And he does that thing where he taps you with his tail."

04 frowned. "He does," he said, softly.

06 bared his teeth.

04 shivered. "I'm sorry! I never mean to do it. I…I just…" He let out a shaky breath. "I can't help myself. I want him *so bad*."

06 frowned. "We all do," he snapped.

04 nodded. "I'm sorry."

06 snorted. He unzipped his uniform pants, and worked his cock out. It was red and throbbing, already damp with sweat, or precum, or both.

The scent hit 04's nose immediately. His eyes widened. His conditioning started to kick in immediately, and he felt himself get hard. His mouth was watering, too. He stared at 06's cock, unable to take his eyes off. He wanted it. He wanted to please him so bad. He needed it. He longed for 06's hot cum firing down his throat. Softly, he whined, looking pitifully up at the other husky.

06 grunted. "Show me you're sorry," he growled.

Nodding dumbly, letting his body and his conditioning take control, 04 opened his muzzle and leaned forward.

06 slept in his bed with him that night, and even though it wasn't really cold enough for co-sleeping yet, 04 appreciated it. They both slept naked, and 06 curled up against his back, holding him, big head and muzzle resting on 04's neck, muscular arm curled over him, hot breath on his ear. 04 knew it was part of their weird little language, to show the other husky there were no real hard feelings, and even though it was a little hot he relished the close contact and the sentiment behind it. He closed

his eyes, exhausted. Even though he'd done nothing but ride in a car most of the day, he slept like the dead.

The next morning at 7:00 am, the shepherds had beaten them into the mess hall, and as soon as he saw them, 04 knew it wasn't an accident.

He frowned. All six of the shepherds were there eating, and their plates were full. He checked his watch. 7:01. The shepherds usually rolled in between 7:00 and 7:05, the dogs' standard breakfast time, and they all got food together. Now they were all already seated. They must have rolled in at quarter till, right after 01 got his food and disappeared back into his quarters, as he always did.

"What the hell," 06 muttered, next to him.

04 looked over the black and tan dogs, all dressed in their uniform slacks and their standard-issue black t-shirts. 05, 08, and 09 were sitting at the table, looking like a textbook Hallmark Card definition of Dog Guilt - ears back, eyes a little wide, refusing to make eye contact. 10 was in the kitchen, working, out of sight.

That left 02 and 03. 02 stared right at him, grinning. 03 glared.

Unlike the huskies, who were more or less identical, the shepherds had a little variation. 03's variation was that he was big, and 02's variation was that he was bigger. 02 essentially acted as leader among the shepherds, another variation between them and the huskies, who acted as a unit.

The huskies tended to be stronger than the shepherds, even though they tended to run smaller. They were also obviously better-suited to colder weather in Alaska, which was why they got picked for general labor. The smarter German shepherds all had technical and precision roles. 02 was bigger than any of the huskies, *and* smart, and he wielded those traits like a weapon.

04 frowned. He ignored the dogs, walking past the tables to the twelve-foot stainless steel table that served as a makeshift barrier between the "kitchen" side of the trailer and its portable metal ranges, ovens, and wash sinks, and the "dining" side of the trailer, which featured three plastic folding tables and an army of folding chairs.

Normally the table was stacked with a buffet-style of steaming trays. Today there were trays, but almost none of the food was left. 10 was at the sink, very deliberately washing big dishes, his back to the group.

"What the fuck?" 06 snapped, out loud.

"Oh, is there nothing left?" 02 boomed, loudly, his mouth full. "Did you miss it when you were too busy adventuring with Master?"

The other huskies turned to square off. 04 glanced left and right. 06 was next to him. 12 and 13 were on his other side. 11 was still missing and probably jacking off in the shower, which he did almost every day. 07 was probably working out with the two big malamutes.

"We didn't even get to go!" 12 protested, next to 04.

06 growled, the husky's lips curling up. "You know damn well that Master picks the rotation and issues his orders. Just like he does for you."

02 stood up, the hulking black and tan monster standing a head taller than any of the rest of them, at least seven feet. 04 thought maybe he was a king shepherd because he was just too big to be a regular shep. He couldn't remember where he'd read that, though. "Yeah," the big dog growled. "And he picks you chumps *every single time* and leaves us here with that fucking cat."

"So I hope you ate in Prudhoe Bay!" chimed in 03. He was smaller than 02 but still bigger than the rest of the sheps, and all of the huskies. His face was mostly all black. 04 shot him a glare and the shepherd's sneer faltered, his ears tilting back, and then returned full-force.

06 started growling, and so did 12. 04 could see 13 squaring up out of the corner of his eye. "If you think you're going to starve us, you're out of your mind," he snarled.

"I'll make more," 10 said, quietly, from across the room. 10 was another normal-sized shep and 04 knew he was afraid of 02, especially when 02 and 03 ganged up, since they were the biggest. His tail was tucked between his legs. Clearly he wasn't thrilled about the plan and 02 had bullied him into it.

"The hell you will," 02 growled.

04 frowned. "You know, you can't throw your weight around like this," he said, icily. "What if Master finds out?"

The room went silent. Even 02's eyebrows shot up. His huge shepherd ears tilted ever-so-slightly backwards in fear. 04 had gone for the jugular, and they all knew it.

After a moment, his face darkened, and 04 suddenly worried he had miscalculated.

"And who's gonna *tell* Master?" the big dog growled, rising to his feet.

"Whoa, hey," 05 said, golden eyes wide. "Leave him alone or we'll all be punished." He looked back and forth between the imposing shepherd and 04.

The big shep took a few steps toward 04. He was huge with muscle, thick from ears to tail. "You're already on thin ice, *04*. Don't think we didn't see you in the trailer. 05 saw you and then your buddy 06 here told us all about it."

04 stared at him, and then glanced to his side to shoot a look at 06.

The other husky's eyebrows shot up, and then he withered. He cowered submissively. *Sorry*, his eyes seemed to say. *I was still mad.*

04 glared at him, and then turned back to the advancing king shepherd. "You can't hurt me," he whispered, his heart pounding. "Master will find out. Master *always* finds out."

The big dog stared daggers into him with his golden eyes, and then scoffed. Picking up his plate, he walked to the corner trash can and dumped in the full plate of food. "You're not even worth the extra calories," he growled, throwing open the connecting hall door with a bang and disappearing into the connection hall. 03 walked swiftly out after him.

04 swallowed, letting out a shaky breath.

At the head of the table, 09 cleared his throat. "Hey, can anybody finish this for me? I'm stuffed."

They turned to look at him. The young shepherd had his head down, his ears pinned back against his head, looking away submissively. He had pushed forward a full plate of food. It was a peace offering.

04 swallowed, and then forced a smile. "Thanks, Nine," he said. He turned. "Twelve, Thirteen, you hungry?"

12 and 13 glanced at each other. "Sure, we'll split it," 12 said. They both moved toward the food.

05 pushed his plate forward. "Here, have mine too!" he said. He brightened, wagging, ears up, clearly relieved the conflict was over. "Does anybody want some Gochujang Jerky?"

06 snorted. "05, *nobody in the world* wants Gochujang Jerky."

They all laughed.

Swallowing, 04 slid into a seat, across from 08, who pushed a full plate across the table to him with submissive ears. 04 forced a smile back and nodded gratefully.

Everything was fine again.

For now.

Exposed

A few days later, after breakfast and lunch when he had finished his requirements for the day, 04 left 06 in the workout trailer and suited up for a run. It was almost 40° out, so he didn't wear much, just a jockstrap and a t-shirt and his athletic shoes. He wouldn't be going more than a few miles from the facility, and there wouldn't be anyone for 15 miles in any direction, and if they did show up the motion sensors would activate and let him know. And if anyone turned the wrong way out of the mining operation, they would get a good show. 04 was lean and muscular, with thick, defined legs, and he looked incredible in a jockstrap.

He exited the door off the workout trailer connection and descended the perforated metal steps to the cold ground. The husky headed around the corner, passing the twenty by thirty foot log cabin that was the original structure at the end of this dirt road. The cabin hadn't been very well insulated, so they had all but abandoned it during the winter months, since the insulation on the prefabricated trailers was much better.

Turning the corner, he ran into 14 and 15, number 07 still in tow. The two malamutes were both seven feet tall, and *massive*, built like Olympic strongmen, and fluffy on top of that. They were both wearing black athletic shorts and white tank tops, as was 07, the husky kitted out like a miniature version of the two huge dogs.

04 looked the three of them over and smelled their musk, immediately looking away, blushing, suddenly self-conscious about his wardrobe choice. They had all seen him naked, and in fact 14 and 15 had both been inside him at the same time before, filling him from either end while 07 sucked him off, but sneaking out with his fluffy ass hanging out still felt scandalous.

14 grinned, massive and toothy. He raised his big mitt-like hands. *"I like your outfit,"* he signed. *"You should wear that more often."* He licked his teeth.

Either 14 or 15 was deaf. 04 couldn't actually remember which of them it was, because neither of them spoke, and both of them communicated only in American sign language. Everyone at the facility had learned ASL, but the two big dogs kept pretty sparse company regardless.

04 raised his paws, blushing. *"Thank you,"* he signed. *"No one was supposed to see me."*

15 grinned. Both of them were grinning evilly at him now. Weren't malamutes supposed to be nice?

"We saw you." He winked. *"Maybe we'll see you later."*

Oh God. 04 felt his face heating up. Both of the malamutes knew that 04 was deeply into them.

04 looked to 07, the husky between the malamutes. *"Maybe you should dress like this,"* he signed. He pointed especially hard on *"You."*

07 shot him a smug look. *"I already know what they like,"* he signed. *"They call you if I get tired."*

Oh Christ. 04 raised his eyebrows, unable to keep the shock off of his face, which had been the reaction 07 wanted. The husky laughed, flashing his teeth, and the three of them disappeared back into the trailers.

Shaking it off, 04 jogged back and forth for a minute to warm up, and then set off on the usual trail.

Between the huskies and the malamutes, they had worn a path in the brush that they all followed. The shepherds mostly stuck to the treadmills, and of course 01 never went outside unless he had to, but the rest of them ran nearly every day during the months when it was feasible. 04 liked to jog through January, but when it was less than -20° even he had to pack it in for the season.

Setting off down the path, the Brooks Range mountains to his right rising gently out of the landscape, the brush already starting to brown, the long, flat, open landscape stretching away, 04 let himself get lost.

Letting his body take over, 04 reflected on how weird things had been since they got back. The shepherds had never banded against them before. This must have been 02's doing, the big lug, but they'd never been at odds like this. 04 thought 02 liked him, and he'd definitely sucked the huge dog off on more than one occasion. What had changed?

Also, 04 himself was feeling on edge. The polar bear would be back any day now. 04 wondered where they would put him. Maybe in the cabin? Master's trailer was tall, with ten-foot ceilings, to accommodate the eight-foot jaguar who occupied the trailer with him. But the trailer was only divided into two suites. And the polar bear seemed to be over nine feet — would he even fit?

Frowning, 04 chugged along. Why did they even need a polar bear? They already had two malamutes and a jaguar, plus an oversized shepherd, for the heavy lifting. Weren't they doing a good job? Maybe it was for security — none of them was exactly skilled in that department, though they did have the motion sensors. But the bear was just a guard. Would he really be an asset?

He thought about the polar bear, frowning, swallowing hard, his bare legs pounding along on the cold ground. He should be excited. Once the polar bear got here, Master would take a few days with him, and then he would be part of the pack. Anytime 04 wanted a taste of ursine he could wander over to wherever they were keeping him and dislocate his jaw around the bear's cock. And yet when he thought of the bear he was filled with apprehension. What was he missing?

Suddenly, 04 realized two things.

First, 04 realized he had totally missed the turnaround back off the main trail. He'd jogged probably four miles down the main road. Startled, he snapped back out of his thoughts.

Second, he realized he wasn't alone.

There was a figure on the horizon, walking down the road toward him, probably another mile down the way. It was a big figure.

It was the bear.

Stunned, 04 stared. He blinked several times. Was he dreaming? He stood still, perfectly still, and just watched.

The figure did not disappear. It was definitely walking toward him. Monster hulking form, long neck, big thick head. It was definitely real, and it was definitely the polar bear.

As he watched with shock and dread, the bear waved. 04 swallowed.

Why hadn't the motion sensors gone off? Frowning, 04 set his jaw. He had better investigate. He wished he'd brought a radio to alert the team.

Setting into a run again, 04 jogged at a gentle pace toward the bear, and five minutes later he had cleared the mile between them.

The bear watched him, looking him over. His eyes widened a little as he saw what 04 was wearing, his gaze dropping to 04's naked legs and the white patches on the insides of his thighs.

The dog frowned, swallowing, fighting a blush. He felt so exposed. The bear had already grabbed him the other day, and now he could see his sheath and balls on full display. And if 04 turned around, the bear would see his naked black-and-white ass, perfectly framed in his jockstrap straps. If he wanted to, he could fuck 04 right here in the scrub. Based on Master's predilections, 04 would probably be guzzling this bear's cum inside the hour, but for now, he was so embarrassed he could barely breathe.

"Hello," the bear said. His eyebrows were still up. He was definitely staring right at 04's dick.

"Sorry," 04 grunted. "We don't get many visitors out here." He forced a smile.

The bear nodded. "I see," he said.

They stared at each other.

"What are you doing here?" 04 asked him.

The bear stared down at him. "The otter offered me a job. I emailed him and he told me to come right away."

04 stared at him. *The otter?* 04 had never heard anyone refer to Master this way. And he was here presumably from his quarters at the mining facility, which was almost sixteen miles away. Without a vehicle.

The husky felt uneasy.

He looked the hulking figure over. The bear was in his uniform slacks and a button-down shirt. He had on a light jacket. He was wearing thick hiking boots, gray with dust, and carrying a duffel bag. "Did…did you *walk?*" he asked.

The bear nodded. He frowned. "Is that a problem? I won't fit in any of your cars."

The husky stared.

"I'm too big," the bear said, unnecessarily.

04 swallowed. He didn't know what to say.

The bear frowned. "I can walk long distances. This is my native climate. He said show up at two. It's only fifteen miles from my mining quarters. Is this a problem?"

04 stammered. "N-no, it's fine. I just didn't expect it."

The bear grunted. "I didn't expect a husky in a jockstrap."

The dog looked away, ears back, feeling his tail tuck between his bare legs. "Okay. I'll walk you the rest of the way."

"Thank you," said the bear. He straightened up.

They walked toward the trailers. They were about four miles out. At a walking pace, 04 did the math in this head — fifteen minutes a mile, four miles, which meant an hour with the bear.

They started off. They walked in silence for ten minutes.

In the distance, the wind whistled softly through the trees. It would be below freezing in just a few weeks.

"*Why* did you come?" 04 heard himself ask, softly.

The bear turned to look down at him. He paused before speaking. "I told you. The otter told me to come. He offered me a job."

Something was still bothering 04. "But you didn't have to come. Why did you come?"

The bear stared at him, gray eyes unblinking, and finally took a breath. "I don't know," he said.

04 pondered that. "Okay," he said.

They walked in silence for another few yards.

"Why do you stay?" the bear asked, suddenly.

Surprised, 04 looked up. "Hm?" he asked.

The bear watched him. 04 felt vulnerable and exposed. "You could work anywhere in this state. It would be easy for a husky to get any job he wanted. Why do you stay out here, with him?"

04 thought about it for a long time, until he realized he didn't have an answer. "I don't know," he said, finally.

The bear nodded thoughtfully. "I see," he said.

They walked in silence for another few minutes.

"Can I touch you?" the bear asked, suddenly.

04 turned to him. "S-sorry?" he asked.

The bear was looking at him. He was staring at the husky's sheath and bare legs again. "Can I touch?" he rumbled. He swallowed. "He made me kiss you the other day." He looked down into the husky's eyes. "It was…incredibly arousing."

04 felt himself heating up. He didn't know what to say. "You remember me? Specifically?"

The bear stared him down with his gray eyes. "Of course I remember," he said, reaching down to squeeze his own crotch.

04 glanced down. The bear was aroused in his uniform slacks.

Staring at him, the bear played with himself.

What was he supposed to do here? What would Master want?

That answer came pretty quickly. Master was the one who had volunteered him in the first place. That would be a yes then. "S-sure," he stammered.

Nodding, the polar bear reached down. He put one huge hand over the husky's package, carefully encircling his mesh-clad balls and sheath, and the other under 04's tail, cupping his entire bare ass.

04 jerked in surprise, writhing in the polar bear's massive paws. "Hnngh!" he grunted.

The bigger man watched him carefully. "Still okay?" he asked.

Letting out a shaky breath, 04 nodded. "S-still okay!" he gasped. Oh fuck. He was getting hard already. The bear's hands were massive and inescapably strong. His cock slipped out of his sheath and fought the mesh netting.

The ursine cupped his balls, digging his fingers in under 04's balls and roughly massaging his perineum. At the same time, he squeezed his ass, hard, and then lifted his hand to grab 04's tail. His hand was so big that 04 had to partially uncurl his tail, and he couldn't possibly escape from the bear.

"Still okay?" he asked again, his voice low. It was almost a growl.

"Unh, ahhh," the husky groaned, squirming in the bear's grasp. "*Yes*," he gasped.

The bear let go of his tail and reached up to cup the back of his head. He leaned down.

04 shivered, trying to pull away, but the bear held him in place.

The huge ursine closed in, his mouth opening, and pressed his huge muzzle up against 04's. His lips were hot and strong, and his tongue came after immediately, pushing 04's lips apart and jamming into his mouth. At the same time, the bear jammed his fingers into 04's jockstrap, freeing his dick from the mesh netting but flattening it against his stomach with the huge palm of his hand.

"*Mmmmhnnngghh*," 04 groaned, the bear's tongue filling his mouth. He writhed in place, between the bear's hand on his head and tongue and the huge flat palm grinding his cock. His body started to take over, and he humped the soft palm of the bear's big hand, and now the polar bear started to growl into his mouth, and that turned him on even more. He started to feel week in the knees and lightheaded, and soon he was thrusting involuntarily at the bear's solid, strong hand, and now the big fucker turned his other hand to gather up his ruff, was actually fucking *scruffing him*, holding him in place while his dog brain made him hump and hump and hump, and then suddenly his balls were emptying and he was grinding as hard as he could against the bear's hand, and the bear was pushing back, and it was wet and hot and slimy and his whole body was quivering.

The bear broke the kiss but held onto him for a long time after he came, holding him steady, while 04 gasped and panted and shivered in place. He stared at the bear, eyes wide, tongue lolling out.

Finally, after what seemed like minutes, 04 felt his heart stop pounding so hard, and he took a long, deep breath and let it out as a shuddering sigh.

The bear straightened up to his full height, proudly, grinning evilly. "I like this place so far," he chuckled, grinning. Lifting his right hand, still holding 04 with the other, he slurped across the palm of his own hand, licking up most of 04's frantic messy orgasm.

The husky watched him, dazed, his mouth dry. What was happening?

The bear pushed his palm into 04's face. "Clean it," he ordered.

Wordlessly, 04 obeyed, licking the rest of his acrid semen off the bear's fat leather paw pad. He could taste himself, his own sweat and cum, and the bear's woody scent.

Why was he following this bear's orders? What was happening? Had he been right to be worried after all?

His concern must have been evident on his face, because the bear's eyebrows slowly raised.

"I told the otter I would be walking. He said you're all conditioned and I could try out anyone I saw on my way in." He frowned. "Was that not okay?"

04 processed that, and let out a shaky sigh. "Oh," he said. "Oh. Okay." It sank in further, and he took another relieved breath. Master was behind this after all. That made him feel much better. "I see. Thank you."

The bear frowned. "Are you okay?"

04 nodded. "Yes! I'm just embarrassed." He forced a smile. "Let's keep moving." He stuffed his drooly cock back into his jockstrap and set off. Hopefully by the time they got back his cock would have retracted into his sheath. Some of his own pre and cum smeared on his hand pads as he manhandled his cock back into his jock. He raised his hand and licked his palm clean.

"Why are you embarrassed? I enjoyed that a great deal," the bear said.

04 glanced at the bear's crotch. He was rock-hard in his uniform pants again. "Do...do you want me to reciprocate?" he asked.

The bear shook his head. "No thank you, I was told I'm not allowed to cum until the otter lets me," he said.

04's eyebrows rose. "Oh! That makes sense. Well! Your hour draws near."

The bear growled. "I'm looking forward to it.

It didn't take them long to reach the cabin.

The structure was a real Alaskan log cabin, hand-built out of huge local pine logs. It was significantly less comfortable than the densely-insulated prefabricated trailers, which was why they hardly ever used it. But it would accommodate all of them, both in terms of space and in height, so 04 wasn't surprised that Master had selected it to break in the nine-foot-plus polar bear.

04 knew to head right to the cabin because he smelled woodsmoke two miles out. The one-room structure had a large stone-and-mortar hearth with a huge fireplace, the only source of heat in the small building, and there was only ever a fire when there was a reason to heat the building above 40°.

04 walked right past their trailers and the water melt tank, but the polar bear next to him looked all around, taking in all of the sights. He seemed to be approving of the accommodations, or at least he was good at hiding his true emotions. 04 couldn't tell which and in a little while, it wouldn't really matter.

The cabin was built into the scrub, on the same slightly-raised flatland as the rest of their facility. It had been there long before their research center, between their trailers and a large unnamed lake that Master sometimes swam in, fed by streams descending from the mountains to the south. Master had thought the cabin was from the early 1900s, but none of them really knew for sure.

The cabin itself was 30 feet on its face, made from medium-sized rough-hewn logs running laterally across its length, the front wall 12 feet tall, with a large lumber door smack in the middle, and only two large windows on either end. It had a simple gable roof, the ridge running the length of the cabin. The roof had been in the worst shape and had taken them an entire summer to replace, first by rebuilding the wooden structure and then sheathing that in pre-insulated metal sheeting. Some of the shepherds were talented carpenters and had led the project, but they had all pitched in to make the cabin habitable. 04 generally felt a sense of pride when he looked at the large structure. Today, however, seeing and smelling the smoke rising gently from the chimney, he felt only dread.

Swallowing, the husky approached the entry door. Raising his hand, he paused, and then knocked loudly.

"Come in!" boomed Master, from inside.

04 felt his heart leap. Some of his anxiety lifting, he reached for the old-fashioned metal hardware of the door. He tripped the bolt and pushed the door open. He stepped in, turning back to nod at the bear.

The room was brightly-lit, with overhead lighting that 14 and 15 had hung from the rafters, but it still took 04's eyes a moment to adjust. He looked for Master first, his pulse quickening as soon as his eyes settled on the otter: short, slim, clad in simple cotton pants and a standard-issue t-shirt.

04 was also surprised to see the shepherds. Every single one of them. 05, 08, 09 and 10 were just milling about, their poses suggesting excitement and anticipation, ears up, tails wagging. 03, the big one, locked eyes with him and frowned. 02, the *biggest* one, saw him and immediately lowered his head aggressively, baring his teeth.

The husky stepped into the room, allowing enough space for the hulking polar bear to step into the open space after him. The door was nine feet tall. The bear still had to duck.

"04!" Master said, brightly, and as always 04 felt his ears tilt back and his tail start wagging. "I like your outfit!" 04 felt his entire body seize up with embarrassment, but Master continued too fast for him to really feel it. "I see you found our guest!" the otter continued. He turned to the bear.

The bear straightened up and looked down at him, eyes a little wide. He didn't seem to know what to do, or even what to say.

04 watched, silently.

The otter beamed. "So glad you could join us!" He grinned toothily. 04 had never thought of otters as scary, but the little lutrine had a set of teeth that could rival any of the canines.' "Did you have any trouble on the way?"

The bear watched him, and shook his head warily. He seemed tense. "N-no, sir," he grunted.

Master smiled. "Glad to hear it." He watched the bear for a moment.

Here it comes, 04 thought.

"Kneel," said the otter, simply.

Watching him, eyes widening, the polar bear slowly lowered himself to his knees.

Now that the bear was down, 04 felt more comfortable looking him over. He looked even more hulking than he had the first time the husky saw him. His shoulders were impossibly broad, and he had the long and sweeping neck of a huge predator. His head and jaw were probably the size of 04's entire chest. Even kneeling, he was still taller than Master.

04 swallowed. He was concerned. The bear was very big. What if he didn't like his programming? It had never happened before, but in this case it would be disastrous. He glanced toward the sheps.

All six of them were watching with laser-like intensity. Even 02 had given up his death glare at 04 and was watching, ears forward, eyes locked, unmoving.

They were prepared to defend Master. 04 felt better.

Master was, as usual, completely unbothered.

"I'm going to touch your face again," he said, grinning evilly.

The bear nodded. "Okay," he said.

Master stepped toward him. "This will…pretty much be the end for you," he said, conversationally. Smiling amiably.

The bear nodded. "Yes, sir," he said, his voice shaking.

The otter stepped forward, raising his arms, and grabbed the kneeling bear's entire face.

The bear's eyes rolled back into his head, and his entire body relaxed. It was stunning to see. 04 hadn't fully realized how tense the polar bear was until he watched him turn to jelly in Master's webbed hands. His hands dropped uselessly to his sides and dangled, and he took a sharp, deep breath, almost a gasp, and let it out as a long, strained sigh.

The otter rubbed the bear's face, running his thumbs along the ursine's huge muzzle, prying his teeth open and tilting his head back, exposing his vulnerable throat.

"Welcome home, 16," the otter growled.

"*Master,*" the bear moaned.

Onboarding

The bear took a few moments for his eyes to stop rolling back into his head. For a long time he looked like he might be at risk of crashing over onto his side, which would not have surprised 04 one bit, because when Master wanted to be in your head, Master got *into your head*. The husky swallowed nervously, watching the massive kneeling polar bear reel, while Master held his head and stared him down.

Finally, the polar bear caught his breath, and some rigidity came back into his huge wide back. He straightened up again, blinking slowly and repeatedly. He seemed dazed, straining to focus his eyes, and it took him a long time to orient himself again.

After almost a minute, the polar bear stopped reeling, and he stared dazedly up at Master, swaying gently. He opened his mouth as if to say something, but didn't say anything at all.

Master smiled at him. "How do you feel?"

The bear had to think for a moment. "Fine, Master," the huge man rumbled. He was still a little unsteady.

"What is your name?" Master asked.

The bear stared at him, thinking. His brow furrowed, and after a moment, he frowned. He closed his mouth, and then opened it again, and then finally, hesitantly, spoke.

"I…I don't know?" he said.

Master beamed proudly down at him. "Your name is *16*. You're part of our family."

The bear blinked, and then smiled happily back. "Yes, Master," he rumbled. "Thank you, Master."

Watching, 04 felt his hackles slowly rise, starting at the back of his neck and traveling down his spine. He repressed a shiver.

Why am I so tense? he thought.

"Rise up, 16, and take your place in your new home!" Master said, releasing the polar bear's huge head.

He took a step back, and the polar bear rose to his full height. 04 actually had to lift his head to watch him. The husky watched, eyes wide.

The bear looked around. He seemed to notice the shepherds for the first time. His eyes settled on 04, too, for just long enough to make the husky's heart beat a little faster.

"Who are they, Master?" the bear asked, his muzzle turned into a severe frown.

"Your packmates!" the otter said, delighted. His face contorted into an evil smile. "Would you like to *meet them?*"

16 looked them all over again. "Very much, Master," he said, staring directly at 04.

The husky felt his mouth go dry. *Oh God*, he thought. *He's gonna fuck me while Master watches and I'm gonna die.* He tried to bite back the whine that was building in his throat.

Master chuckled. "I'm afraid that one is not part of your initiation," he said.

The polar bear turned back to the otter. "Yes, sir," he said. He looked eagerly toward the shepherds. "Who should I... meet, Master?"

The otter gestured to the line of dogs against the back wall. "Go take your pick."

"Yes, *sir*," the bear said, eagerly. He immediately walked over to the row of shepherds at the back of the cabin.

He started with 02. The king shepherd was a foot taller than most of the shepherds, pushing seven feet, thick and mean. He raised his upper lip as soon as the polar bear came near him, furrowing his brow. A low, dangerous, terrifying growl emanated from his throat.

A growl?! 04 felt his eyebrows rise in shock. Stunned, he glanced at Master to see how the otter would react. Master's brow furrowed, ever so slightly, but otherwise the otter gave no indication that anything was wrong.

16 didn't even react, just stared the shepherd in the eyes, and silently moved on. He came to 03 next, the 6'6" shepherd watching him with slightly wide eyes.

The polar bear leaned in and down, suddenly, sharply, too fast, and sniffed loudly. It was a deep inhalation and the sound was explosive in the cabin.

All of them jumped. 04 felt himself flinch in surprise. 03 jerked back so hard he hit the wall behind him, golden eyes wide in his face of black fur. He gasped.

02 barked, deafeningly loud, making everyone flinch again, lunging forward, stopping just before hitting the bear. 16 turned his head, but otherwise didn't react. They stared at each other from inches away.

04 felt his skin crawling. What was happening?! He stared at Master for guidance. The otter just watched, though now his frown was obvious.

02 started growling again.

"Easy," said 16, and moved on to the next dog.

It was a long time before 04's heart stopped pounding.

The room was tense as 16 went down the rest of the line. He did lean in to sniff 05, 08, and 09, though he did it slower and without further incident. They mostly just watched him warily.

Then he came to 10, the chef shepherd, who was already blushing and wouldn't make eye contact. His tail was between his legs but his ears weren't tilted back. Instead, he was squirming in place, transferring his weight back and forth from foot to foot.

04 blinked, watching him, and then cracked a smile. 10 was definitely a size queen, like 04 himself, though he guessed the dog had a bear fetish that they were all just finding out about now.

Including 16, apparently. The bear leaned his huge head in, dipping his massive nose under 10's chin, snuffling gently. At the same time, he reached forward with his big mitts and gently grasped both of 10's flanks.

The shepherd squirmed. 04 could tell he was trying with all his might not to whine submissively. The shepherd's tail popped out from between his legs and started wagging.

"Nnnnngh," the shepherd whimpered, involuntarily. He was already hard in his uniform pants.

"This one," said 16, with an evil little smile.

Master watched him. "Why?" he asked.

16 stared at the dog. "He's nervous. But mostly excited. He wants this."

The otter nodded. "Very good." He smiled and turned to the rest of the dogs. "The rest of you will get your turn. In the meantime, 10 and 16, please step forward."

Still smirking, the bear took center stage in the middle of the wooden floor. 10 trailed after him, panting gently, his tongue poking out. 05, 08 and 09 gave him approving smiles. 09 clapped him on the back as he stepped away. 02 and 03 didn't react positively but at least they didn't start shit, either.

The mood was jovial now. 10 was about to get his world rocked and they all knew it. His erection tented his pants as he walked.

"Face each other," Master ordered.

They did. 16 stared down into 10's eyes. The much-smaller shepherd squirmed under his gaze. He alternated between gritting his teeth and panting.

"16, undress your new friend."

"Yes, Master," 16 growled, cracking a smile. He reached for the smaller dog.

Staring up at him, eyes wide, 10 shivered. He was clearly still into it but he was also staring down the barrel of a nine-foot-tall polar bear who had been told to strip him.

"I'll be gentle," 16 told him, reaching for the hem of the dog's shirt.

The shepherd raised his arms. 04 noticed that he was shivering now, head to toe. 16 grasped the sides of the dog's shirt with his huge hands and pulled upward, tugging the dog's shirt up over his head without even lifting his own arms over his head.

Reflexively, involuntarily, 04 let his eyes roam over 10's shirtless body. The shepherd was not especially ripped but thickly muscled, beefy, the only shepherd besides 02 with a belly. He was a beautiful black and tan and 04 drank in the sight of him. On some level, he knew they were conditioned to be in love with one another's bodies, but he couldn't fight it any more than he could forget his number. He could tell it was working on the other dogs, too, because there wasn't a pair of golden eyes on anything but 10 as the bear stripped him.

16 reached down for the dog's belt clasp and quickly worked it open. 10 started panting faster now, fast and frightened, squirming in the huge bear's grasp, especially as the bear carefully lowered his fly and opened his pants. 16 crouched down to unlace the dog's boots, again working quickly and precisely.

"Step out of your boots," he told 10. "Put your hands on my shoulders."

10 complied instantly, nodding even as he was doing it. He put his shaking hands on the bear's shoulders, breathing hard, and worked his way out of his boots. Left first, and 04 was surprised to see 10 was wearing his boots with no socks. Then right. He stumbled as he did it.

"It's okay," 16 told him, deep voice lowered to a whisper. "I won't hurt you." He looked earnestly up at the shepherd, staring into his eyes.

10's golden eyes widened. He nodded, taking a deep breath, and even managed a weak smile.

16 stared at him, the faintest hint of a smile in his eyes. "There it is." Reaching up, he slid his massive thumbs down into 10's pants, and gently but firmly tugged downward.

16 went slowly and carefully, but he was still so strong that 10 had to struggle to stay standing as his pants were yanked forcibly down off of him. He writhed in place, gritting his teeth, shivering, and 04 was actually concerned for a moment. Then he caught a glimpse of red as 10 turned to step out of his pants, and realized the shepherd was rock-hard, fully out of his sheath.

16 straightened up, and as 04 watched the hulking bear and the helpless, exposed, aroused shepherd, he had to swallow. He was feeling pretty full in the sheath himself, and he didn't have anything more than a jockstrap to cover it up. The husky felt the dull throb of arousal pulsing in his chest, and his stomach, and his sheath.

They all stared at the naked shepherd. 10 squirmed under their collective gaze, exposed. Amazingly, this seemed to make him grow harder, and now his cock started throbbing with his heartbeat. He looked away, blushing furiously.

The cabin was starting to fill with the smell of horny dog musk. 04 took and released several long breaths, willing himself to stay soft, so there wouldn't be *two* rock-hard dog cocks on display.

16 turned to look at Master, and the bear's head was so big that the movement made 04 snap his head up to look at him.

"Now you," Master said, smiling pleasantly.

16 nodded, reached for his belt, and practically flung his clothes off. He undressed with impressive speed, pulling out his belt, carefully folding his uniform pants, and folding his shirt on top of it. He set them on a pile on top of his boots and straightened up.

The massive naked white polar bear looked more like a marble statue than a living creature. He straightened up and stared down at Master. The bear's musculature was massive. He was shockingly trim for an ursine, and 04 let his eyes linger for a long time on the trim slab of the polar bear's chest, glide down his visible abdominal muscles, and settle on his naked fluffy crotch. His sheath was fat and full but he wasn't yet out of it; the sheath alone was the size of a 12oz aluminum can. The cock inside would probably be terrifying. 04 stared at the bear's sheath and tremendous, heavy dangling balls, and had to remind himself to breathe. He could smell the bear now, too, a sharp musky scent that overlaid all of their dog scents, and he felt arousal deep in his guts.

"Now what, Master?" 16 asked, casually.

The otter beamed. "Pleasure your new friend," he said, simply.

16 processed that, nodded, and then turned to the shepherd. "Yes, *sir*," he said, again.

10 let out a soft, sharp whine. Nervously, the shepherd curled his hands into fists.

16 lowered his head to look the shepherd in the eye. "Anything you *don't* want me to do?" he asked.

"I-I'm fine!" the smaller dog barked. "I'm just nervous because you're so big! It's an *evolutionary defense mechanism!*" he sputtered.

16 cracked a smile. "That's okay. I'll go slow." He reached up for the dog's face and cupped the shepherd's chin — and his entire head, in fact — in his humongous bear paws. He stroked 10's head and rubbed his temples, effortlessly palming the shepherd's entire head.

10's entire body stiffened, but as soon as the bear started petting him, his nostrils flared, and 04 could tell that the shepherd was deeply inhaling the bear's scent. The dog's eyes gradually un-widened, and then slowly unfocused.

04 thought of how good the bear smelled up close. *10's done for*, he thought, cracking a smile.

16 rubbed harder, ruffling the dog's face ruff, squeezing him gently, and 10's eyes slid slowly shut, his mouth opening. "Haaaaahhhhh," he breathed, quietly. His eyebrows went up in surprise, though his eyes stayed half-closed in pleasure.

16 leaned in and nibbled gently at the side of the dogs' face. 10 whimpered, tilting his head over, exposing his throat. 16 let his paws slide down 10's arms, holding the dog in place, and 04 saw the shepherd shiver. He arched his back, staring at the huge bear, as if in disbelief that this was happening.

04 felt his own sheath start to part. His cock was starting to slide out. The jockstrap would mostly restrict him from getting fully hard but it would be painfully obvious. He tried not to squirm, shifting left and right on his big husky feet.

16 lowered himself to his knees now, pulling 10 toward him, sliding his paws around behind the dog. 10's arms were still pinned at his side, and 04 could tell the polar bear was using his claws, dragging them through the shepherd's black fur, grazing his skin. 16 suddenly squeezed, holding 10's back and ass and crushing the dog up against him, and dipped his massive head, nibbling delicately at the side of the shepherd's throat.

10 gasped, high and sharp. He squirmed in place, and then started to struggle, writhing between the bear's massive arms and his huge wide torso. 04 would have leapt in to help him, but 10 was whimpering now, almost squeaking, and the sounds he was making were unquestionably sexual. Based on the position, he would be grinding his throbbing cock against the bear's perfect abs, as 16 held him firmly in place. 10 was squeezing his eyes shut now, gritting his teeth, whining sharply, and 04 absolutely knew he was in heaven.

The husky opened his mouth to let himself pant. He was fully hard now, his cock tenting the front of his jockstrap. He stood perfectly still, hoping no one would notice.

Looking to the rest of the shepherds, he found them in a similar state. All of them were hard, even 02, who shifted uncomfortably to accommodate his huge meat stick. A few of the dogs were openly playing with themselves.

04 glanced at Master. The otter just watched, his face betraying nothing, perfectly still and perfectly silent.

16 growled lightly — it was a play growl, 04 knew, because serious bear growls were existentially terrifying — and shuffled his huge head in to nibble harder on 10's neck. 10 squeaked and tilted his head away, moaning, and now 04 could see that he was definitely humping against the bear's meaty torso.

"Good boy," 16 growled into 10's fur. The dog gasped, tilting his head back.

Master nodded, and the movement made 04 turn to face him.

The otter turned to look at him. His red eyes fixated on the husky.

04 felt his heart leap into his throat.

Master looked around for a moment, and then found the bear's duffel bag. "04, please come here," he said.

04 looked around. None of the other dogs had even acknowledged that something was happening. They were just watching their compatriot being defiled. 10 and 16 were still enthusiastically going at it. No one else had reacted in any way.

The husky tore his eyes away and quickly walked to Master. "S-," His voice faltered. He had to clear his throat. "S-sir?" he finally croaked out.

Master was crouched over the bear's bag, digging through it. He pulled out a huge, oversized, smartphone — an older one, by the look of it — and pressed a button. The phone lit up, unlocked. Satisfied, Master put the giant phone back in the bag. He straightened up, all smiles.

"04, I hate to pull you away from the fun, but would you please go bring this to 01?"

04 felt his eyes widen. Take it to 01? He pictured the massive angry jaguar scowling at him. "S-s-sir?" he stammered.

Master smiled at him. "It's okay. He'll be waiting for you. He's waiting for 16's information so he can do a little research. It's the rest of his onboarding." He waggled his eyebrows. "I hate to tear you away from the party. But based on the husky cum I smell on you, you had your fun already." He raised an eyebrow mischievously, smirking.

Horrified, 04 lowered his eyes. "Yes, Master. Right away, Master." Avoiding eye contact, he reached for the bag.

"04," Master said.

The husky died a little inside. He looked up. "Y-yes, Master?" he asked.

The otter was staring directly at him. "You're a good boy." He reached up to cup 04's muzzle. "You're a perfect little bitch dog and I love you."

The words hit 04 like an ocean wave. He reeled, absorbing Master's praise, his head swimming as the words poured over him like hot wax, sinking into him, warming him. His head spun.

Perfect little bitch dog.

"Th-thank—" 04 gasped. He struggled to get the words out. He swayed, dizzily, and he could barely breathe. "Thank you, Master," he gasped, blinking back tears.

The otter beamed back at him and it warmed 04 up from within.

Unable to keep the smile off his face, 04 hefted the huge, heavy oversized bag, and opened the door into the cold arctic air.

Inside 01's lab, as always, it was stiflingly hot.

The black jaguar was at his desk. He looked up as 04 opened the door, yellow eyes wide and annoyed. He wasn't wearing the usual sweatshirt-and-parka combo that 04 saw him in almost year-round. Inside his lab, he wore only a t-shirt and a pair of their standard-issue small cotton workout shorts, his beefy legs and huge broad panther feet bare on display. It was the only time that 04 could see the jaguar's naturally thick and muscular body, though he hardly ever dared to look.

He walked in and sniffed deeply, reflexively. The room was full of 01's scent, which to 04 smelled like a combination of warming spices — ginger and cloves and coriander.

"Don't any of you ever *knock?*" growled the big cat.

04 felt his ears fold back against his head. "I'm sorry, sir. Master said you would be waiting."

The jaguar stared at him. His eyes darted to the enormous duffel bag that 04 was holding. "Is that the bear's?"

04 nodded.

01 nodded back at him. "Okay. Come in then, 06. You're letting the heat out."

04 frowned. "I'm 04."

The jaguar's eyebrows furrowed. "Fine. Come in, 04, you're letting the heat out."

Frowning, 04 stepped into the room. He had to turn sideways to fit the bag through the door.

He had barely gotten it through the narrow hallway. 01's lab, which was also his quarters, was half of the Master's trailer. There was a hallway running the length of the trailer, giving both quarters an exit into the main connection hallway instead of exiting to the frigid Arctic exterior, but the space was small and awkward. It was also perfectly ambient, which made 04 a little annoyed; the connecting hallway was probably 65°, so he didn't see why 01 was complaining, except of course 01's lab was probably closer to 85°.

He staggered in. The room was twelve by twelve. 01 had a desk with four computer monitors, where he did…something 04 knew absolutely nothing about. There was a stainless-steel lab table, and a lot of equipment that 04 absolutely did not recognize. In one corner was 01's bed, which was huge, since 01 was easily eight feet tall, towering over 04 and all of the dogs, even 02 and the malamutes. The space was filled with plants, including what 04 thought was a huge monstera nearly grazing the ceiling, and lit by one big window in each side wall. The windows were covered over with water vapor, lending them a bright, frosted glass look.

01 rolled over in his chair. "Bring that over here," he ordered.

04 set the bag down on the floor in front of him, crouching behind it. He swallowed, struggling to keep his tongue in his mouth, as he already felt the urge to pant. 04 much preferred the 40° outside to the sweltering heat of 01's lab.

The jaguar reached his massive hands into the bag, digging out the phone immediately. It had looked like a tablet in Master's hands, but in 01's huge cat paws it just looked like a normal cellphone.

04 must have stared at it a little too long because 01 looked at him. The husky felt himself wither.

"Go sit on the sofa," 01 ordered.

Nodding, 04 scrambled to his feet and moved over to the couch.

It was huge, scaled for someone 01's size, and probably ten or twenty years old. 04 hefted himself up onto the cushion. He sat, trying not to pant.

01 dug through boxes until he found a connector. He plugged the phone into his computer and started tapping keys.

Roasting, 04 opened his mouth a little. He tried to pant quietly.

01 noticed immediately. He glanced at the dog, face severe and blank.

The husky grimaced. "Sorry, sir," he rumbled.

"You may remove your shirt," the jaguar told him.

04 felt his heart swell. "Thank you, sir!" he burst. Writhing out of his shirt, he pulled it off and dropped it next to him, and immediately felt much better as his fur could finally radiate some of the heat he was holding. He sat back on the couch, clad only in his jockstrap, his mouth half-open, relaxing.

Rolling his eyes, 01 went back to his work. His fingers flew over his keyboard, and after a moment a number of windows opened up. They had little icons that looked like phone apps.

01 started with the camera gallery. He pulled the window up to his biggest monitor and dragged the photo folder up, filled with previews, viewing them 16 at a time. 04 watched silently from the couch. The sofa was big and soft and the heat was making him tired. 04 was a little scared of 01 but he liked him a lot. The thought of taking a nap on the big jaguar's sofa while the cat worked filled him with another kind of warmth. But he knew 01 wouldn't like that, so he willed himself to stay awake.

The bear didn't have many photos. Almost none of them were of people. There were a lot of photos of the Alaskan landscape. 01 scrolled down, and 04 could tell what season the pictures had been taken because there was a clear change from the beautiful wild garden that was Alaska's short summer, to the gray wintery snowscape of the winters. As he watched, year after year passed by. 04 counted at least five different seasonal cycles.

Buildings, vehicles, supply shipments, documents. Occasionally a person. Occasionally some pornography. Pretty vanilla stuff, though 04 noticed both men and women. Mountains. Ships on the dock. Tiny quarters on a fishing boat. Lots of seascapes.

04 worried. Something was bothering him. Something about the bear, how they'd just picked him up from the mine. How close the mine was. But he couldn't think of it. It was like a name or a place he was trying to remember.

The jaguar brought up a beautiful picture of a rainbow over the ocean, with the bear in front of it. His one and only selfie.

01 glanced back at the husky. "Not a terribly exciting fellow, this polar bear."

04 blinked slowly. "Blue collar jobs. No family. No close friends."

The big cat raised an eyebrow. "Hm," he said. "Some of you *do* pay attention."

It was a backhanded compliment, but a compliment nonetheless. 04 leaned back on his tail so 01 wouldn't hear him wagging.

01 pulled open another window from 16's phone and dragged it onto the larger screen. 04 saw a series of questions.

> *I am happy with how my life has turned*
> *out.*
> *1. Strongly Agree*
> *2. Mostly Agree*
> *3. Neither Agree Nor Disagree*
> *4. Disagree*
> *5. Strongly Disagree*

The bear had selected choice 5.

04 only saw one page, but all of the questions were like that.

> *I feel confident in the choices I have*
> *made.*
> *When I make a decision, I stick by it.*
> *I have control over my life.*
> *Someone would miss me if I was gone.*

04 felt a chill at the last question. Once again, the last choice had been selected: ***Strongly Disagree.***

01 glanced back over his shoulder and caught the husky staring. 04 felt himself shrivel. He tried to sink into the couch.

"Since you're watching over my shoulder," the jaguar rumbled, "You might as well come up here."

Ears back, 04 pried himself off the sofa and slunk to where 01 was perched in his chair. He stood next to him, trying not to lower his head too far so he wouldn't embarrass himself with a full submission display.

The huge jaguar turned to him, and very slowly, looked him up and down his nearly-naked form. 04 was suddenly acutely aware that he was standing in front of the facility's second in command in only his jockstrap.

01 stared, sniffing deeply, leaning his big head in. "Out running, were we?" He stared at the husky's bare chest, his nostrils flaring.

04 felt himself shrivel. "Sorry, sir," he mumbled.

01 blinked. He seemed surprised. "I wasn't complaining," he grumbled. "You're just…very…concentrated." He looked up into the dog's eyes, and then turned to show him the screen. "What I'm looking at now is an assessment test. It's very common in psychological evaluation, but not very reliable. We use it to gauge general life satisfaction."

He flipped to the next screen. The questions changed.

> *I feel happy most of the time.*
> *I am often unable to be consoled.*
> *When change happens, I recover quickly.*
> *Sometimes, I want to die.*

That was the last question on the page. 04 couldn't see the answer. He was glad.

01 tapped down a few more screens. 04 glanced at the scroll bar. The screen was only scrolled down a quarter of the page.

The husky frowned. "How many questions are there?"

01 shrugged. "Usually a hundred."

The husky turned to him. "D…did I take a test like this?" He stared. "For my…onboarding?"

01 cracked a humorless smile. "No. Your *onboarding* was…a little different."

The husky thought about that, and nodded. "Oh," he said, softly.

"The rest of the phone research is very basic. Just looking for red flags." With astonishing speed, 01 checked every app's storage files. The bear didn't have any social media so 01 didn't have anything to look at there. His browser history was all vanilla porn or very basic informational searches. 04 stared. The bear didn't seem to have much going on.

The last thing 01 opened was a questionnaire with information like the bear's full name, last addresses, and social security number.

"Background check," 04 said, before he could stop himself.

01 nodded. "Very good. That's the last stage we handle here." He opened a program called PERSONA SEARCH and started entering the bear's information.

The husky frowned. "Why are you manually entering this? He could have just sent it to us."

01 grunted. "Too much of a trail. If someone does come looking for our dear bear friend, it would be far too good a clue that he transmitted his social security number and credit history a week before he dropped off the face of the earth."

04 couldn't keep the frown off his face. "But he emailed Master. I heard him say it. There's *already* a trail." He took his eyes off the screen and turned to the jaguar.

The big cat raised his eyebrows. "He sure did."

They stared at each other.

He agrees with me, 04 thought.

The thought made him worry.

01 looked at him another second longer, and then went back to entering information.

04 let out a shaky breath. He felt worse now than he did before.

01 glanced at him. "Don't worry. It hasn't backfired yet. At least I convinced Master to do a thorough personality check before he claimed anyone else." He hit a button and results started scrolling.

04's ears perked. "Huh? When does that happen?"

01 glanced at him, cracking a small smile. "It's happening right now."

04 stared at him, and then thought back to what he'd seen in the cabin.

Master had told the bear to "test out" anyone he'd seen on the way in. He'd noted the results. Master had directed the bear to choose a shepherd, which had predictably resulted in the bear getting snarled at by 02, and then watched how he handled it. Master had observed what the bear's preferences were and seen how the bear handled a shy, nervous shepherd.

It hadn't been playtime. It had been an evaluation.

He stared in wonder.

01 was still scrolling. "Hmm, I'm starting to see why Master picked this bear up off the street. No family, no business connections, no address for more than a year, no solid career. He won't be missed. He certainly can pick them."

04 frowned. "He'll be missed by the gold mine."

01 glanced at him. "He'll put in his notice as if he's leaving the job. Standard practice. Master made you all do it. Then he'll be part of our happy family."

The husky snorted skeptically.

01 paused, and then slowly turned to face the dog.

04 felt himself wilt. He fought the urge to curl himself into a ball.

He'd thought that 01 would be mad, but he wasn't. In fact, the cat was *curious.* This, of course, was worse.

The jaguar stared at him. "Tell me why you did that."

The husky writhed under the cat's gaze. "I'm sorry, sir," he said, hurriedly. "It won't happen again."

The jaguar leaned forward. "Has Master told you everything is fine?"

04 stared at him. "I...I can't remember?"

The jaguar nodded slowly. Now he looked concerned.

01. Was looking at him. *With concern.*

04 felt his ears flatten against his head. Now he did dip his muzzle, hunching his head. As much as he tried to still his body, he felt himself begin to shiver.

The jaguar's eyebrows rose. He was studying 04 intently now.

04 felt a crushing sense of guilt. It was getting hard to breathe. "I'm sorry," he whispered. "I'm sorry. Can I please go? I'll come back later. P-please. I just have to g—"

"Look at me," 01 interrupted. He pointed at his eyes. "Look me in the eyes." He leaned forward.

Cowering, 04 did as he was instructed. He wanted to curl into a ball instead of making eye contact with the jaguar. 01 was tall, and seated, they were more or less at eye level. The husky stared into the jaguar's yellow eyes.

"Good," 01 told him. "Keep looking into my eyes. *Sleepy puppy.*"

The words washed over 04. He straightened up, surprised, his eyebrows rising. The feelings of panic started to drain out of him like 10's dirty dishwater, the gray cloudiness swirling down the drain.

"Wh...what?" he breathed. Something was happening. 01 was doing something to him. "Wh—"

"Sssshhh," the jaguar cut him off. "Keep looking. *Sleepy puppy.*"

04 jerked gently again, his body jolting, and when he stopped moving, he felt completely at ease. In fact, he was starting to feel numb.

He stared into the jaguar's eyes. They were beautiful. He didn't want to look away now. 01 was beautiful, and 04 loved staring at him. He stared, holding perfectly still, his mouth slightly opening. Things were getting hazy. He felt so much better.

"That's a good boy," the jaguar purred. "Keep looking. Such a good boy. Take a deep breath and hold it."

04 inhaled and held it. He was feeling warm and relaxed. The big jaguar reached up and touched the sides of 04's face, and then his shoulders, and then his bare sides, and 04 was slightly surprised to find himself frozen in place. The jaguar pushed him gently, but his body just would not move out of position, almost reflexively. His body felt heavy and lethargic and immobile.

"Let it out," 01 ordered, and 04 exhaled. As the breath left him, so did the last of his energy, and he stood perfectly still. His eyes wouldn't even stay all the way open now, and his vision occluded as his eyes slid half-shut. He was so relaxed. He felt amazing.

Still he stared at the big cat, and it occurred to him that he was slipping under, and 01 wasn't supposed to be able to *do* that, only *Master* was, and while this wasn't the same kind of brute-force takeover that Master exerted, 01 was absolutely unequivocally taking control of the husky's mind and body. He noted this the way he might note the current weather, because it was getting harder and harder to think, and 04's thoughts got hazier and hazier, and everything was lost in the warm, comforting, cat-spiced fog that was completely overtaking him.

Watching him, the cat rumbled. He reached up and stroked 04's face. "Repeat after me," he said. "You are a good and obedient dog."

04 stared at him. He could barely stand, eyes half closed, ears drooping. "I am a good and obedient dog," he murmured. The words sapped even more of his energy. All of his resistance was gone.

"It feels good and right to give me control," the cat instructed. He touched the dog's shoulders.

"It feels good and right to give you control," the husky mumbled back. His arms dangled uselessly at his sides, tingling from the jaguar's touch. He was 01's now. He would do anything the cat told him to do. He fought to keep his eyes open, even as slits, because the jaguar had told him to keep looking. His eyes were so beautiful. They compelled him.

"You hear me and obey."

04 swayed gently. Hearing the words filled him with dull pleasure. It was so hard to speak, but it felt good to say the refrain back. "I hear you and obey," he rumbled.

"Good, good dog," the jaguar told him, squeezing his cheek ruffs and roughly rubbing his head. "Good *sleepy puppy*." The jaguar's paws were huge and all but enveloped his head. 04 barely felt it. He couldn't think and he couldn't feel his body. He only knew pleasure and 01's will.

The jaguar sat back. He just watched 04 for a moment, staring at the tranced husky.

04 just stared back, swaying gently on his feet. He awaited his next orders.

"Now then," 01 said. The jaguar reached up to stroke his chin. "04...you're a very good dog. Your Master and I need your help with something. Tell me you'll obey."

The words sent a charge of pleasure through 04's entire body. "I will obey," he breathed.

01 nodded. "Good, then. Close your eyes."

04 complied, instantly.

"Good. Now, I need you to access your mind. Think of it like the bear's phone. I need to plug into you and get some information. Tell me your mind belongs to me."

04 let out a shallow breath. "My mind belongs to you."

"Very good. I want you to observe your mind before you, on a screen, just like we were both looking at. A list of programs, all with their own data. Can you see it, 04?"

04 swayed, processing this. In front of him appeared a screen, one icon at the top followed by a series of icons below it. At the top, instead of a phone logo, he saw a stylized husky face. There was a little "04" superimposed over it.

"I see it," he rumbled.

"Excellent. Now, 04, one of these programs has an error in it. It's giving you trouble."

04 felt himself frown. There was a little red exclamation point in a triangle over the husky icon now.

"Very good. You see what I mean. Now, 04…I need to know where the trouble is coming from. Tell me if you understand."

"I understand," 04 said.

"Is it 02?" the jaguar asked. "Open up the apps and tell me."

04 frowned. As he watched, a folder called DOGS opened up, followed by a subfolder called SHEPHERD DOGS. Inside that folder were thumbnails of all the dog's faces. 02's was first. He was frowning.

04's limited intellect couldn't tell if that was what the jaguar meant. "I…I don't know," he whispered, agitated.

"Scan it for errors," the jaguar offered. His voice was confident, and it calmed the husky.

As he watched, a little icon appeared over 02's face. SCANNING, it said, in a green computery font. A little progress bar climbed toward full.

```
Scanning...
====
25%...
50%...
75%...
100%...
====
SCAN COMPLETE. NO ERRORS
FOUND.
```

Eyes still closed, 04 furrowed his brow. "No error," he whispered.

"Hm," the jaguar said, in front of him. "Expand your scan to the entire residency."

04 watched as the **SHEPHERD** file closed, and then the **DOGS** file, in a main file called **PACK**. The scan appeared again.

He watched, silently.

Suddenly, a little red exclamation point appeared. **ERROR**, the text said.

04 gasped. "Error," he said.

"Mmm," the jaguar grunted. "Open folders until you find the problem."

"Yes, sir," 04 whispered back. He did. **PACK**, opened. **SHEPHERD DOGS** was clear. **HUSKY DOGS** was clear. **MALAMUTES** was clear. 01 was clear. The last folder had a big red **X**.

It was 16's face.

"Bear," 04 growled.

"Hmmmm," 01 mused. "Run a diagnostic. Tell me what the problem is."

04 watched as this happened by itself.

DIAGNOSTIC...
====
10%...
25%...
50%...
75%...
90%...
100%
====
ERROR: DANGER TO MASTER.

04 gasped. "Danger to Master," he whispered.

01 was close, leaning forward. "Diagnose danger," he said.

DIAGNOSTIC...
====
10%...
25%...
====
ERROR: ACCESS DENIED.

The husky felt his heart pounding. "Access denied," he whimpered.

"Administrator credentials 01," the jaguar growled. 04 felt strong paws roughly grasp the sides of his face again. 01's thumbs were over his muzzle, tilting his head gently upward, exposing his throat. "Override Infallible Master protocol."

DIAGNOSTIC...
====
10%...
25%...

04 watched, his heart pounding.

50%...
75%...
90%...
100%...

Text filled the screen.

MASTER BEING TOO RISKY MASTER BEING TOO RISKY MASTER BEING TOO RISKY MASTER BEING TOO RISKY MASTER BEING TOO RISKY MASTER BEING TOO RISKY MASTER BEING TOO RISKY MASTER BEING TOO RISKY MASTER BEING TOO RISKY MASTER BEING TOO RISKY MASTER BEING TOO RISKY MASTER BEING TOO RISKY MASTER BEING TOO RISKY MASTER BEING TOO RISKY

04 snapped his eyes open. "*Master's being too risky!*" he gasped.

01 recoiled, golden eyes wide, eyebrows up, ears back, mouth open. He looked as scared as 04 had ever seen him.

The husky barely noticed. "Master's being too risky!" he repeated. "He just picked that bear up off the street! The mine is too close. We don't know what's going on there!" He gasped. He couldn't catch his breath. "He already left an electronic trail and now he's here! We're *walking distance* down the r-r-road! Someone will come for him and *find us!*" He gasped, his tongue lolling out. How could this happen? Master didn't make mistakes. Master was perfect. 04 couldn't bear the thought of questioning him. He felt horrible, miserable, agony deep in his guts. He knew he was a bad dog for even considering this. He couldn't breathe. His tongue lolled out of his mouth, and he couldn't get enough air. He couldn't breathe. He couldn't breathe. He couldn't breathe.

"It's okay, it's okay, it's okay!" 01 assured him, grabbing his shoulders. He gathered up the husky and squeezed him. "*Sleepy puppy! Sleepy puppy!*"

04 writhed in his grasp. "*It's not okay! Master is in danger!*"

"Sssshhh," 01 growled, tightening his grasp. He was so strong, bear-hugging the husky, pinning his arms to his sides. It was terrifying *and* comforting at the same time. "Master is fine! Master's in the cabin! Master has all his good dogs to protect him! *Sleepy puppy!*"

04 jerked, squirming in 01's arms, his arms pinned to his sides. His legs gave out, and now 01 was holding all of his weight. 04's body and brain were trying to shut down, but there was a hole in his heart that prevented him from fully relaxing. "I'm a bad dog," he whimpered. "I've doubted Master."

"It's okay. You're a good, good dog," 01 purred into his ear. "You're just concerned for Master. Sometimes Master makes mistakes."

"No he doesn't," whimpered 04. He buried his nose against 01's chest.

"Of course he does," 01 said. "But you can't see it because of your programming. No wonder you were so agitated. You poor sweet dog. But you can relax now, *sleepy puppy*. I'm going to help you."

04 felt himself starting to slip again. "You...you will?" He was having trouble keeping his eyes open. The warmth of 01's body was starting to seep through 04's thick fur.

"Yes, good boy. I hereby grant you a one-time exception to your programming. Please raise your concerns to your Master so you can help keep him safe. Administrator clearance 01."

"Thank you," 04 mumbled. "We're...we're all in danger."

04 didn't notice, but the jaguar was silent for a long time after that.

When 01 did finally start talking again, his voice was shaky. "F...first thing tomorrow, okay, 04? See Master first thing in the morning, tomorrow."

"First thing tomorrow," the husky mumbled back.

"Good boy," the jaguar said, into his ear. He was still holding the dog's entire body weight. "Here, let's calm you down. Stand up, *sleepy puppy*," he ordered. The jaguar turned 04 around, facing away from him, and gently lifted the dog onto his feet.

04 put his feet under him as best he could. His footing wasn't sure but he did stay upright, gently swaying. Standing up and holding his eyes open was taking way too much energy, so he finally closed his eyes.

01 pressed up against him, still seated in his rolling chair. He scooted forward on the seat and straddled the husky, his thick thighs on either side of 04's hips, and reached around him, squeezing the smaller dog. He flattened out his palms, rubbing them up and down the dog's fluffy stomach.

04 writhed in pleasure. He lifted his head up, moaning.

"*There we go*. What a good boy," 01 rumbled. He rubbed 04's entire body with his huge jaguar palms, stroking his entire stomach and chest, the underside of his throat, the front of his legs, his bulge.

04 squirmed in pleasure, and stood gently at attention.

After a moment he felt thick jaguar claws slide in between the strap of his jock and his hips. 01 gently lifted the pouch off of his sheath and balls, and carefully tugged the strap down over 04's muscular legs. It cleared his big quads and dropped onto the floor.

Dazed, eyes closed, 04 stood in 01's quarters, completely naked.

A moment later the cat's hands were back on him, again from behind, but now more gentle and deliberate. 01's fingerpads traveled over his stomach, and then chest, and then they diverged. 01's left hand settled under 04's muzzle, roughly holding his entire lower jaw in place. The cat's right hand settled on the husky's sheath.

04 squirmed, letting out a quiet grunt, writhing under the cat's ministrations. The hand on his jaw tightened, almost painfully, lifting his head and exposing his throat, and the other hand gently massaged his sheath.

It felt good and the heat and the cat's scent quickly overwhelmed him. Even tranced, 04's cock slid smoothly out of his fat sheath and into 01's waiting paw.

01 slowly and gently stroked the dog's shaft. "See?" he rumbled. "Would a bad boy get a reward like this?"

"Nnnh!" 04 gasped. He tried to hump 01's hand, but he was trapped between the cat's thick thighs and his iron grip. He had no choice but to stand there and take it at the pace 01 was setting.

"Answer me," 01 ordered. "Would I do this for a bad dog?"

"No," 04 grunted. "Only a good dog."

"Say you're a good dog," 01 growled in his ear. He wouldn't speed up. Same achingly slow pace.

"I-I'm…I'm a good dog!" 04 gasped.

"Good. Good dog. Good *sleepy puppy*," 01 purred in his ear.

04 felt himself sliding, deeper and deeper. He felt like he was falling out of his body.

01 went on and on and on. 04 felt his body and his thoughts get further and further away. He might have been asleep, or deep in trance, or dreaming, he didn't know which, but he did know that 01 just held him in place and edged him for a long, long time.

"Mmmmm, you like me, don't you, *sleepy puppy?*" the jaguar finally rumbled.

04 roused from the depths of his stasis. "I love you," he rumbled.

"Oh, that's so nice of you," 01 rumbled. "Would you…feel better…if I fucked you, sweet puppy?"

04 let out a shallow breath. "Yes, sir," he answered without opening his eyes.

"Well," 01 whispered. "The good dog is going to get a reward now."

01's hands left him, but only for a few moments.

Then he felt rough hands on him, all over him, under his tail. Slick lube. Working all over him, then into him. He was so relaxed. The sensations felt so good. Huge hands slid under his arms and his body grew light as he was lifted off of his feet.

He dangled for a moment, and then he came down on something hard, directly under his tail. 04 could barely feel his body, but he knew what this was — 01's rigid monster cock. There was resistance as 01 lined him up, and then a bending, and then a sudden rush as the cat's impossibly thick member impaled him. 04 was completely limp and felt almost completely numb, but he felt a stretching, and then incredible fullness. He kept sliding down, down, down, until it seemed that his entire insides were pushed aside for 01's invading shaft, and only then did he settle against the cat's warm lap.

Strong, big arms curled around 04's chest again, and he leaned back against the jaguar. His whole world was fullness and pleasure. 01 whispered things to him, things that never reached 04's conscious mind, and the magic the cat was making in his brain mixed with the dull, throbbing, inexorable pleasure from his guts, and 04 floated on a cloud of ecstasy. The only sense that was telling him anything was his nose, and his nose was telling him all about the jaguar, and bliss.

01's whispering increased in urgency, and 04 felt his body respond. He pushed back against the cat, and he felt the jaguar grasp his thighs and push 04's muscular husky butt down onto his member, grinding the dog into his lap, and 04 just floated along as if caught in a warm rushing wave. 01 was in control of 04's body now, as well as his mind, and the husky loved him and trusted him and patiently waited for release.

Some part of 04's brain was aware that he had done a good job when the cat grunted and seized and pushed him down and held him there. Then there was more whispering in his ear and 04 was shocked to find himself climaxing, writhing in the jaguar's grasp but failing altogether to escape. He felt his climax splatter his stomach and chest, and he smelled both of their semen.

"Good dog," 01 grunted in his ear. "Good, good d-dog," he gasped, shivering. "Go to sleep now, *sleepy puppy.*"

04 went to sleep.

"Wake up, 04," someone said, gently shaking him awake.

04 sleepily opened his eyes. He was warm and somewhere soft. He slowly blinked awake.

A massive black jaguar was staring at him from a few inches away.

04 awoke with a start. He looked around, wide-eyed. He was on 01's sofa, in his jock and shirt. Oh God, he'd fallen asleep after all. "I'm so sorry, sir!" he burst, jerking his head up, eyes wide. *"Please forgive me!"*

01 cracked a rare smile. "It's okay, 04. The check is done. Can you bring it over to Master?"

04 wriggled to a sitting position. "Yes, sir!" He scrambled off the sofa. His entire body was sore, and for a moment, his legs gave out. Jesus, how long had he been asleep? His legs were killing him. Insanely, his asshole felt sore. He struggled to stay on his feet. Why did his whole body ache?

01 frowned at him. "Please relax," he said. "You were out for a while."

04 swallowed. "I'm sorry, sir. It'll never happen again."

The jaguar blinked at him. "Do you remember anything else?"

04 thought. He had watched the background check and then…fallen asleep? "N-no, sir?"

The jaguar seemed to be considering, for several long moments, and then cracked a little smile. "We had sex, 04. You stripped down to your jockstrap, and I—" The jaguar swallowed. He actually looked a little flushed. "I really just liked that a lot," he said.

04 stared at him, blankly, and then suddenly the memories came rushing back to him. Sinking down on 01's huge jaguar meat. His scents. The feeling of the cat's paws on 04's body.

The husky stared, eyes wide. "I-I-I-I…I can't believe I forgot sir, I'm so sorry." He was blushing with his whole face and he could feel the heat in his chest too. Holy shit. 01 had fucked him. He stared at the cat in disbelief. His mouth opened reflexively and he started panting. The afterglow washed back over him. His whole body remembered the sensation at once.

The cat smiled at him. He was so handsome. "It's okay, 04. The heat is probably getting to you." He leaned back in his crouch. "And…don't worry. I'm just another drone. I'm just like you."

04 swallowed. "Y-yes, sir. I knew that." Right? Of course he knew that. "I just…" He looked at the cat. "I just didn't think you liked me, sir."

01 looked at him, and slowly frowned. He was quiet for a long moment. Finally, he spoke. "I like you just fine, 04. I like all of you. I just…this place…the things he's doing here…" The jaguar got a faraway look in his eyes, and trailed off.

04 didn't know what to say to that, so he didn't say anything.

01 suddenly brightened. "Anyway! Please bring this report to Master." He held up a sheaf of papers. "And…thank you for raising your concerns. Please raise them to Master." He smiled. "We appreciate your concern for our well-being."

04 felt his heart swell, and he nodded. He felt so much better than he had when he walked in. The sex had been good, but the relief was better.

"Thank you, sir!" 04 burst. He beamed, wagging, and gratefully accepted the papers from the jaguar.

01 smiled at him. "That'll be all, 04."

Smiling, the husky nodded and headed for the door.

When he got back to the cabin, three of the shepherds were tapped out. 05, 08, and 09 were seated or laying against the back wall. 05 had a Gatorade. 08 looked like he was on the verge of unconsciousness. 10 looked exhausted but was sitting and watching, his ears drooping, his face and chest wet and matted with…something.

The massive polar bear was on all fours, a fallen deity. 03 was crouching, humping the bear's mouth. 02 was on top of the bear, robotically fucking him, growling softly and pumping like an oil derrick. 02 was seven feet tall but he looked so small humping the much-larger bear. Any other third party wouldn't even have been visible between the two huge shepherds.

16 was on his hands and knees, panting, slobbering on 03's cock, his eyes unfocused but maniacally eager, his face and chest fur matted with spit, sweat, and cum. 04 could finally see the bear's huge black cock swinging underneath him, rock-hard and dripping like a leaky faucet, and surmised with some alarm that Master had still not let him cum. 02's relentless pounding was squelching with every thrust, and 04 could see that lube and cum had dripped down both of the polar bear's inner thighs, down to his knees. He looked crazed, horny, and ecstatic.

Eyes wide, 04 turned to Master.

The otter gave him a big grin. "You missed quite a show, 04," he said. He looked the husky over, his nostrils flaring, and sniffed him. He leaned in, and 04 knew the otter could smell 01's hands all over him. "Hmm. Or maybe you didn't," he said, raising his eyebrows, amused.

04 swallowed. "Show still seems to be going, Master." Clearing his throat, he handed over 01's report. "Here you are, Master."

"Thank you, 04!" Master took the papers and looked down. He took his time reading the first page.

04 watched Master for a moment, and then turned his head to watch 02 and 03 defile the polar bear. The bear didn't have to stretch his mouth to accommodate 03's cock, and in fact he seemed to be smiling. His eyes were unfocused but happy. On top of him, 02 was panting, pounding him, dripping sweat and drool onto the back of the polar bear's neck.

04 was fairly spent, but the show was exciting, nonetheless. He stared, amazed, until Master cleared his throat.

The husky turned to look at him. The small otter was smiling. "Well! It seems we'll have a new addition to the pack."

04 felt his heart start pounding. He forced a smile, but the information had a...finality to it. He thought of begging Master not to go through with it. But he couldn't think of why he would want that. So he just kept his mouth shut.

If the otter noticed, he didn't react. Instead, he walked past 04, toward the messy sex pile in the center of the cabin.

"02! 03! That's enough!" Master said.

03 disengaged immediately, panting hard, his tongue lolling out. He was rock-hard, his cock dripping pre and bear spit all over the floor. He looked relieved to be tagged out.

02 stopped but didn't move. "But Master! I haven't cum!" the huge shepherd protested.

The otter frowned. "You can cum whenever you want. I give you all free rein. Get off the bear."

02 stared at the Master, his brow furrowed, his eyes dangerous. He didn't move.

04 felt his hackles rise. What the fuck? He looked around in disbelief. All of the other dogs had noticed. They were all watching with varying levels of discomfort.

Finally, 03 cleared his throat. "C'mon, 02," he said. "You can fuck me at our quarters." He tried to pass it off casually but 04 could hear his voice shaking.

02 stared defiantly at Master for another long moment, and then finally pulled out of the polar bear.

The bear barely reacted as the huge shepherd pulled his thick cock out of him. He just held himself, still on all fours, looking up at Master, fur matted to his skin, his huge blue tongue hanging out.

Master stared at 02 for another moment, and then stepped up to the bear. He smiled down at him.

The bear looked up at Master, tongue lolling out like a dog, his eyes unfocused. "Master," he rumbled.

"Hello, 16," Master said. "How do you feel?"

The bear beamed up at him. "Wonderful, Master," he rasped.

The otter smiled. He reached down to gently hold the bear's wet, messy head. 04 raised his eyebrows. Let it never be said that the Master minded getting dirty.

"16, it just so happens we have an opening on our team for a security agent. Would you be interested in joining our family to help keep us safe?"

The bear nodded eagerly. "Yes, Master!"

The otter grinned. "Well then, welcome to the team."

The bear grinned massively. His eyes still weren't quite focused, and he looked a little frenetic. 04 watched him, taking a deep breath.

"Stand up, 16," Master instructed.

The bear nodded, lifting himself to his knees, staggering to his feet. He swayed gently. 04 wondered how long he had been on all fours. How long had 04 been gone? He felt like it had been hours.

The massive polar bear stood there, arms relaxed at his side, eyes swimming. He looked eagerly down at Master, a stupid, happy look on his face. He was still fully erect.

04 liked the bear's body but he absolutely couldn't keep his eyes off of 16's cock. It was black, as 04 knew the bear's skin was under his fur, and at least a foot long. The bear's meat was at least as thick around as a wine bottle. He was impressively hard and still leaking, dripping a steady stream of milky white pre down the length of his shaft.

Master, to 04's surprise, leaned over and went right after it.

The otter didn't have to kneel, just sort of crouched, and took the upper half of the bear's cock in his hands. He leaned forward, opening his mouth widely, barely able to get his jaws around the bear's cockhead.

16 gasped, gritting his teeth. His eyes suddenly cleared, and he stared down in plain disbelief at the small otter blowing him. "M-Master!" he gasped.

The otter grunted, making a quiet gagging noise, and dipped his head an inch or two lower, pumping the bear's shaft as he went.

16 gasped, clamping his huge hands into fists at his sides. He squirmed, his entire body tensing, and 04 could tell he was trying not to move, which was probably a good idea if he didn't want to knock down his new boss.

04 stared in disbelief. He knew Master liked to party, but he didn't expect to see him blow a nine-foot polar bear. He looked at the other dogs. The shepherds were all

staring in varying degrees of astonishment. 09 was sitting up now, his jaw hanging open. "Go, *Master!*" he cheered.

After 09 cheered, the rest of them started in, with the exception of 02, who was still scowling. Even 03 was grinning. 04 couldn't believe what he was seeing, but he couldn't help but smile, either. It was mostly barking and howling, but it was *celebratory*.

16 grunted, and then groaned, and then growled deep in his chest, which filled the cabin with deep reverberating sound. "M-master!" he growled. "*I'm close!*" 04 was frankly stunned the bear had lasted this long, after his hours-long sexual adventure.

The small otter doubled down, putting one hand under the bear's heavy dangling balls. He looked up with his searching red eyes, jaw straining.

The bear groaned, gritting his teeth as if in severe pain, and his entire body shivered as he let loose. "*Aaannnggghghhh!*" he snarled.

04 looked down at Master, concerned.

The otter gulped down the first mouthful, but the volume was just too great. He gagged and yanked his head back, and the next blast of cum hit him right in the face. It was like a jet of water from one of 10's kitchen sprayers, and it blasted all over him. He was still pumping, and the bear was still cumming, gushing rope after rope of stunningly thick bear cum into the otter's face, soaking his fur and gushing down his shirt and pants. The cabin already smelled like a sex dungeon, but the fresh acrid scent of so much new semen hit 04's nostrils immediately.

"*YEAHHHH!*" howled 09, throwing one arm up in triumph, and everyone cheered. The bear came for a long time, holding himself frozen in place — grunting and growling and shivering. He didn't buck his hips, but his naked white ass flexed as he strained to hold perfectly still.

Finally, the bear stopped cumming. Panting, tongue hanging out, he looked down. So did 04.

Master looked like he had fallen face-first in wet cement. He squeezed one eye shut. "Owwwww," he groaned, flexing his jaw.

04 and 08 rushed up to Master's side. "Master, are you all right?!" 08 produced a towel. "Sir, close your eyes!"

The otter took a deep breath, gasping. He closed his eyes and let 08 towel the worst of it off of him. "I'm fine! I'm fine!" 08 finished toweling him. The otter's brown fur was still matted to his face with pearly-white semen. "I got overexcited. I really should leave this to you boys."

They exchanged glances.

"Master, that was *amazing*," 09 said, his eyes wide and appreciative.

The otter chuckled. "Was it? Do you boys like your new coworker?"

"Yes Master!" chorused five of the six sheps. 04 looked up at the bear, who was smiling amiably, and still breathing hard.

"Um!" Master announced. He coughed, licking his teeth. "16, I would like to formally welcome you to our facility. Please give whatever notice you need to give at your prior employment and see us as soon as you can."

The bear smiled down at him. "I can start right now, Master!" he said.

04 felt all of his anxiety return in one sharp wave. His stomach dropped. He looked at the otter.

"Oh!" Master said. He pondered. "Well, then. Uh!" He looked around. "These are your quarters. 08, 09, 05, will you help 16 get settled with bedding and such?"

The shepherds in question loudly accepted the order.

Master looked up at 16. "Do you know how to operate and maintain a fireplace? I'm sorry to say this cabin is the only place we have that will accommodate a man of your stature. We have bedding for you, but the cabin doesn't have electric heat yet."

The bear nodded. "No problem, Master. I am a polar bear, after all," he said, smiling.

Master grinned up at him. "Very good. Now then! I hate to leave you, but I somewhat urgently need to take a swim." He smiled. "Your initiation gift to me is starting to dry in my fur."

The bear nodded. "Very good, Master!"

"All right. Everyone else, dismissed!" Master announced.

The shepherds began to file out. Master turned to go.

"Master," 04 said.

The otter turned.

04 swallowed. "Permission to guard you while you swim?"

The otter blinked at him. "Why?" he asked, genuinely confused.

04 forced a smile. "Just want to keep you safe, Master."

The otter's brow furrowed. "I suppose that's fine." He looked down at 04's bare legs. "Maybe you can join me. You have some jaguar to wash off, I think."

04 felt embarrassment overcome his concern. "Y-yes, Master," he said, reddening.

Grinning mercilessly, despite his current condition, the otter chuckled.

RECALIBRATION

The next day, 04 went to see Master in his quarters.

Master didn't necessarily care what the dogs smelled like, and in fact loved to pick them off on their way back from the gym trailer, but 04 wanted to be taken seriously, so he showered freshly and put on uniform pants and a black uniform button-down. 04 had finally gotten a good night's sleep for the first time in days, and he woke up well-rested and pleasantly-sore from 01's manhandling, especially under his tail. He felt good in general, and he felt *great* that he would finally be able to air his concerns to Master.

He thought about *what* he was going to say: the bear was too close, they didn't know anything about the mine, what if he'd left a trail that led back to them? 04 didn't know any details about what was really going on at Master's facility, but he knew they had to stay hidden.

He crossed through the chilly connection hall from the husky quarters, passed the fire doors for the gym and mess trailers, and peered through the door into Master's trailer.

04 entered and knocked on Master's door for a minute, but didn't get an answer, positive or negative. Unless Master was off with one of the dogs somewhere in the facility, that left the research trailer.

Swallowing, 04 returned to the connection hallway and walked ten feet across to the research trailer. His good mood was already starting to erode. Anxiously, he covered his points in his mind: unknown entity, electronic trail, too close.

He opened the door to the research trailer and all of it left his mind like fog blowing off the lake in a storm.

The research trailer had always been creepy to 04. It was a repurposed deployable field hospital, so it was always a little colder than the rest of the trailers. The entire thing was open with nothing to divide it into sections but dangling curtains, and parts of it were currently in use for several of Master's and 01's desks, bookshelves, tall work cabinets with stools, a microscope, several more pieces of lab equipment that 04 did not recognize, general storage, and even a few collapsible gurneys. It had a disheveled, mismatched, cluttered look that 04 hated, especially compared to the brutally-efficient, perfectly-sectioned, purpose-built other trailers.

What immediately grabbed 04's attention, however, was the far end.

This end *had* been a field hospital operating room, which they used for standard medical care - both 13 and 08 were some kind of advanced medic (though they both felt like fully-fledged doctors to 04) and they did most of their medical care on site. It had a huge padded gurney in the center, sized for even the largest of them, with a colossal, imposing surgical light suspended over the ceiling.

On this gurney was 02, completely naked, arms at his side, restrained at his wrists and his ankles. He was laid out flat, staring straight up, eyes wide, mouth open, focused on a small flatscreen monitor on a mechanical arm suspended directly over his face. 04 couldn't see what was on the monitor, but it was so bright it lit up 02's face. He was completely relaxed, his hulking body limp and helpless. 02 was a huge, hulking beast, thickly muscled but not defined, with a gentle curve of a belly and a fat sheath prominently on display. The big king shepherd could easily lift 04 over his head, and seeing him restrained like this wasn't completely unprovocative. 04 knew it was his conditioning, but he felt guilty for it just the same.

Staring, 04 also noticed a device encircling 02's big head, directly next to his huge ears, a large white device with two black pads that looked like RF readers but twice the size, extending down either side of 02's head. 04 couldn't tell what they were but it looked serious. He also noticed that 02's far arm had an IV line trailing up to a hanging bag full of bright green liquid that 04 absolutely could not identify.

He stared, horrified, and slowly felt his hackles rise. They'd never been given drugs before.

A curtain pulled back, and 04 flinched.

Master stared at him. The little otter was wearing a lab coat, which he didn't often do, and glasses, which 04 hadn't known he had. He had a bright and ready smile. "04! What brings you here?"

The husky stared at him, eyes wide, and then turned his head. "I...I..." He couldn't keep his eyes off the restrained shepherd.

Master watched 04 for a second, turning to follow his gaze. He had what appeared to be a moment of recognition. "Oh," he said, flatly. "Mmmm." He frowned, turning his head. "Don't be worried about that. It...looks worse than it is." He grimaced.

"Wh-wh-what's happening to him?" 04 asked. He'd never seen 02 so still. He was definitely breathing but he was making no attempt to move. Just staring straight up at whatever was on the monitor.

Master smiled brightly. "Just…some new techniques we're trying out."

04 swallowed. "I-is…is this my fault?" He grimaced.

Master looked shocked. "Wh…is what your fault?"

04 swallowed a whimper. "Whatever's happening to him. Is this because of the fight? In the mess hall?"

Master stared at him for a moment, and then he softened. "Oh." As 04 expected, Master knew exactly what he was talking about. "No, of course not. That was just…part of a larger pattern." He smiled.

04 frowned. He glanced at the spaced-out shepherd. There had been a pattern. 02 had been growing steadily more…difficult. He'd been unpleasant, and vindictive. They'd all noticed it. The husky swallowed. "Will he be…okay?"

Master smiled sympathetically and let out a long breath. "Of course. This is just a little experiment! This is why we're here, after all."

04 turned to look at him. He stared.

It took him a moment to work up the nerve to speak. "Why…why we're here…?" he repeated, tentatively.

Master started to answer, but the door to the trailer suddenly opened. Master looked over 04's shoulder at the door behind him. 04 whirled in place.

01 was standing in the doorway, the large jaguar wearing a lab coat that 04 could have used as a bedspread. He had a laptop computer under his arm, and he looked up, surprised, eyebrows up. After a moment his expression softened. He stepped into the room, closing the door behind him. "04," he said, slowly. He looked at the laid-out shepherd, and then back. "I'm sorry," he said. "This…wasn't on the schedule."

04 turned back to Master. The otter's eyes were surprised. He looked back and forth between the jaguar and the husky.

01 cleared his throat. "I asked 04 to come see you today. He has…some concerns."

Master stared at the cat for a long time, and then slowly turned to the husky. 04 felt his tail tuck between his legs.

The otter stared at him. "04…is something the matter?" he asked. His tone was gentle. His body language was open. He was responsive. *Why do I feel so terrified?* 04 wondered, straining to keep his ears from flattening against his head.

"Go ahead, 04," the big cat prompted. "Master knows you just want to keep us all safe. It's okay."

The otter watched 01 say this, and then turned to the husky, frowning with concern.

04 took a deep breath. "I have concerns about the bear, Master."

The otter's eyebrows shot up. "16?" he asked.

04 nodded. "Yes, Master. Well…not about *him*. Just…our proximity to the mine." He swallowed. "We just don't know anything about them, Master, and they're very, very close. They're between us and the highway. The bear emailed you, and we don't know the security status of his phone. There might be a trail that leads right to us. I…" He sighed. "I have a bad feeling, Master."

The otter listened to all of this, eyebrows up, mouth slightly opened. "Oh," he said, finally. He looked down, processing all of that.

04 stood patiently in front of him.

"Well," Master said, looking between the husky and the cat. He seemed…at a loss for words.

04 felt his anxiety come creeping back.

Master gathered his thoughts and turned to 01. "I thought we talked about this," he said.

04 raised his eyebrows.

01 nodded. "We did. And I was satisfied at that point. Until I heard from 04."

Master narrowed his eyes. He flashed his sharp little mustelid teeth for a moment. "As you know, this is all under control."

The jaguar stared at him. "Is it?" he asked, icily.

04 felt all the blood drain out of his face. He stared at the two of them, frozen. He had never heard any of them talk to Master like this before. He couldn't move.

The otter seemed unphased, if a little annoyed. "Of course it is," he snapped. "Have we ever had a problem before?"

01 frowned. "Have you ever seen one of the dogs concerned?" he countered.

They both looked at 04. The husky felt his ears flatten against his head.

"Especially *him*, of all of them," 01 said.

04 stared, his eyes widening. Him? What did *that* mean?

Master frowned. He was looking at 04, but not really focusing on him. He seemed to be deep in thought.

01 took a deep breath. "You can ignore my concerns at your prerogative, but if you ignore *his* gut feeling, I have a feeling you do so at all of our peril."

04 couldn't believe this was happening. He looked back and forth between the Master and 01. What did any of this mean?!

The otter looked up at 04, over his glasses, and took a deep breath. Without moving his head, he looked to 01, and then back to 04.

"*Shit*," he said, finally.

04 felt his eyebrows leap up.

Master turned to the jaguar. "Shit," he said again. "You're right. Of course you're right." He thought for a moment. "Um. How much security experience did you turn up in 16's profile?"

01's eyebrows rose. "Uh?" He thought about it. "A lot. Mostly down in Fairbanks. Some up in Prudhoe Bay. Some oil rig experience. One other mining company."

Master nodded. "Good. Find out what he thinks about our setup. Anything he thinks we're lacking, let's consider implementing." He considered. "And see how you feel about it. If you don't have confidence in what he's telling you, let's consider bringing in…outside experience."

01's eyes widened. He looked like he was trying to keep an enraged expression off his face, and only partially succeeding.

Master smiled smugly. "But we'll start with the bear. Sound good?" He looked to both the jaguar and the dog.

01 considered. "Sounds good, sir," he said. He sounded genuine. "Thank you…Master."

Master looked at 04. "Any concerns about the bear himself?"

04 blinked. "No, sir. Just…just what might follow him here." He swallowed.

Master and 01 exchanged a glance.

"Understood, 04." Master smiled. "Thank you for raising your concerns. Anything else bothering you at the moment?"

Involuntarily, 04's eyes flicked to the laid-out shepherd. 02 hadn't moved the entire time. He was just lying there, limp, naked.

Master again followed his gaze, and again, astonishingly, only seemed to remember the helpless king shepherd once he was looking at him. "Ah. Right." He walked toward the dog, waving his arm at 04. "Come here, 04."

04's eyes widened. Immediately, his heart started pounding. He looked toward 01.

The jaguar nodded. He gestured with his muzzle.

Swallowing, 04 loped hesitantly to the far end of the lab, where Master was already standing.

02 looked even more dazed up close. The dog was laid out, eyes half-open, mouth parted, staring up at the monitor a foot away from his face. 04 could see what was on the screen now – a brightly-colored spiral, swimming slowly in unending circles. He could see the bright pink spiral reflected in the shepherd's eyes, giving him a swirly-eyed expression. 04 shivered.

"Come closer!" Master insisted, overly-cheerful. "He can hear you, you know. He knows you're here."

04 looked at the absolutely blank expression on the giant shepherd's face, and then up at Master. "Really?" he asked, dubiously. It didn't seem possible.

Master chuckled. "Sure!" He stepped around to 04's side of the gurney. "Here." He took 04's big husky left hand in his small webbed paws, and hefted it onto 02's soft tummy. He guided 04 into rubbing in a big, gentle circle.

The shepherd started to squirm, gently coming to life, as if rousing from sleep.

Eyes widening, 04 took over and rubbed 02's tummy in a big, lazy circle.

02's eyes lidded to slits and he arched his back, groaning softly. He took a deep breath and let it out as a long, contented sigh.

04 felt himself start to wag.

Master moved around to the base of the gurney, where 02's huge black bare feet were shackled in place by massive leather straps around his thick ankles. The otter raised his hands and dragged his claws down the leather balls of 02's feet, twiddling his fingers on the dog's fat heels.

02 writhed in place, exhaling sharply. He didn't take his eyes off the monitor, but he did start to squirm in discomfort. His mouth opened and his tongue poked out, and he even started panting for a moment.

"See?" Master asked him. He beamed. "Nothing to worry about. You all just…need to be a certain way," he said. "Like the equipment here! You all need to be…in spec. And 02 was getting out of spec. And when a piece of laboratory equipment gets out of spec, you recalibrate it! 02 is being…recalibrated." He offered 04 a smile.

The husky stared at him. He wasn't sure he liked that analogy. He glanced to 01. The jaguar was frowning.

04 turned back to Master to ask something else, but when he turned back, the otter was staring directly at him. His red eyes were intense, and 04 immediately forgot what he was talking about. He couldn't look away. He couldn't even breathe.

He just stared.

"You have nothing to worry about, 04," the otter told him. "Everything is fine."

04 couldn't catch his breath. "I have...nothing to worry about," he repeated back. "Everything...is fine." He was starting to feel hazy. Master's eyes floated in front of him.

The otter stared at him another few moments, and then broke the gaze. He turned away, amiably. "Here, you'll love this." He moved to the head of the gurney.

04 started awake, blinking. His head felt fuzzy. What was happening? He felt warm. His heart was pounding.

"The programming comes in several...flavors," Master said. He picked up a computer tablet attached by USB cable to the monitor over 02's face. "You'll like this one." He tapped the pad several times.

The light over 02's face blinked out, and then changed color to cerulean. 02 blinked lazily a few times, and then his brow furrowed, as he struggled to make sense out of whatever was in front of him. Then, his eyes slowly widened, and his mouth opened.

The shepherd's body came alive. He began squirming, his thick legs and arms tensing. He curled his huge paws into fists. The shepherd started tugging gently against the restraints, his arms and legs flexing gorgeously. The leather creaked, and the gurney made several loud metallic popping noises as it struggled to hold the massive shepherd in place.

02 let out a little groan, gritting his teeth. His package started to swell, and as 04 watched, the shepherd's fat fuzzy sheath opened up and his huge king shepherd cock slid out. He never took his eyes off the monitor, but his expression was intense and focused. He grunted, biting back a whine, and tugged his arms, flashing his teeth. His cock was fully hard now, and he arched his back and then bucked his hips. He stank of arousal now, restrained in place, mind completely under Master's control, helpless. His cock throbbed against his belly, the tip already glistening.

04 stared at it.

Master appeared at his side. "I'm sure 02 would like it if you would help him out right now, 04," he purred. He reached up and 04 felt the otter gently drumming his fingers on the back of his head.

04 stared at the dog's throbbing cock. He wanted it. He *needed it*. He was going into a trance again, he could feel it, but that wasn't going to stop him from planting his muzzle around 02's member and sucking him dry.

Master gently pushed his head downward, toward 02's meat, and 04 let him, and as his nose filled with the scent of 02's cock and he reflexively opened his muzzle, he knew everything was going to be okay. He leaned forward and took 02 into his mouth, and everything slowly faded out.

Someone was gently shaking him.

04 slowly felt himself stir awake. It was chilly, just how he liked it, and he was snuggled in a big soft comforter. He groaned in annoyance.

"04, buddy. Come on," coaxed someone. Firm hands shook his shoulder.

"Nnnnnnnawrooorooooorooooo," 04 grumbled. He was too comfortable. Reluctantly, he opened his eyes.

06 was staring at him, nose to nose. "Hey," he grunted, leaning forward to lick 04's face.

04 grunted in annoyance, but lifted his head. He let 06 lick him for a few moments, as he blinked himself awake.

Bed. He was in bed.

04 snapped fully awake. He was in *bed?* He opened his eyes, and looked around. This wasn't his bed. This wasn't his room.

He looked around. "A-am I in…your bed?" he asked, tentatively.

06 stared at him, and then exhaled in visible relief. "Thank God. You're finally back with us. You were totally out of it all day yesterday."

04 stared at him. "All *day?* What day is it?"

06 frowned. "The twenty ninth."

04 felt his heart start pounding. "The twenty ninth?" He'd lost the entire day after talking to Master. "Wh-what happened to me?"

The other husky swallowed. "I don't know. I found you passed out on the couch in the common area yesterday morning. You weren't talking sense. Something about being in danger and something happening to 02. I could barely get you to eat and then eventually I put you to bed. 13 checked you out and he said you were fine, physically, and I couldn't think of anything else to do." He grimaced.

04 watched him. He had no reason to believe 06 would lie to him. "Thank you for taking care of me." He thought about what 06 said. *Something happening to 02.*

Abruptly, it all came back to him. 02 laid out on the table. The IV. The device.

He inhaled shakily. "D-d-did 02 come back to the pack?" he asked, his voice shaking.

06 stared at him. He took a deep breath, and then let it out slowly. "Well..." He swallowed. "You...probably just need to see for yourself."

04 felt his heart drop into his stomach.

The walk to the shepherd trailer was a short one, but it felt like the deserted Alaskan highway.

By the time they crossed the short connector hallway, 04's adrenaline was racing. His heart was pounding in his chest and he just let his tongue loll out so he could start panting.

06 glanced back at him with a frown.

They crossed to the fire door on the other side, and after a short knock, 06 let himself into the common area in the shepherd trailer. It was exactly like the huskies' trailer, but mirrored.

03 was sitting in a folding chair at their little plastic table. He looked up as they came in, his worried golden eyes standing out in his black face. The shepherd looked at 06 and then 04. His ears weren't flat, but they were ratcheted anxiously backward.

02 was at the table, too. He looked healthy and strong, sat upright, friendly, and attentive. He smiled at them when they came in: ears forward, confident, attentive. 04 had been naked in 06's bed and only put on a pair of shorts, and 02 actually looked the muscular husky up and down. His ears tilted back and he gave 04 a little bashful smirk.

04 stared. He felt cautiously optimistic. 02 looked fine. 02 looked *great*, actually. What the fuck had happened?

"Hey," 03 said. The shepherd had focused on 04 and had been staring at him since he walked in. "How...are you?" he asked, hesitantly. His voice was slow and concerned.

"Fine," 04 said. He was still looking at 02. "How is *he*?"

03 opened his mouth, but didn't say anything.

02 turned his big head to 03, and then back to 04. He was still smiling a big friendly smile. They could all hear his tail wagging behind him.

"I'm fine," 02 said, a big grin on his muzzle. He sounded great, until he continued talking.

His next words made 04's blood drain out of his face.

"I'm 02," he said, with a smile. "Who are you?"

BLOODSTREAM

The next few weeks passed with relative calm.

The day after 04 woke up in 06's bed after losing half a day, Master called an all-staff meeting, and told them that each of them would have to meet with 01 for a short "evaluation." 04's was scheduled last.

He was terrified the entire day, mostly hanging around the mess hall, so he could help 10 with dish duty and also stress-eat, but then his time finally came up. The evaluation was easy, and it passed in a blur. 04 couldn't even remember what they had talked about. He only remembered walking out with a warm, fuzzy feeling that lasted a long time.

His euphoria lasted *days*, in fact. He started sleeping in 06's room and they were having an incredible amount of sex. 04 found himself having sex with a *lot* of people. It was like someone had converted his anxiety directly into pure husky horniness. He fucked 06 in his bed, he let 06 fuck him, he sucked 10 off under his apron in the mess hall, he let the malamutes spitroast him while 07 watched him and masturbated, and he even climbed on top of 11 and pounded him when he knew everybody else would say he was being too rough (11 pronounced him "acceptably energetic"). He hung around Master in hopes of being chosen for the otter's release (and it worked a few times). He even thought about blowing the new polar bear like Master had, but he couldn't work up the nerve.

His mysterious horniness lasted a full week before he could calm down again, and even then, he was still way above his normal arousal level. But he finally felt normal and relaxed again for the first time in weeks, if a little fuzzy. Things went well for another two weeks after that.

Whatever Master had done to 02 had removed a lot of the tension from their lives. The huge shepherd was either with 16 learning about the facility - he genuinely did not remember a single thing prior to his "recalibration" - or with 03 and the other sheps. He steered clear of the huskies, but he wasn't unfriendly. He actually seemed to be a little bit shy, and he could barely tell the huskies apart. He only seemed to know who 04 was, and actually appeared to be nursing a little bit of a crush on him. He was sweet and calm and friendly, and it was like night and day.

04 wondered how much of his newfound relaxation was the result of 02's recalibration. He hadn't realized how much of an incendiary force the big dog had become. 02's buddy 03 certainly seemed a lot calmer now, so maybe that was the reason all of 04's tension was gone. It was a mystery he idly wondered about, dimly and dully, sometimes, when he was running, or on the second supply run to Prudhoe Bay, or on dish duty in the mess. But he wasn't too concerned.

It was mid-October now, and the sun didn't rise until 9 or 9:15 in the morning and was down by 6:30 pm. It often didn't get above freezing anymore, and the nights were as cold as 15° or 20°. There was already snow on the ground — only a few inches, but more would be coming. The lake wasn't completely frozen over but it would be soon; they were already storing water because there wasn't quite enough snow on the ground yet to fully rely on the melt tank. At night they could see the northern lights more and more frequently as night chipped away at more and more of the daylight hours.

All of them were clinging to the last vestiges of the fall, spending as much time outside as they could before the month of darkness coming in December. Temperatures would be 20° below zero in February and March. 04 still went for a daily run, though he had to wear pants and a coat. The harsh arctic winter marched relentlessly toward them.

16 was integrating well. Chef 10 never seemed to leave the polar bear's side after that first night, and once 16 "met" the huskies, 11 quickly peeled off too. One of the two of them was almost always with the polar bear, and now 11 was often helping in the kitchen. 04 couldn't remember a single time he had seen 10 and 11 interact prior to 16's arrival, but now the bear had seemingly brought the slim husky and the beefy chef shepherd together as much as he had drawn them to himself. It was rare to see any of them without at least one of the other two. The dogs were easy and relaxed with one another.

For some reason 04 couldn't recall, they were doing a security overhaul of the entire facility, and 16 was leading it. Shortly after 16's initiation, Master took 01 and 16 down to Fairbanks, after taking two benches out of the Suburban so the big jaguar and polar bear could fit inside. When they came back they had a trailer full of crates. 04 had helped unload them, and the boxes were *heavy*. A lot of them held electronics equipment. Many of them were marked "LIVE AMMUNITION" and he recognized several long rifle cases.

Right after that a bank of monitors went up in the research trailer, and another in the mess, showing live security feed around their facility and the surrounding area. Two of the cameras were mounted on their trailers, trained on the road. One of them was all the way down the access road twenty miles away, filming their turnoff to the Dalton Highway. The only thing they couldn't see was the…what was it? There was some other kind of facility on the road with them. He couldn't quite remember what it was, though. It was probably fine.

In addition to the cameras and monitors, 16 was now certifying many of them with firearms. They set up a shooting range behind the cabin and he had at least two of them practicing there once a day. 03 and 05 were the best at it, with 14 and 15 close behind, though 04 was pretty good too. The guns felt heavy and familiar in his hands and he loaded and cleaned them with ease. A few of the dogs, including 06, were scared to even touch them, so they got to be exempt. Idly, 04 wondered what the reason was for the overhaul, but nothing came to mind so he just didn't worry about it. Once he got over his horniness, everything felt dull and relaxed to him. Dull and relaxed and calm.

16 learned sign language in record time, and the malamutes began to hang out in his cabin, bringing 07 along with them. They had a spare bed in one of their quarters that they brought to 16's cabin to use as a makeshift lounge space. 04 originally thought it was because of the structure's high ceilings, since both 14 and 15 were seven feet tall and their ears almost grazed the ceilings in the trailers, but later he tagged along with 06 and found out why.

16 kept the fire going all the time in his cabin, and true to his word, Master had procured electric heating. Now that it was lived-in, the cabin was a delight. It could hold all of them, and many nights it did. Even on their 20° evenings the cabin was warm and cozy and inviting. They had already been storing some of the extra bedding in the cabin, and they moved in some of the extra furniture. 12 could sew, and with a few of the other dogs' help, they made cushions out of old fabric.

It was a nice little space. One night 10 had made little bread treats that he served with marinara sauce, and another night he made some kind of fruit crumble in a cast-iron dutch oven, right on the fire, which made the cabin smell amazing. 01 surprised them all by setting up some of his equipment as a projector with little speakers, using a sheet as a projector screen. They watched a movie from the 1960s called *Mirage*. 04 couldn't remember the last time he had seen a movie, and while the plot was difficult to follow, he just sat, wedged in between 05 and 06, enjoying their warmth, and watched. The cabin took on an almost dorm-like feel, and in two weeks, most of them went from hanging out in their own rooms at night after-shift, or the tiny gathering area in the front of the husky and shepherd trailers, to hanging out in 16's cabin.

It was on one of these nights, amidst the smell of baking apples and woodsmoke, that 04 had his next horrible revelation.

Most of their duties were restricted to weekdays and the weekend was generally reserved for relaxing, which Master said was important. Three weeks after 16's initiation and 02's wipe, it was a Friday night.

04 finished mopping the mess hall, his last task of the day, at 6:30, just as the sun was going down. 10 had been in there baking something, some kind of biscuits or pastries based on the scent, and scurried off with a huge sheet tray right as 04 was finishing up. 04 headed back to the husky trailer to pick up 06.

06 was napping, sprawled out on his bed, half covered by a blanket that was so twisted it looked like it was trying to suffocate him like a snake. His foot was hanging off the bed and he was snoring, mouth wide open.

04 walked in, cracking a smile. "Wake uuuuuppp," he cooed. He sat down in 06's chair, which was so close to the bed in the cramped space that he could easily reach the bed. He reached forward and rubbed 06's bare belly. 04 *loved* 06's belly. He ate a lot but he worked out even more, and the other husky had a perfect flat tummy. He stroked the dog's belly from his chest to his waist.

06 groaned. "Hawroooooooooooooooooooo," he whined. "Gimme another half hour."

04 chuckled. "No, we're gonna miss the food. 10 said he has a surprise. It smelled really good." He curled his fingers and scratched 06 through his fur.

06 stretched, his muscular arms up over his head, and 04 could feel the other dog's taut belly stretch. He felt his abs, feeling up his stomach. 06 was naked, and his scent filled 04's nose.

Swallowing hard, he let his paw slide down to 06's sheath, and then to his balls.

"Unngh!" 06 grunted. He lifted himself up onto his elbows and looked down at 04, surprised, blinking sleepily.

Swallowing, feeling his heart pounding, 04 stared guiltily back at him. He felt his ears tilt back. "You mind if I, ah…" He rolled 06's balls in his hands, rubbing his sheath with his thumb. The other dog was stiffening under his grip.

06 took a deep breath and let it out as a shivering exhale. "Yeah, man, go ahead," he grunted, watching 04 intently. "Suck it. Suck me off." He wanted it now. Sex had been the furthest thing on his mind ten seconds ago, but now he *wanted* 04.

The thought made 04 shiver. Nodding, he lowered his head to 06's waist and planted his muzzle on the dog's fuzzy sheath, coaxing the dog's cock out with his hand, into his waiting mouth.

He got a little fuzzy, as he always did, his conditioning taking over his mind and his body, but he was still present for the act. 04 loved blowing 06, because the dog writhed and squirmed like he was getting a full body massage. 06 reached down and held 04's head down against his perfect belly, and bucked his hips, gently fucking 04's waiting muzzle. His hands were strong on 04's head and his enthusiasm made it so exciting.

06 came quickly, and 04 lapped up every drop. After he finally finished cumming, 06 stroked his head for half a minute. When 04 lifted his head, he was calm and relaxed and felt so happy. He was hard in his pants, but he didn't feel the need to jack off, because he knew he would just be horny again in another twenty minutes.

06 was panting, staring at him, tongue lolling out. "Man. What's got *into* you?"

04 swallowed, frowning. The taste of 06's acrid cum filled his mouth and nose. "I don't know. I just can't help myself lately." He licked his chops and his nose.

06 sat up. He rolled his shoulders and stretched his neck. Slowly, he climbed out of bed and began searching for clothes to put on, his naked form within touching distance of 04 at all times. The room was filled with his scent, and it washed over 04. He tried not to notice how beautiful 06 was, the bright whites of his fur, the inky blacks. He just sat and observed.

06 finished putting on black sweatpants and a white t-shirt. He stopped in front of 04, stared at him, and reached out to take 04's muzzle in his hands. He stroked 04's face, rubbing the base of his jaw, holding his muzzle and reaching up to stroke his head. 04 was mildly surprised at the gesture, but it felt *amazing*, and after a moment he just closed his eyes and tried to keep his head up. 06's hands felt wonderful on his fur, and 04 felt so relaxed he could have fallen asleep.

Slowly, 06's hands stopped moving, and 04 half-opened his eyes.

06 was staring at him, frowning, his blue eyes filled with concern. "Are you okay, buddy?" he asked, softly.

04 stared up at him. He didn't know how to answer, so he finally answered honestly. "I don't know," he said.

That didn't seem to make 06 feel any better. He stood, watching 04 with his brow furrowed in concern, and then finally nodded. "Okay," he said, softly. "Let's go."

Nodding, 04 stood up. He swayed a little on his feet but it didn't take him long to get his bearings again.

The connection hall had lights, but not many, and it was already dark outside, so the hall was dim.

04 trailed after 06, following him, watching his tail idly wag, and almost bumped into him when the dog stopped before he got to the rear exterior door.

He stumbled.

06 turned back and smiled playfully at him as he disappeared through the fire door into Master and 01's trailer. He scampered off down the narrow connection hallway.

Eyes widening, 04 felt his heart start pounding. "What are you doing?!" he hissed, dashing after the other husky.

Turning, grinning evilly, a glint in his eye, 06 walked four more steps and knocked loudly on 01's door.

04 felt his blood turn to ice. He watched, horrified.

"*Coming*," growled a deep, threatening voice inside.

"What are you doing?!" he hissed, again.

06 beamed at him. "Something you'll thank me for!"

The door opened. It was dark in the connection hall, and the occupant was lit from behind, accompanied by a wave of air so hot it was almost steamy. A wave of jaguar scent came with it, warming and spicy, and 04 felt his entire body respond.

It was 01, of course, and while 04 was used to the big jaguar wearing the tight little shorts that barely covered his massive quads and bulge, he was *not* ready for the fact that 01 wasn't wearing anything else.

Bare-chested, muscular and triangular, his thick muscles in perfect relief under his glistening black fur, 01 stared at them with confusion. "Oh. I thought you were Master." He frowned severely. He had a perfect flat stomach and wide, muscular shoulders. "Good evening, 04." He squinted at 06. "12."

06 beamed. "Close enough."

The jaguar stared down at them. "Why are *you* here?"

04 cringed.

06 was unphased. "Why are you here? You should come to 16's cabin." He wagged delightedly. "There's food and there's going to be a movie. Come hang out!"

01 frowned severely. He looked back and forth between them.

"You don't have to come if you don't want to," 04 blurted.

The jaguar stared at him for a moment.

04 resisted the urge to cower. He felt his ears fold back and couldn't un-fold them.

The jaguar's face softened. "I don't…not want to come." He sighed. "The cabin is just very cold."

06 smiled vacantly at him. "It's a lot better now. With the fire going and all of us in there it's pretty warm. And it's pretty relaxed so you can always wrap up in a blanket."

01 considered, dubiously.

The husky beamed. "And it'll be *really* warm if you wrap up in a blanket with two naked huskies."

04 turned to him, horrified.

01's eyes slowly widened, and then he actually looked embarrassed. He looked away, his face flushing.

06 just smiled, wagging innocently. "Here…feel how warm we are," he said, reaching forward and putting his hands flat on 01's beefy chest.

01 jerked, but didn't pull away. He stared at 06, shocked.

"*06! What are you doing!*" 04 hissed. He stared at the dog's flat hands on the big cat's perfect chest. He was horrified and aroused. His heart was pounding and his dick was about to slide out of his sheath.

06 just smiled pleasantly up at the jaguar. "Do you feel it?"

Eyes wide, breathing shallowly, 01 nodded down at him.

06 beamed. "Do you want to feel 04, too?" he asked, innocently. "Just to check?" he said, with a smile.

01 stared at him, his golden eyes wide. He slowly turned his eyes to 04.

04 looked up at him. He swallowed, trying not to cower. His body wanted to bend into a submissive pretzel.

Silently, 01 opened his hand. He gently extended it to 04, fingers open. The way he would take a child's hand.

04's eyes widened.

01 watched him. Calmly. Relaxed. No expectations. 04 knew he could have played it off. 01 wouldn't have minded. He was reaching out.

04 looked down. Silently, he took the big jaguar's hand.

01 had probably expected him just to hold it, but 04 was feeling trusting and a little horny, so he lifted the huge cat's hand — it was *heavy*, even just guiding it — and

put 01's palm up against his face and throat. He looked away as he did it, blushing hotly.

01 made a soft, barely-perceptible chuff, and gently curled his fingers, cradling 04's muzzle and face in his hand. Silently, he stroked 04's face with his thumb.

Shivering, 04 resisted the urge to nuzzle and lick 01's palm. He just stood there, breathing hard, feeling the warmth of 01's soft leather paw pads, the strength of his huge hand, taking in his scent. He was flooded by the memory of the cat's big hands all over his exposed chest and stomach, the cat's thick fingers carefully tugging his jockstrap down his legs, leaving him exposed. He shivered.

They stood like that for what seemed like a long time.

Then, quietly, 01 took his hand back. He looked back and forth between the two of them — 06, and then 04, and then 06 again.

"I will come," he said. He gave them one final look, stepped awkwardly backwards, and closed the door to his room in their faces.

06 laughed. He turned to 04. "I like him!" He headed off down the corridor.

04 raised his lips in a snarl. "What's the matter with you?!" he snapped. His entire body was burning. He was sweating, even in just his t-shirt.

They left the rear door of the connection hall, descended the safety-grate metal steps to ground level, and walked around Master's trailer toward the cabin.

It was already dark outside, and the night air was probably around 20° and windy, which helped cool 04 off. He looked up. The northern lights were visible as a gentle glow. There was still a little moon left and it made them hard to see.

"Seriously, what is the matter with you?" 04 demanded, as they rounded the corner of Master and 01's trailer.

06 beamed at him, raising one eyebrow. "You should be thanking me. If we play our cards right, one or both of us could be scoring the jaguar tonight." He shrugged. "You're the horny one. I'm just planning ahead…I know if I don't run interference for you, you'll sneak off and fuck 11 again."

04 stared, and then let out a long sigh. "God. I fucked him so hard last night he actually said I did a good job."

06 let out a low whistle. "Wow! And your competition is a polar bear. That's pretty good."

04 smiled, and then let out a little sigh. "Thanks. I wish I knew what was going on with me."

06 smiled. "Don't worry! I'm sure the answer is right around the corner."

They rounded the corner to the cabin.

As soon as they opened the front door, 04 could smell food, and it smelled *amazing*. He smelled the pastries he had smelled in the mess, and then apples baking again. And something with chocolate? A few of the dogs were in front of the fireplace making smores. It looked warm and cozy and inviting. The only light was from the fire and the projector and a few little oil lanterns.

10 appeared in front of them with a little pastry in each hand. The big shepherd was beaming. "Welcome!" he said. "Open up!"

06 and 04 both opened their mouths without question. 10 popped a little pastry into each of their muzzles.

They chewed. It was a delicious buttery flaky pastry and there was some kind of delightful little meat preserve inside. It tasted beefy and chewy and spicy and peppery and it was fucking *amazing*. The meat was pleasantly leathery, like a dog chew, and had a nice spice that lit up his tongue. The taste was a little familiar.

"Is that…" 04 pondered. "*Gochujang jerky?*" Horrified, he looked around for 05. The shepherd was sitting on a cushion by the fire. He spotted them and waved.

10 laughed. "It's okay. He donated a pack to me. I told him I could make them better."

04 looked back at 05. The shepherd had a plate of the little pastries. The ones on his plate had the beef sticking out of both ends, 04 noted. Like a little hot dog.

"You were right," 04 said. "Can I eat fifteen more of those?"

06 nodded his agreement.

10 lit up. "Yes! I made so many." He beamed, wagging. "Come on in and get a drink."

They both walked in and stomped the snow off their boots. The floor of the cabin was wood plank, and 16 kept it fastidiously clean.

04 observed the huge polar bear across the room. They had a table in here now, too, and he was seated at it, with 02 and 03. 11 was there too, pressed so close to the bear he was cuddled up against him. 16 waved, and 04 swallowed his nervousness and waved back. 08 and 09 were here too, at the stove with 05. 09 was strumming an acoustic guitar, a surprise gift from Master on the last supply run. 14 and 15 were already finishing up a movie with the closed captions on and the volume blasting, curled up on 16's massive bed in the corner. For half a second, 04 thought the malamutes had left their buddy 07 behind, and then he spotted a husky tail poking out of the mass of fluffy malamute fur. He smiled.

10 appeared in front of them with two red plastic cups. "Here!" he said, holding them out.

04 and 06 each took one. 04 smelled apple cider (from concentrate, like most of their food), sugar, spices, and something sharp and acrid that immediately hit his nose.

His eyes widened. "10!" he said. "Is there liquor in this?! What if Master finds ou—"

The beefy shepherd grinned. "It's okay! Master said we could. We each have a two-shot ration." He lowered his head conspiratorially. "Do you want both of your shots right now?"

04 raised his eyebrows. He blinked. "Uh, no thanks," he said. "I'll come find you later."

10 beamed, his tongue lolling out. He seemed like maybe he'd had more than his allotted ration. "Great!" he said. A timer dinged up near the fireplace. "Oh, gotta get that. Get settled!" He loped away.

04 glanced to 06 to say something and found the other husky staring at his cup with one of his ears back. He looked up. He looked *sick*.

04 stared. "Wh…are you okay?" he asked, softly.

06 opened his mouth to say something. He was still staring at his cup with something like horror. "I—" he started, but didn't follow it up with anything.

04 looked down at his cup. He could smell the alcohol wafting off of it. Oh.

He reached forward and took the cup out of the other husky's hand. "Oh, hey, here, give me that." He took it away from 06. "You don't have to drink if you don't want to."

06's relief was palpable and instantaneous. The other husky sighed, his flattened ear rising up. He exhaled, long and slow, and straightened his shoulders. He smiled brightly. "Thanks, 04. I don't know what came over me."

04 poured the other husky's drink into his own cup. "Here, see? All gone!" He nested the cups in his hand. "Do you want me to get rid of mine?"

06 shook his head. "No! No, enjoy it. I'm so sorry." He shook his head, taking another breath and letting it out as a shaky sigh. "That was weird!" He smiled. "I'm gonna go get some more of those little meat puffs. You wanna sit somewhere?"

04 nodded. "Sure, buddy," he said, with a warm smile.

06 wandered away, his tail wagging cutely behind him, and 04 looked around. There was a long wooden bench along the entrance wall that would have a good view of the room. He elected to stay there.

04 walked over and sat, setting his cup down next to him. He looked toward the corner, where the dogs had started a new movie. This one was in black and white with

a loud orchestral score. It was still in the opening credits and he saw the word *Spellbound* and the name Alfred Hitchcock, which meant nothing to him. Idly, he watched.

As he waited, 12 and 13 walked in, apparently fresh from a run, as they were both steaming. Once 01 showed up — *if* he showed — they would have a full house, leaving only Master alone in the trailer network.

06 reappeared with a plastic plate full of little pastries. He also had two scoops of some kind of baked apple thing. It all smelled amazing, and 04 was instantly wagging and drooling.

"Oh, my God," he said. "I cannot believe what 10 can do with canned apples."

06 chuckled. "Right?" He grinned. "Open!"

04 opened his mouth, and 06 stuck a pastry in. He chewed, and this one was even better than the first. His senses came alive.

06 gestured at the movie. There were several attractive 1940s people onscreen. It looked like it was supposed to be inside a hospital or asylum of some kind, but based on how everyone looked it might as well have been a supper club. Things looked beautiful and tense. "You wanna watch?"

04 frowned. "No, this looks like it'll give you nightmares." He turned back.

06 stared at him, and looked away, frowning. "That only happened once."

04 cracked a smile. "We've only seen one movie." He looked around for something else. "Maybe we can get 09 to sing." He looked around for the young shepherd.

Across the room, 04 saw 09's ears perk up. He lasered in on him.

04 smiled. Setting his drink down, he mimed playing a guitar.

09 straightened up, cleared his throat, and immediately began singing.

04 didn't recognize the tune at all, but he did vastly enjoy it. Together with 06, he listened to 09 sing from across the cabin, mixed in with sweeping orchestral score and the weird clippy non-accent that all movie stars had in the '40s. 10 came by to top off their drinks, and 04 took both of them again. Pleasantly buzzed, with a full belly, 04 sat, and listened, and leaned against 06.

The door clunked, and then pulled open. 04 glanced over and saw an empty doorway, and was about to get up, assuming the wind had pulled the door open, when he realized that it was 01, all black and dressed in a big black parka. He saw the big cat's golden eyes and felt his entire body tense.

01 walked in, a lot closer to the nine-foot tall door than any of the dogs were, and looked around. A lot of the conversation dropped off, and 09 even stopped playing for a moment, before embarrassedly resuming.

01 looked around, and had just enough time to nod at 04 and 06, before chef 10 appeared in front of him with a pastry and a plastic cup. "Hi!" the dog said, wagging, and 04 surmised that 10 was definitely over his ration.

Wide-eyed, the jaguar accepted the food. He delicately sniffed the pastry and then bit half of it off. He chewed slowly, and then frowned, his eyes narrowing. "Did...did you put *meat* in this bread?"

Wincing, 10 nodded guiltily.

01 stared at him, eyes wide and intense. "It is AMAZING."

10 beamed and loped away.

01 looked around, and after a moment, actually shrugged out of his parka. He hung it on the rack by the door. He walked up to 04 and 06 and just nodded.

"You're right," he rumbled. "It is fairly warm in here."

06 beamed at him. "So I guess you won't be needing any husky heaters, then," he said, wagging mischievously.

The jaguar stared at him for a long time, raising his drink to his lips. He took a long pull without breaking eye contact.

"I didn't say that," he said, expression betraying nothing.

04 felt his heart start pounding.

06 stared up at him, and then grinned. "Well. It's supposed to be a cold night, sir," he said.

The big cat nodded. "As always." He glanced at 04, then back at 06, then took a look around. His eyes settled on the projector. "Has it been playing long?" he asked.

"Nope!" 06 chirped. "Just started."

01 turned back to them. "I believe I will watch. I will...let you know if I get cold."

06 beamed at him. "I'll be waiting!"

01 nodded at 04, and then headed for 16's bed in the corner. He eyed the shoe pile, and reluctantly stooped to remove his boots. He was wearing a pair of thick wool socks that 04 had remembered receiving with his gear kit but had never actually worn.

Nimbly, 01 climbed up on 16's bed and nestled his way into the corner. Looking up to the screen, he settled in.

06 turned to 04 and waggled his eyebrows.

04 chuckled. "I don't know how you can be so bold with him. I'm still a little scared of him."

06 smiled amiably at him and let out a little sigh. "04, he likes you. He *fucked* you, man. He's never fucked me."

04 snorted. "Yeah, well, seems like you might need to update that status after tonight."

06 chuckled and reached down to squeeze his arm.

They went back to listening.

After three or four songs 09 took a break and accepted a drink. He was a handsome kid. He sat with his back to the huge stone fireplace, ringed by 12 and 13, two huskies, and 08, another shepherd. 04 always loved seeing the huskies and the shepherds mix, and this warmed his heart. Guzzling a cup of water, 09 passed the guitar to 12. 04 idly watched as the older husky took the guitar, tuned it, and then started playing something in a minor key.

It was complex, scales, in a minor key, and it made something short in 04's brain. Wide-eyed, he stared.

12 started singing, and 04 knew what he was going to sing before he sang it. "*I've been spinning now for time, couple bottles by my side, I got sinnin' on my mind...sippin' on red wine...*"

04 felt his entire body tense. He knew this song.

12 had a beautiful voice but it made 04's blood run cold. "*I've been sitting here for ages...ripping out pages...how'd I get so faded? How'd I get so faded?*"

He swallowed. The fur on his arms was standing up. Why did he know this?

12 sang on, closing his eyes. '*Oh, nono don't, leave me lonely now...if you loved me how'd you never learn? Ooh, colored crimson in my eyes, one or two could take my mind...*"

It came to him, suddenly. His ex-girlfriend had liked this song. It was Ed Sheeran. She'd bought this album and played it every time they drove together somewhere. She'd make him put the windows down in his Jeep and blast the entire album, even though it was his car, and *Sing* was the only good track off that album and even that wasn't very good.

All of his fur stood up.

"*This is how it ends...I feel the chemicals...burn in my...bloodstream.*"

Had he ever remembered anything before? He thought frantically about it, trying to hold still.

"*Fading out again...I feel the chemicals...burn in my...bloodstream...*"

09 whooped. 04 flinched.

06 finally noticed. He turned his head. "Hey, are you okay?"

12 continued with the rest of the song. 04 tried to ignore his hackles rising.

He swallowed. "I'm fine," he said. But he didn't feel fine. He *felt* like his haze of stupidity and horniness were lifting like fog on the lake blowing away in a stiff wind.

Lifting his drink, he swallowed, and frowned.

As 12 droned on about "*tell me when it kicks in,*" 04 looked around. He had a clear head now, and something was bothering him. Something was wrong. 12's guitar riffs drilled into his brain as he looked around for the threat.

His eyes settled on the polar bear.

16 was in the far left of the cabin, the opposite end of where the movie was taking place. He was seated at a bench in front of a tall table, with 11, the slim husky cuddled up next to him. As 04 watched, the polar bear stood, gently sliding 11 off the bench. They walked across the cabin, and as they passed by the fire, 16 tugged on 10's arm. The shepherd was fussing over some food and drinks on the hearth. 16 tugged him away, leaned way down, held him tight, and closed their muzzles together. 04 watched the moment 10 started squirming, and he knew 16 was probably choking the dog with his tongue. He writhed, remembering the feeling of 16's huge tongue in *his* mouth, stretching his jaw and blocking his throat.

10 thrashed in the bear's grip, holding hard on to 16's arms, until the polar bear disengaged, and then shivered, panting, his own tongue lolling out. He looked shocked, but horny, panting with a dazed expression.

04 let out a shaky breath.

16 rumbled something in 10's ear, and 10 looked reluctantly back at the food, before 11 slipped his arm in 10's arm, sidling up to him, and together the two guided the chef shepherd away from the food. 04 watched them pile into a blanket and add themselves to the movie cuddle pile.

"*What's happening in the movie?*" 11 signed.

"*These people are all crazy,*" 15 signed back. The malamute was smiling. "*Good so far.*"

Frowning, 04 turned away. 16 didn't seem like a threat, just a big horny monster. The bear could easily cause any amount of trouble that he wanted to. Instead, he was acting as a friendly party host. 04 hadn't had the nerve to seek out his company since he got here, but that was intimidation at his size because they would probably end up having sex, and not evaluation of him as a threat.

Right?

"All the voices in my mind," 12 sang, "Calling out across the line…all the voices in my mind…calling out across the line…" It went on, and on, perfectly faithful to a rendition that 04 had heard a hundred times, in a life he didn't remember.

But did he?

He thought of 02, who didn't even seem to think he'd had a life before the facility. Idly, he looked around to find him.

The biggest shepherd was still at the table. As 04 turned, he saw the huge dog staring directly at him. His eyebrows shot upward.

Blushing, 02 looked away, immediately. He hung his head, ears back, face red.

04 watched him. It was suddenly clear to him that the huge shepherd did have a crush on him after all. Surprised, he stared. 02 looked back up, his head dipped submissively. They made eye contact. The king shepherd risked a shy smile, and then immediately looked away again.

04 pondered, resisting the urge to frown and instead smiling politely back. 02 was important, too. Had he really forgotten about the dog strapped to the gurney, the mysterious green liquid draining slowly into him? 03 had kept 02 on a pretty tight leash since his recalibration. 04 should probably go check on the big dog. 02 clearly wasn't going to mind the company.

06 chuckled next to him. "Yo, we are *definitely* gonna score tonight."

04 turned to say something about 02 but to his surprise, 06 was looking the other way. 04 followed his gaze.

He was looking at 01, who was staring right at the two of them, golden eyes in the darkness. He glanced away.

06 turned to him, grinning. "I think our big cat might need a little warming up. That's the fourth time I've caught him staring." He raised an eyebrow, beaming. "You wanna go for it?"

04 looked over again. The big jaguar was staring at him. This time, he didn't look away. Just watched for a few moments. After a moment, he shifted his gaze to 06. His gaze was long and piercing.

04 swallowed, his fur standing on end. His heart was racing. "It doesn't look like he's gonna be picky on who he gets." He swallowed. "This was your idea. You should go over there."

06 raised one eyebrow. "Me?" He frowned. "*Just* me? What are *you* gonna do?"

"Um," 04 said.

He had to decide. 01 might have valuable information about what was going on in the facility. He would definitely head back to the lab if 04 and 06 pushed. But wasn't that using him for information? 04 felt terrible about it just as the big panther seemed to be warming up to them. And 04 still hadn't really had extensive contact with 16, and the big polar bear was friendly and always up for more company. He might reveal something too. But 02 could be a good lead if 04 wanted more details on the weirdest thing currently happening in the facility. And 04 was starting to genuinely miss talking to him.

In the end, he decided to follow the lead he was least scared of. He raised his eyes to 02, on the other side of the cabin.

06 followed his gaze. This time they both caught the big shepherd staring.

04 turned back. "I feel like I need to go make up with 02. It's been *so weird* since he got...back."

06 turned back to 04. "Oh, wow! Mr. Popularity. Okay, go bag that big dog. Do you mind if I take the big cat?" He smiled. "We can meet back here in an hour and switch."

04 laughed, despite himself. 06 always could always get a chuckle out of him. "In an hour you're gonna be in bed with an ice pack under your tail." He smiled.

06 raised one eyebrow. "Jesus, here's hoping. Okay, friend. Let's go!"

"You first!" 04 told him. He wanted to see how things would go, in case 06 needed backup.

06 grinned. "Thanks, buddy. You've always got my back." He leaned forward and gave 04 a sweet little lick, winked, and lifted himself to his feet. Tail wagging, he loped over to the movie pile, straight for the big jaguar in the corner.

"Hey," he said, kicking his boots off. "Mind if I join you?"

01's eyebrows rose. He swallowed. His attention was fully on 06 and he actually looked a little nervous.

Insanely, 04 felt a little pang of jealousy. He pointed his ears as hard as he could, and could just make out the rumble of the big cat's deep voice.

"Not at all. Good evening," he rumbled.

"It's about to be!" 06 said, crawling up onto the bed, and dropping into the blanket pile next to the big cat.

04 smiled, resolved himself, slammed the rest of his drink, set the empty cup down on the bench, and stood up to walk to the big table.

As soon as 02 saw him coming, the huge shepherd reacted like he'd been caught in the trash can. He straightened up, ears perfectly erect, and watched, eyes wide. 03 was next to him, the dark-faced shepherd seated in the corner of the cabin. They were alone at the table, facing into the cabin, maybe ten feet from the guitar circle, alone. 03 caught a glance of 04 and frowned.

12 started playing *Shape of You* now, and it made 04's ears ring like he was standing inside a church bell.

He ignored it. He walked up to the end of the table and looked up at 02. He needed to talk to the big shepherd. He ignored 03, who was already staring daggers into him.

"Hey," he said to 02, his voice low. "Mind if I join you? Or do you want to keep just staring at each other all night?" He smiled in what he hoped was a sultry way, and not forced.

The shepherd stared at him, and then lowered his head, ears tilting back. 04 could immediately hear his tail wagging, *whump whump whump whump* against the log wall behind him. "Sorry for staring," he said, smiling bashfully.

04 smiled, and it was authentic. 02 was adorable, shy, and awkward. He'd been like this before, when they were all new to the facility. Just a big goofy shepherd. "Don't be sorry," 04 said. "You can stare. I don't see you talking to many of the huskies."

02 smiled at him, beaming. "I try to leave you alone. 03 says you're all *really*, really, busy."

04's smile froze on his face. He stared, and slowly turned to the other shepherd. "Really," he said, icily.

03 stared balefully back at him, his golden eyes narrowed in his mostly-black face. The other shepherd was a big man, too, shorter than 02 but still six inches taller than 04, broad-shouldered, narrow-waisted, and thick with muscle. He would have been terrifying if 04 hadn't felt such contempt for him.

So it *wasn't* a coincidence that 04 hadn't crossed paths with 02. 03 was keeping him away on purpose. And 04 knew exactly why — the first night 02 had "arrived," 04 had asked him what he thought were very general questions about his "prior posting." 02 hadn't been able to answer and had gotten upset. 04 had dropped it but clearly 03 was holding a grudge. Maybe it was because he was a little buzzed, but if he'd been closer to 03, he would have been tempted to slap him across his stupid angry face.

Redoubling his smile, he turned back to 02. The big dog was clueless about the animosity at the table.

"Well!" 04 announced. "I'm never too busy for a big handsome shepherd. In fact…" He reached down for the hem of his shirt, yanked upward on it, and shrugged out of his shirt, arching his back to show off his perfect stomach and meaty chest. He lifted the shirt over his chest, showing off his ripped arms. "You can stare all you want." He smirked at the two dogs.

02 stared at him in stunned silence. Mouth hanging open, the huge shepherd's amber eyes followed the curves of 04's lithe black and white body. As he watched, his tongue began to poke out as he panted gently. Next to him, 03's face screwed into a mask of fury.

"Anyway," 04 said, leaning against the table. It was sized for 16, or at least 02, and came up nearly to his chest. "Anybody got a drink left?"

Wordlessly, his eyes not leaving the husky's muscular chest, 02 reached for his drink and slid it right up next to the husky.

Smiling, 04 reached for it. He put his hand on top of 02's huge paw and held it there.

02's eyes widened.

"Thanks," 04 said, quietly. He picked up the plastic cup and lifted it to his lips. He drank it faster than he intended to. The alcohol and cider went sharply down his throat.

03 rumbled in disapproval. "You're over your ration," he grunted.

04 gave him a side-eye. He was definitely feeling the buzz. "Master didn't say we couldn't exchange. I used to drink ten times this much in college."

03 was so surprised by that statement that he momentarily seemed to forget to be enraged.

04 ignored him. He focused on the big shepherd, hitting him with a thousand-watt smile.

02 finally made eye contact again, surprised. He stared into the husky's blue eyes.

"So, you're hanging out with 03, huh?" 04 rumbled. He leaned on the table, putting his hand down on 02's big mitt again. "That's kinda funny. 02 and 03?"

The dog stared dopily back at him, and then broke into a grin. "I guess," he said. "I never thought of it." He started wagging again.

04 nodded severely. "You know, we used to have another 02," he said, softly.

02 stared. After a moment, his golden eyes widened. "R-really?" he said, quietly.

03 was staring daggers into him. 04 ignored him.

"Yeah," 04 said. He was definitely feeling the booze. He felt the insane urge to keep picking at the scab. "A big king shepherd. Just like you."

The king shepherd watched 04. His brow furrowed. "Really?" He swallowed. "W-what…what happened to him?" he asked, hesitantly.

04 took a deep breath, and let it out as a long sigh. "Don't know. He was just gone one day," he said, sadly.

"*Stop it*," snapped 03, sharply.

04 frowned. "You're staying in his room," he said, with a concerned frown.

02 recoiled, pulling his hand back. He actually looked scared. "Wh-what?!" he asked, a scared whine creeping into his voice.

04 frowned. He instantly felt bad.

"*04, I'm warning you*," 03 growled, leaning forward.

04 glanced at him, frowning. He turned back to the big dog. "I'm sorry. I'm teasing. We…" He swallowed, and forced a smile. "We never had an 02 before you."

02 stared at him, and then turned to 03, eyebrows up and ears back, scared.

03's face instantly softened. "It's true." He turned to 04. "The husky is just being *an asshole*."

02 let out a shaky, relieved sigh. He turned back to 04. His ears were still flat against his head.

"Hey, *I'm* sorry," 04 said. He frowned. "C'mere." He reached up with both hands.

Dipping his head submissively, 02 leaned downward toward him.

"Aww, 02, I'm sorry!" 04 sighed. He reached up to stroke the big dog's huge fuzzy face and ears. "I'm so sorry. I was just teasing. I thought it would be funny." He held 02's chin and stroked him with his other hand.

02 stared soulfully up at him. "I'm sorry I got scared," he mumbled.

04 felt his heart breaking. "No, I'm sorry. I didn't mean for that to be mean." He squeezed 02's head and leaned up to kiss his nose.

02's eyebrows rose at that, and his big ears flopped up, and he looked shyly away.

04 let out a long sigh. He didn't know why he'd pushed the big dog. Well, yes he did, because asshole 02 would have deserved it. But new sweet 02 didn't. "I'm so sorry. I didn't realize you'd spook so easily."

02 swallowed, ears back again. "It's okay," he said, softly. "It was worth it, for the kiss." He looked away, blushing, hiding a little smile.

04 stared, surprised.

02 turned to look back at him, head still dipped a little, and offered him another shy little smile.

04 stared back. His heart was pounding.

On some level, he knew it was his conditioning, and the promise of size-difference sex. But on another level, this was 02, and 04 was feeling things he hadn't felt in a long time.

He'd missed 02, he suddenly realized.

04 was at a loss for words for a moment, and then he managed to stammer out a reply. He forced a flirty smile. "Yeah?" he asked.

Shyly, 02 nodded.

God, it was *cute*. 04 couldn't help but smile, genuinely. "You want another one?"

Excited, 02 nodded. His ears were up now and 04 could hear his tail wagging.

Beaming, 04 leaned in and stood on his tiptoes. 02 leaned down, and their muzzles connected, and they kissed. 04 closed his eyes, enjoying 02's taste, his nostrils full of the big dog's scent, and they opened their mouths at the same time, their tongues working against one another, and 04 let out a long, rumbling growl as his sheath filled up and his cock spilled out into his sweatpants.

They broke the kiss after a long few moments. 04 stared in mild surprise. 02 stared worshipfully back at him, in absolute bliss.

Mouth still open, 04 took a long breath. He shook his head, looked at 02, looked at the stunned 03, and then swallowed. He looked down and he was obviously, painfully hard into his sweatpants. "C-can I sit between you guys?" he said, softly.

What was happening? What was he feeling? Was this more of his mysterious induced horniness? It felt different for some reason. What was happening to him?

02 wagged. "Sure!" he said. 03 didn't say anything.

02 scooted out of the way and 04 clambered up on the high bench. The table came up to his chest, because of course it did. This was 16's cabin and the table was sized for him. 04 scooted further in, the table level with his armpits. He glanced warily at 03 to his left. The big dog narrowed his eyes. 02 slipped back in.

Even with the angry 03 directly next to him, 04 felt a little more secure in the corner with 02 between him and everyone else in the cabin.

He looked out over the table.

12 had turned the guitar back over to 09 who was playing a song 04 didn't recognize at all. 08 had wandered over to watch the movie. 07 was now in 14's lap, and 04 was not at all surprised to see the husky was completely naked, his cock half out of his sheath as 14 idly rubbed the dog's belly and inner thighs. 15 had a hand on 07's belly, too. He looked for 06, and it took him a moment to find him, because he was nestled up against 01's side, with the panther's big arm circled around him. The panther was nuzzling the top of 06's head.

It all felt surreal, and wrong. 04 was drunk, he suddenly realized. He was drunk and this was all wrong.

04 frowned at the table. "How the fuck was 11 sitting here?" he snapped. "This is a table for *giants*."

For the first time, 03 laughed. "How do you think? He was sitting in 16's lap," he chuckled. He smirked at the husky.

04 turned to glare at him, and then pivoted 180° to 02.

"Gimmie a boost," he grunted at the big shepherd.

02 looked surprised, and then shy again. Smiling, he scooted a little closer.

04 clambered up onto the dog's left leg, straddling 02's left thigh with his asscheeks, and could finally see at a reasonable height. He spotted another unattended red plastic cup and reached for it. Without a second thought, he downed the contents. It was lukewarm cider and it burned going down.

Pushed forward by 02's musclegut, 04 started to slide off the shepherd's lap. "Ope!" 02 said.

04 turned and looked up at him. "You better *hold* me," he said. He looked up at 02.

02 looked down at him from inches away. Silently, the big dog put his arms loosely around 04's bare chest. He was looking less nervous and more intense by the moment.

04 narrowed his eyes. "I said hold me," he snapped, putting his hands over 02's big paws. He put 02's left hand under his arm, tight across his bare stomach, and his right hand on his own thigh. He felt the heat immediately.

He stared up at 02 from inches away.

02 stared down at him, golden eyes hesitant and searching.

They both felt something.

04 was shocked. *I'm gonna fuck this dog tonight*, he thought.

He tilted his muzzle up, just an inch or two, not nearly enough to reach the shepherd, but it was enough to signal his willingness, and that was all the sign that 02 needed.

The shepherd leaned down, opening his mouth, and as soon as their muzzles met 02's tongue was inside his mouth. 04 sucked, hard, closing his eyes, pushing back hard against the shepherd's warm lips, and 02's arms tightened around him, *really* tightened. He held him hard and strong, and 04 shivered and squirmed and pushed his muzzle hard against 02 like he was trying to shove him away. He heard himself whimper in pleasure, and he swam in his alcoholic haze and warmth and 02's wonderful scent.

I missed him so much, he thought. They'd used to do this. When they were new. Before 02 had gotten mean.

They kissed for a long time, and 04 could feel his heart pounding and feel his dick throbbing. He took 02's hand and pulled it over his crotch, so the shepherd could feel too, and 02 growled into his mouth and rubbed his cock, hard, and 04 writhed and shivered in his grasp, whimpering and grunting and growling.

It went on seemingly forever, and then 03 started growling.

They both broke the kiss.

Dazed, surprised, 04 turned.

The other shepherd was glaring at him, lip raised, ears forward, eyes murderous. Not at them. At *him.*

"At least let me out of the god damn bench first," he growled.

04 stared at him. He resisted the urge to narrow his eyes.

03 and 04 had never really been *friends,* but he had always been *civil,* until 02 had started to go off the rails and turned the shepherds into a mean little gang. 03 had always been all business, calm, even-keeled, except when Master or one of the other dogs had worked him up into a sweaty, horny fervor. Those occasions seemed to be the only times that 03 was truly enjoying himself.

Now 04 did narrow his eyes. Well. If 03 needed a good fucking, 04 was going to *provide.*

"Pull your buddy in," he said, to 02.

03's brow furrowed, in anger and confusion, and then 02's arm left 04's shoulder and reached for 03. He reached the other shepherd easily, and then effortlessly yanked him over. 03 flailed, eyes wide in surprise, and 02 grabbed him by the *scruff,* and yanked him bodily right up against 04. 03 was big, but 02 was bigger.

"What the fuck are you doing, 04?!" 03 hissed, baring his teeth.

Setting his eyes, 04 reached for the other shepherd's crotch.

"Don't you *dare!*" 03 growled, his face a mask of shock and anger.

04 settled his strong hands into 03's crotch, pressing his sweatpants down hard, and as expected he found the shepherd already hard. Staring at him, he squeezed his cock, and began massaging.

"Don't... *don't!*" hissed 03, but his eyes were already sliding half-shut under 04's ministration. "You little black and white fucker," he groaned, squirming in place. He was so hard under 04's hand. It was hard to massage the dog's fat cock left-handed, but 04 worked into a rhythm, pumping 03's cock as best he could through the dog's sweatpants. "I...hate...you..." he gasped, his muzzle opening and his tongue spilling out. He had a longer coat than the other sheps, and it lent him a bearded, dignified look, which made it all the more exciting when his arousal overcame him like this.

04 pivoted, turning to him. He massaged the dazed dog's cock for another few seconds, staring at him. Slowly, he leaned in.

"Get off me," 03 groaned, his muzzle slightly open, his eyes closed almost to slits. 04 hadn't been this close to 03 in months, close enough to smell the musky woodsmoke aroma of the big shepherd as he slowly lost control to his arousal. It was a familiar scent and, surprisingly, it made 04's heart twinge with longing.

"I missed him, but I missed *you*, too," 04 told him, and then leaned in and their muzzles connected.

03 leaned hard into the kiss, immediately, mouth opening, and 04 basked in his taste, similar to 02 but so distinctly different, his tongue, thicker and rougher, his aggressive kissing as he ground his hips and cock against 04's hand. 04 knew 03's scent as well as he knew his own.

04 reached into 02's lap with his other hand, feeling for the dog's crotch, making the huge dog under him jump, and found 02's huge cock hard and fully out of his sheath. 02 let out a shaky, excited breath, and 04 had a much easier time pumping the huge dog's thick meat through his sweatpants, because he was right-handed. 02 shivered, his entire big body quaking, and he clamped his massive paw down on 04's dick so hard he almost cut off blood flow. 02 wasn't coordinated enough to jack and be jacked at the same time, 04 knew from experience, so he just serviced the big dogs.

Fully drunk now, half-naked, sucking face with 03, sandwiched between the two biggest shepherds with *both* of their dicks in his hands, 04 just writhed in place, brain hazy, body singing, mind gone. It felt good, and right, and familiar.

They did that for a long time, and then 04 literally started to run out of air, so he broke the kiss. 03 stared at him from inches away, panting. Over his shoulder, 02 was panting and also drooling.

He wanted them.

He wanted them both.

"Let's go fuck," 04 said. His voice sounded distant and raspy, even to himself.

03 stared at him, dazed. He nodded. "Okay," he said, softly.

04 turned to 02. "*Yes*," the big dog said, loudly, forcefully.

04 couldn't help but smile. "Your place, big dog. My room is too little for the two of you."

02 nodded with seriousness, looked around, and slid out of the bench. He was still fully erect in his sweatpants, 04 nodded, and the shepherd absolutely reeked of precum.

As he followed 02 to the door, feeling the floor roll gently underneath him, he looked over to the movie pile, looking for his friend. He found 06 in 01's lap, straddling the big panther, facing him. 06's shirt was off, too, and they were making out.

Just before the door closed, 04 saw 01's eyes open. The jaguar looked directly at him.

And then the door closed, and he was outside.

The walk back to the trailers was a short one but the cold air seemed to cool 03 off.

02 was not cooled off *at all*. The big shepherd was panting, even on the walk, and he kept glancing back at 04 to make sure he was behind him. His fat cock was still hard, too, tenting his uniform pants. He looked intense and excited, wagging.

Carrying his shirt, 04 chuckled. He was still pretty buzzed and feeling pretty good. "Wow, you're ready to go." He turned to 03 as they were climbing the perforated metal steps to the connection hall. "Have you not been taking care of your boy? He looks like he really needs to fuck." He wagged idly behind himself.

03 glanced at him. "We haven't done anything since he…got here."

04 stared. "R…really?"

03 bored holes into his eyes. "*Yes*," he snapped. "We *just met*. Don't you remember when *you* were new, 04?" he asked, pointedly.

04 thought about that. He tried to remember when they had first arrived at the facility. They were clearly the first ones to inhabit it. There had been a lot of work, and it had just been the three of them, plus Master, 01, and 05. They hadn't even acquired 06 yet. 04 was the only husky.

He thought about that. He remembered being in his room, alone in the husky trailer, jacking off every night, fantasizing about the other dogs, and of course Master had periodically dropped by his room, and when Master was around, everything got really fuzzy and horny and he woke up feeling great with a sore asshole. But it probably had been a while before he'd actually worked up the nerve to seek out any of the other dogs on his own.

Probably…about three weeks.

Huh.

The two dog trailers were at the end of the connection hallway. 02 fast-walked past all the other trailers to the shepherd trailer, checking twice to make sure 03 and 04 were following, and hurriedly opened the door. 04 chuckled. Big dog needed a *release*.

Both trailers had six small rooms and two big rooms. In the husky trailer, 14 and 15 got the big rooms, since the malamutes were each seven feet tall. In the shepherd trailer, 02 and 03 got the big rooms, even though 03 was only six and a half feet, though the way Master was picking up new arrivals lately, 04 wondered if he would be getting pre-empted soon.

02's room was at the end of the hall, with a door at a 45-degree angle opposite 03's door. The thin door opened into the room and 02 walked in, ducking in the doorframe. He loped quickly into the room and turned around.

His room was mostly bed, as all of their rooms were, though the beds in the end-rooms were up against the far wall, to accommodate the fact that two eight foot beds spaced end-to-end occupied the entire width of the trailer. On the other wall was a tiny closet, a small desk with a chair, and a miniscule sink.

"Well, here we are," 02 said, smiling nervously.

"Here we are," 04 said, grinning, walking forward and pressing himself up against the big dog's belly. He looked goofily up at him.

02 looked surprised, and then intense. He cautiously lowered his head to 04's muzzle.

The husky closed his eyes and met the shepherd's muzzle, and they kissed long, and loudly, and wetly.

04 put his hands up and stroked 02's belly, hard, running his paws up and down the shepherd's sides. 02 had a pronounced potbelly, and 04 fucking *loved it*, and it had been probably six months since 02 had let him touch it.

02 squirmed away from him. "Ssstopppp," the shepherd whined. He looked away, smiling bashfully. "I don't have a six-pack like the rest of you."

The husky recoiled, eyes wide. "Are you kidding? That's why you're so fuckin' *hot*." He reached for the hem of the dog's shirt and yanked on it. "Off, please."

02 blushed, smiling awkwardly, and reluctantly tugged off his shirt. His huge body moved dangerously in the space, like a giant mechanical arm operating in a broom closet. His arms grazed the ceiling as the shirt came off his big frame.

02 was built like a powerlifter, with a pronounced belly and a thick, beefy musculature to match. His belly was big and soft and white, his white fur running up to the underside of his throat. 04 drank in the sight of him, his buzzed head reeling and his cock throbbing. He'd known what 02 looked like, of course, but it hit so different when he wasn't scared of him. "Flex for me," he ordered, dazed.

Smiling shyly, 02 lifted both his arms and flexed both of his biceps. He looked as wide as Master was tall. His arms looked like slabs of beef.

"Wh-what do you think?" he asked, shyly.

Wordlessly, 04 slid to his knees.

02's eyebrows shot up. Behind 04, 03 groaned and let out an annoyed breath.

04 licked his chops, letting his tongue show. "C'mere," he said.

02 stared at him, and then slowly stepped toward him. He stood over him, his mouth open, panting. A few little drops of drool came off of 02's tongue and spattered down on 04's face. It made the husky's heart pound. The big dog stank of arousal and there was a big fat bulge in his sweats.

His mouth flooding with saliva, 04 reached up for 02's pants and curled his fingers in under the waistband of 02's sweatpants. He gently tugged downward, exposing the white fluffy fur under 02's belly, soft and wet and matted down by sweat and elastic, and then yanked the dog's pants down, all the way to his knees.

02 groaned as his cock came free and squirmed in place, panting. He wasn't wearing underwear, and his cock bounced up and hit 04 in the chin, which is what the husky had wanted. 02 had a big fat beautiful cock, nine or ten inches, deep red with a perfect round head, and 04 loved it. He leaned in and rubbed his muzzle up against it, drinking in the scent of sweat and dog and cock, closing his eyes. As he nuzzled, he reached up and curled his fingers around the dog's fat shaft, squeezing and massaging, putting his other hand on 02's muscular leg to steady the two of them.

"*Aaaaaaaahnngghh!*" 02 gasped. He shivered.

04 let his eyes slide close and aimed the cock at his mouth. He opened wide and slowly lunged. 02's cock was salty and filled his muzzle, flattening his tongue against the base of his jaw. 04 pushed his head forward, choking himself on the fat meat until he felt his gag reflex kick in. He strained to keep his jaw open, moaning and slurping.

"*Oh God,*" 02 moaned. He shivered.

04 guzzled 02's dick for a few long moments, filling his nostrils, letting his head swim with 02's familiar scent, before he remembered the other dog in the room.

Reluctantly disengaging from 02's member, 04 idly pumped the dog's slick, fat cock. He turned his head to see what 03 was doing.

The other shepherd was behind him, glaring. He had his arms crossed and he looked mad.

04 shuffled, on his knees. He was between the two of them. He scooted past 02 in the narrow space between the bed and the desk. Reaching up, he wiped drool away from his muzzle with the back of his paw.

"Grab your friend," he ordered, raspily.

02 stared at him, nodded wordlessly, and crossed the room in a step. He parked next to 03 and put a big bare arm over his shoulders, holding him.

"*Hey!*" 03 snapped. "What's the big idea?"

04 crossed to him and was on the dog's waistline in a second.

"Don't even *think* about—" 03 started.

04 snarled at him. He pulled the other shepherd's pants down, hard. 03 was wearing standard-issue black briefs, which 04 quickly tugged down, too. He wasn't fully hard, but he wasn't soft, either. The muscular dog was about halfway out of his sheath, and 04 leaned forward and put his muzzle around the dog's entire cock and sheath.

03 stiffened, growling, and 02 tightened his grip around the dog's broad shoulders. 04 held his hips, holding the dog in place against his squirming, and suckled hard, massaging the dog's sheath and shaft with his tongue, and 03's cock slowly and inexorably slid out of his sheath, thickening, into 04's muzzle, until the husky had to slide off the shepherd's sheath and just suck his shaft.

03 let out a shaky breath, pumping his hips gently into 04's muzzle, and the husky knew he had him. He looked up, into 03's eyes, and saw the shepherd's eyes narrowed in his black face. His mouth was open, though, and he was panting.

Slowly, he pulled off of 03's dick, making eye contact with him as he did it.

03 stared down into 04's blue eyes, and silently, he shivered.

04 turned back to 02, smiling up at him, and reached up to take the dog's cock in his left hand as he sank down on his cock. He kept his right hand on 03's throbbing member, one of the dog's dicks in each of his hands, and sucked, slowly bobbing up and down on one of their dicks, and then the other, trailing streamers of husky drool every time he went back and forth, his own cock hard and leaking in his pants, blissed out and rumbling.

His conditioning wasn't kicking in, because he was in control here. He had two of the biggest dogs here, with their pants around their knees, holding perfectly still for him, both watching him intently to see what he would do next. He relished their combined scents, the two big dogs' smells mingling in his nose, with the acrid smell of precum and the meaty scents of their two fat dicks, enhanced by his saliva all over both of them. 02 squeezed 03 hard, grinding against him, and 03 stood in place, hands curled into fists at his sides, grunting and shivering.

04 went back and forth for a long time, feeling them get closer and closer, enjoying the milky, perfumy scent of precum on his tongue, until finally, his jaw started to cramp, and he pulled off.

Panting, rolling his neck, he sat back on his haunches, dazed.

"Are you okay?" 02 asked, immediately.

04 looked up at him, reaching up to wipe at his slobbery muzzle with the back of his hand. "You two smell good together," he rumbled.

Staring down at him, 02 blushed.

"Get on the bed," 04 told him. "But first, get naked."

Nodding, 02 immediately yanked his pants down, and then stopped to hurriedly unlace his boots and clunk out of them. 03 just frowned.

04 stared at him, dropping his pants. He was rock-hard too, not that that was a surprise. "Didn't you hear me? Your boy wants to fuck. You don't want to upset the new guy, do you, 03?" He glared.

03 frowned, and reached for the hem of his shirt.

"Wait," 04 told him.

The big shepherd stopped.

Slowly, 04 reached for the dog's shirt. He lifted it up, exposing 03's perfect muscular belly, dragging his hands up the dog's wide flanks. Growling, 03 lifted his arms, and 04 tugged the broad-shouldered shepherd's shirt off, standing on his very tiptoes so he could pull the shirt over the tall shepherd's head.

When he pulled the shirt off, the dog underneath looked enraged. But 04 was still buzzed, and he was getting used to it. He smiled. 03 was thick and muscular, and it was worth it to see him shirtless.

03 rolled his golden eyes. "Let's just get this over with." He slid his pants down, and 04 noted he was still rock-hard.

There was a crash as 02 flopped onto the bed. He beamed back at 04, his huge shepherd ears tilted slightly backwards in embarrassment.

04 grinned at him. He slid out of his own pants, ejecting his boots in one step each, and scrambled up onto 02's tall bed. He crawled toward the shepherd and then climbed him like a mountain.

"*Oof!*" 02 grunted as the husky flattened himself on his belly, and then there was a husky tongue halfway down his throat and he couldn't say anything. "Mmmm-*mmmm*," he moaned, sucking on 04's tongue, and then he lifted his huge hands and ran them up and down 04's back.

04 shivered under the meaty dog's big mitts, arching his back and humping. They were both hard, and their dicks were grinding against one another.

The bed rocked, and 04 glanced to see that 03 had climbed on, *too*, and was watching the two of them make out with a frown.

04 glanced at him, and then slid down off 02's belly, sliding into the small space between the shepherds, pressed up between them.

03 leaned into it, and too late 04 realized his back was to the other shepherd.

03 engaged immediately, chuckling evilly and leaning hard against him, his cock digging up against 04's ass. "Oh, wow, presenting to me already?" he asked. He ground suggestively against 04's fluffy butt.

04 squirmed, turning to flash his teeth at 03.

03 narrowed his eyes. "Now, now," he said. "You don't want to upset the new guy, do you, 04?" He reached forward and dug his big hand in between 04's legs, digging his fingers up into 04's perineum. It was hard. It was too hard.

"*Arrrrp!*" 04 yelped, twitching. He snarled at 03, showing his teeth.

The shepherd was grinning evilly at him. "Oh, sorry," he said. "I guess I got too excited."

04 narrowed his eyes. He frowned. *I should really Sleepy Puppy this jerk, he thought.*

He stopped.

Confused, alarmed, his heart pounding, he stared.

Sleepy puppy.

He knew that. He knew what would happen. 03 would shut down, and then he would follow orders.

04's heart started pounding. What was this command? Where had it come from? It didn't make any sense, and yet 04 knew it to be true. Any of them would respond to that. He didn't know why it was true, or where it had come from, but he knew with complete certainty that it would work. It was like he was remembering a thought from someone else's brain.

03 stared at him, shocked. He seemed to know the mood had changed.

02 picked up on it immediately. He frowned. "Y-you okay?" he asked, hesitantly. He sat up on his elbows.

04 looked at him, wide-eyed.

03 frowned. "What's the matter with you?"

The husky looked back and forth between the two of them. "Wh…I…" He pondered. His head was reeling. He was still a little drunk but now he felt like the world was escaping him. "Can I ask you both something?"

02 looked concerned now. 03 looked confused and annoyed.

04 swallowed. "Does the phrase *Sleepy puppy* mean anything to you?"

The effect on them was startling and immediate.

On his right, 03 recoiled as if slapped. He blinked, surprised, and his mouth dropped open. He reeled, dazed, his eyes confused and unfocused. Immediately, his eyelids started to drift shut. He let out a soft, confused, nonsensical noise.

On his left, 02 just…dropped. The big dog immediately went limp, dropping lifelessly back onto the bed, making it shake. He lay there as if unconscious, his mouth hanging open, his eyes half-closed, his pupils rolled back into his head. His tongue was lolled limply out of the side of his mouth.

Heart pounding, 04 stared at them. A surge of adrenaline filled him. What had he done to them?!

03 had been hit less hard than 02. He was still somewhat conscious, though he was struggling.

And that made sense. That's how the command would work. 03 had a lot more going on in his brain. 02 only had three weeks' worth of thoughts, most of it commands, and the order had turned his brain off immediately.

04 wriggled around and gently shook 03. "Hey!" he said. "Hey, snap out of it! Come back to me!" He reached up and lightly smacked the dog's muzzle.

"Hhhh…ahhhngnghh," 03 stammered, his head rolling. He blinked, wide and exaggerated. He seemed to be trying to get his eyes to focus. "Whhhh…"

"Wake up!" 04 whimpered. He slapped 03 again, harder. Oh, God. What if he couldn't reverse this? "Please! 03!" he whined.

03 finally seemed to notice him. He blinked, long and slow, and after another few more blinks he seemed to really *see* 04 again.

"Wh…" he stammered. He took a few deep breaths. "What," he whispered.

"I'm so sorry!" 04 whined. "I didn't know it would do that!"

03 took a deep breath. He still seemed to be having trouble getting his eyes to focus. "M...my head. It all went blank." He took a few deep breaths. He finally looked over 04 and saw 02. He gasped.

04 turned. 02 was still flat on the bed, his arms at his sides, unresponsive.

03 scrambled off the bed, to his feet. He leaned over, filling the room. "What did you do to him?! To *us?!*" he demanded.

04 swallowed. "I used a trigger phrase." He scooted off the bed and dropped off, standing next to 03. He was scared. He put his hands up and wrapped his arms around himself.

03 stared at him, his eyes wide. "What the fuck is a *trigger phrase?*"

04 shivered. "It's a phrase that activates some of our conditioning. I think there's a lot of them." He swallowed. He felt his ears wiggle and realized he was shaking.

03 stared at him. He looked confused and skeptical, on the verge of a scowl, like he was trying to decide if he should be mad or not. "Where did you learn it?"

04 swallowed. "I don't know. I'm starting to remember things." He swallowed. "What do *you* remember from your life before...here? Before Alaska?"

03 frowned. He was a handsome dog, and he still looked handsome, even upset. "N...nothing," he finally said. "Master took all our memories. I only remember this place." He zeroed his gaze on 04 and narrowed his yellow eyes. For some reason, possibly because he was the only shepherd with a completely-black face, he looked terrifying when he did this. "What do you remember?" he asked, in a low and dangerous voice.

04 stared at him. Finally, he looked away. "I remembered something about that song earlier. I had a girlfriend who used to listen to it a lot."

03 stared at him like he'd grown caribou antlers. The dog's eyes widened, and he opened his mouth to say something, and then closed it.

04 looked away, scowling. "Don't look at me like that. I didn't ask for this." He hugged himself a little tighter, watching the zonked dog on the bed. 02 still stared up at nothing.

03 took a deep breath, and finally swallowed. "You should talk to Master."

04 let out a long sigh. "I don't think so."

03 looked *horrified*. "04, you're talking *crazy*. You have to tell him."

04 glanced at him. "I feel like I did already, and they put me in this weird horny trance." He shook his head. "I told them what was going on and they just made me dumb and horny for three weeks."

03 snorted. "I hadn't noticed a difference."

04 winced. He glanced at 03 to try to see if it was a joke. The other dog was staring blankly back at him. It didn't feel like a joke. He looked back away.

03 cleared his throat. "Anyway, what's wrong with being dumb and horny? That's kind of our whole deal here, in case you hadn't noticed."

04 turned to him. "I don't think we're *safe*," he snapped. "I feel like something is wrong."

03 stared at him, eyes wide. "W-why? What's wrong?" he asked, softly.

04 didn't look at him. "I don't know," he said.

03 groaned. "*Great*," he said. "I'm glad you had a good reason."

04 glanced at him, and then lowered his head.

03 was silent for a moment, and then let out a long sigh. "Hey, I'm…sorry," he grunted. "This is all just a lot, you know?" He frowned. "Can you wake him up?"

04 looked at him. He took a deep breath. "I want to ask him some questions first."

03 stared at him. "Wh…what? No! Wake him up!" He leaned forward, mad. "Wake him up right now!"

04 lifted his head, curling his paws into gentle fists. "Look, 03, something is wrong here. I need to try to see if I can find out what's going on."

03 looked him up and down, frowning. "I could just yell for help right now, you know," he said. "Master would hear me. I could get him in here to fix whatever you've done."

04 felt the blood drain out of his face as he processed that. He stared at 03, frozen.

03 watched him, the big shepherd's anger slowly melting to confusion, and then to concern, as he slowly realized the extent of 04's terror.

"Hey," he finally said, softly. "Relax." He swallowed. "Jesus. You're really spooked, aren't you." He watched 04 with a furrowed brow.

"*Something is wrong,*" 04 told him.

Eyes widening, 03 watched him. Now he really looked scared. He took a deep breath. "Okay. Ask him questions. But *hurry up*," he snapped. "And don't hurt him."

04 side-eyed him. "I would *never*," he snapped. He turned to the bed.

02 was still sprawled right where he had fallen. His chest gently rose and fell.

"02," he said. "Can you hear me?"

"Yes," the shepherd said, immediately. His voice was raspy but loud, and immediate. They both jumped.

"Are you still hypnotized, 02?"

The shepherd answered without opening his eyes. "Yes, sir."

04 swallowed. "Go deeper, *sleepy puppy*," he ordered.

Next to him, 03 gasped. He pulled his head back and swayed.

02 twitched a little. His entire big body shivered.

"Good boy," 04 told him. "Tell me you're a good boy," he added. He knew that would deepen 02's trance.

"I'm a good boy," 02 mumbled, from the bed.

Next to him, 03 violently shook his head. 04 hadn't even been talking to him but the dog was clearly trying to snap himself out of a new trance.

04 put a hand on 03's arm. "03, wake up."

03's eyes immediately snapped open. He stared at 04, shocked.

The husky turned back to the other shepherd. "02, tell me your mind belongs to me."

02 answered without hesitation. "My mind belongs to you," he rumbled.

"It feels good and right to obey. Doesn't it, 02? It gives you incredible pleasure to follow my orders." 04 didn't know where the words were coming from, but they kept coming. He knew how to do this. He'd been through it a thousand times.

02 began to gently squirm. "It feels good and right to obey," the big dog whispered, shivering. His sheath started to plump and his fat cock slowly started to slide out.

"02, I need to ask you a few questions. Tell me you'll answer whatever I want," he ordered. His voice was clear, confident. He knew what he was doing.

"I'll answer whatever you want," 02 mumbled.

"It will bring you pleasure to answer me," 04 told him. "Every question you answer, your body will fill with pleasure."

"It will bring me pleasure," 02 mumbled. Eyes still closed, he arched his back a little. His cock hardened fully, sliding all the way out.

Next to 04, 03 let out a soft, shuddery breath.

04 nodded. "Good." He reached up and rubbed his eyes. "How far back do your memories go, 02?"

02 answered immediately. "This unit has memories lasting twenty-two days."

04 lowered his hands. He turned to look at 03.

The other shepherd was staring in shock, his ears back, his mouth open.

04 swallowed. "How far back do your orders go?" he asked.

02 answered immediately again. "22 days, sir."

04 felt his face getting hot. "02...when were you born?"

02 didn't open his eyes. "22 days ago, sir."

The husky looked at 03 again. Now the big dog looked scared.

He cleared his throat. "02, you're obviously older than 22 days old. What were you before...this?"

02's brow furrowed. "This unit has been online for 22 days, sir."

04 took a shaky breath. His heart was pounding and the hair on his arms was starting to stand up. The computer terminology all felt familiar to him. "02, what is your programming to account for the time before..." He struggled. "The time before...this unit was...online."

02 immediately piped up. "Programming is as follows: I have arrived at Master's facility anew. My life before here doesn't matter. The dogs are friends. Master is my master. 01 is just another drone just like me. I was a bad dog in my previous life and it's an honor to be reborn to serve Master."

04 just stared.

Slowly, he turned to 03. The other shepherd's mouth was open, and his eyes were wide with horror.

04 frowned. "Still think we're safe?"

03 didn't answer, just watched 02 with increasing concern.

04 cleared his throat. "Unit 02, I need information from before you...came online. I need information about your life from before that period."

Emotionlessly, 02 took a breath. "This unit is not authorized to recall that information," he said.

04 stared blankly at him, and then he remembered the prompt.

"02, I need to access information from your previous life. Administrator clearance 01."

In the husky's peripheral vision, 03 turned to him.

"Access granted," 02 said, in a singsong voice. "Proceed with your inquiry."

04 turned to look at 03. The big shepherd was staring at him with something between wonder and horror.

He turned back to the prone dog. "Unit 02, what was your post before this station?"

02 continued staring mindlessly up at the ceiling, eyes narrowed almost to slits. "Answer not found," he said, emotionlessly.

04 frowned. "Where did you live before Alaska?"

"Answer not found."

04 narrowed his eyes. "What was your name before 02? Your occupation? Your marital status?"

"Answer not found. Answer not found. Answer not found."

04 growled softly. "We're not getting *anywhere*." He turned to 03. "I need to put you under."

03 snapped his head back, eyes wide. "What?! Why?" he demanded.

04 narrowed his eyes. "You're the control group. I want to see if I can access your memories from before the facility." He swallowed. "While we still can."

03's ears folded back and he showed his teeth. He glared down at 04. "No way! Fuck you!"

04 rolled his eyes. "Jesus, 03. Doesn't this terrify you?" He gestured at the passed-out king shepherd. "What if he was just the start? What if *we're next?*"

03's eyebrows shot up. "Why would we be next?!"

04 threw his hands up. "I don't know, maybe because *he's 02, and you're 03 and I'm 04?! You idiot?!!?*"

03 opened his mouth to snap back, but he didn't have a rebuttal for that. He just stared at 04 and eventually closed his mouth.

The husky let out a weary sigh. "Come on. We're wasting time. Don't you trust me?"

03 made a face. "Of course not!" he snapped.

That stung a little. 04 narrowed his eyes. "You know, I don't have to *ask* you this," he said, dangerously. "I can just *do* it to you. I have a free pass to turn your brain off whenever I want."

03 stared at him, and slowly, his eyes widened. He watched 04, his ears folding back, and after a moment his mouth opened. His tongue poked out, just a little, as he started softly panting. He watched him, silently, his mind seemingly racing.

04 furrowed his brow. The big shepherd looked scared, but he almost looked…turned on, too.

The husky felt his jaw drop open. "Oh my God. Are you *into this?!*"

03 actually recoiled his head in shock. "What?! *Of course not!*" he hissed.

04 frowned at him. He pondered. "I mean, it would make sense. We're probably *all* conditioned to be into it." He stepped forward, reaching up to gently touch 03's bare chest.

The big dog flinched, but made no attempt to pull away. He just watched 04, with increasingly-widening eyes.

04 watched him back. "Are you sure you don't like the idea, 03?" he asked, softly, seductively. He trailed his hand down 03's chest, over his flat belly. "You don't want me poking around in your head? Doing whatever I wanted to you?"

03's eyes widened and his brow furrowed. He showed his teeth, like he was going to bite. He didn't move away, at all. "I don't want you in my head," he whispered, shakily.

04 glanced down. The shepherd's cock was threatening to make an appearance again. His sheath was plump and already starting to part.

The husky raised an eyebrow, smiled genially. "I don't know, friend...I could give you some fun *new* commands." He stroked 03's belly and then reached up to feel for one of his nipples. He felt the dog's nipple harden under his fingertips, poking through his fur. "What do you think of that?" He looked up at him with his blue eyes and stared.

03 shivered, watching him. His cock started to slide out of his sheath. "S-stop it," he whispered.

"I could make you *my* servant," 04 told him, letting his hand slide down to gently brush 03's cock.

The big shepherd shivered. He was breathing heavily now. His tongue poked out. He watched 04 from inches away, terrified and aroused, frozen.

04 reached up and gently took the dog's big muzzle in his hands. "Listen," he said. "I have never been more sure about anything that we need answers."

03 watched him, his golden eyes intense and frightened, and eventually he swallowed, and nodded. "O-okay," he whispered.

04 squeezed his face. "I won't do anything weird. I promise." He released the dog. "Lay down."

Turning away, the shepherd let out a shaky breath. He climbed back onto the bed, glanced nervously at the unresponsive 02, and lay on his back, staring up at the ceiling.

He looked scared.

04 leaned in, frowning sympathetically. He touched 03's belly. The big dog flinched.

The husky sighed. "It's okay," he said, softly. "It's gonna be okay. This is good." He patted his chest.

03 frowned severely and glared up at him. "Yeah, and what if *you're* programmed to do this to me? What if this is why you have a bad feeling?" He stared daggers into 04.

The husky didn't have an answer to that. He opened his mouth and then closed it.

"Just get it over with," 03 grumbled. He frowned. "But if you do anything weird to me, I swear to God I'll kick your little black and white ass so hard that—"

"*Sleepy puppy*," 04 snapped at him.

03 flinched as if struck. His eyes immediately unfocused. He stared in 04's general direction, stunned.

04 frowned at him. It was unnerving. 03 looked like he had been stabbed and his brain and body were in the process of realizing it. "*Sleepy puppy!*" he said, again.

03 flinched, staring in his general direction, and tried to respond. His eyes were confused, searching. He lay on the bed, reeling, stunned. "Hhhhhh," he gasped, meaninglessly.

04 leaned forward and stroked the dog's face. "Go to sleep, *sleepy puppy*," he said.

03 jerked one final time, his eyes rolling back into his head, his mouth opening, and finally went out, his arms going limp at his sides. As he did it, he exhaled, letting out a long vocalization. "Aaaaahhhhh-hhhhhhhh," he hissed, and then he was out.

04 swallowed. The dog had sounded like he was dying.

Shivering, he stared. Okay. This was *fine*. Right? Yes. This was good.

The two biggest shepherds lay stretched out, naked, and helpless before him, unresponsive.

He shivered. This was fine.

Okay.

He cleared his throat. "Unit 03, tell me you're a good boy."

03 stiffened on the bed. His tongue retracted into his mouth as he prepared to speak. "I'm a good boy, sir," he mumbled. He shivered a little in apparent pleasure.

04 nodded. He took 03 through a few more prompts. 03 repeated everything dutifully back to him, his big body gently quivering with delight.

04 stared at him. *How many times have I laid on a gurney and repeated back these same prompts?* he wondered. He couldn't recall any specific time, or in fact, even any details at all. But in his heart he knew it to be dozens. Or hundreds. How else did he know all of these scripts?

He watched the big helpless dog.

"Unit 03, status report," he said.

03 answered immediately. "Status: optimal," he mumbled.

04 watched him. "Anything to report?"

"Nothing to report, sir," 03 said, perfectly evenly. He was totally devoid of emotion. His voice actually sounded different when he wasn't angry, 04 realized. He frowned.

He stared at the prone dog. "Have you noticed anything strange at the facility?"

03 processed for a moment. "02's memories deleted. New bear." He paused. "New security. Motion sensors tripped."

04 felt his heart catch in his chest. "Wh-what?!" he asked. "When did the motion sensors trip?"

03 answered emotionlessly. "Eight days ago."

The husky stared. Jesus, he'd been out of it. That settled it — Master and 01 had *done* something to him. He swallowed. "What happened?"

03's brow furrowed. "Clarify request."

04 thought for a moment. "Describe the timeline of the motion sensors activation."

His eyes closed, 03 narrated emotionlessly at the ceiling. "Motion sensor 3 tripped at 8:31 pm. Motion sensor 11 tripped at 9:45 pm. Motion sensor 8 tripped at 11:07 pm. No intruders located. No further incidents."

04 couldn't believe what he was hearing. "Does Master know?"

03 grunted. "16 alerted Master."

04 stared. His mind was racing. Why hadn't 03 mentioned this? Why hadn't *anyone* mentioned it?

This was presumably a new system that was installed as part of 16's security upgrade. It was entirely possible — even *plausible* — that these were false alarms triggered by a new system in its first Alaska winter.

And yet...

He swallowed. "Why didn't you tell me about the motion sensor breaches?" he asked.

"I don't like you," 03 answered, immediately.

04 stared at him, stunned. After a moment, he grimaced. He felt that one in the pit of his stomach.

"Wh...why not?" he asked, softly.

03's brow furrowed. "Always causing trouble," he said.

04 watched the dog.

After a moment, he shook his head. "Are you concerned about 02?" he asked.

"No," 03 answered, immediately.

04 bit back a growl. "*Why not?*" he snarled.

03 was silent for a few moments.

"Inquiry unclear," he said, finally.

04 stared.

He was stalling on the questions he really wanted to ask, he realized.

He sighed.

"Unit 03...how far back do *your* memories go?" he asked.

03 answered immediately. "One thousand, two hundred, and forty-nine days, sir."

04 felt his blood run cold.

That was over three years. The fur on his arms started to stand up.

"Wh-wh-where did you live before Alaska?" he asked.

03 answered without hesitation. "*Tampa*, Florida, United States," he said.

04 stared at him. Tampa? That was almost as far away as you could get from Alaska and still be in the US. More importantly, 03 *knew* he was from Tampa.

He swallowed, his heart pounding. "What was your occupation?" he asked, his voice shaking.

"Law enforcement officer," 03 answered.

04 stared at him. 03 was a cop from Florida.

He could see it.

All his fur was standing on end. He could feel his heart beating in his throat.

"What...what was your name?" he whispered.

"Access denied," 03 told him.

04 stared. He knew the override. He could use it.

Silently, shaking, he stared at the big, helpless dog.

Finally, he shook his head. No. He wouldn't do it. He already had his answer — 03 still had *his* memories, though they were locked away. 02's memories were completely gone. He'd been wiped. Formatted. Factory reset. The only thing in his mind was what Master and 01 had put there in the last three weeks. Something was happening.

He looked down at the two prone shepherds. It was time to wake them up.

"02, 03, can you hear me?"

"I hear and obey," they both said, in unison.

04 watched them. This power was terrifying but also kind of exciting.

He looked down at 03, broad-shouldered, muscular, helpless. Hadn't 03 been turned on by this whole thing? The husky considered, and then remembered he could just ask.

He cleared his throat.

"03, do you like the idea of me poking around in your head?"

03 answered as clear as a bell. "Yes, sir. I love it."

04 stared at him. "03, are you *aroused* by the idea of me poking around in your head? Asserting my control?"

03 squirmed ever-so-slightly. "Y-yes, sir," he answered, a very slight tremor in his voice. He arched his back, almost imperceptibly, and his soft sheath began to plump up.

04 immediately felt his own cock stir. His mouth felt dry. "Would you like me to give you a command?" he asked, his voice raspy. "Would you like me to make you *do things,* 03?"

The big shepherd began to squirm. "Yes, sir. Very much," he said. His arms lay flat at his sides but his red cockhead began to poke out of his sheath.

04 stared. "Okay. Uh." He thought for a moment. "Listen to me, 03. Here is your command. When I tell you to kneel, your body will take over and kneel. When I tell you to beg, your body will take over and lift your hands and arms into a begging posture. You'll beg like a good boy and you won't be able to move until I release you from that position. Do you understand?"

03 squeezed his eyes shut, squirming gently in place. "Yes, sir," he said, his voice low and deep.

"Do you *like* that?" 04 asked, hesitantly.

"Very much, sir," 03 said, shivering.

04 nodded. "Very good. When you wake up, you'll have no memory of these questions, or that command. But you'll still have to obey them. Do you understand?"

"Yes, sir," whispered the shepherd.

04 watched him. "Good." He stared.

He stared for a long time.

Finally, he took a deep breath. "03...wake up," he said.

The big shepherd woke up very slowly. First his mouth opened, and then his eyes slid hesitantly open. He lay there, breathing through his mouth, eyes half open, and looked quizzically around the room. He moved slowly and he seemed to be disoriented.

04 leaned forward and gently stroked his chest. "Hey," he rumbled. "How are you feeling?"

03 groaned, blinking sleepily at him. "Wh...whozza..."

Frowning, 04 leaned forward and licked 03's face. He put his hands on the big dog's chest and did it over and over again. Surprisingly, 03 let him.

Finally, 03 started to stir, lifting his arm to rub at his eyes. He blinked a lot, looking around, eyes bleary. "Unnnnnghh," he said. "Jesus."

04 stared at him with tightened lips. "Are you okay?" he asked.

Slowly, dazed, 03 nodded. "Yeah. That's...that really puts you out," he said, dazed.

04 sighed. "I'm sorry."

03 squeezed one eye shut and looked at him with the other. "I'm okay. Wh...what did you find out?" he asked.

04 stared at him. "Do you want to know what your job was before you came to Alaska?"

Now, 03's eyes both snapped open. He stared at 04 with absolute, undisguised horror. "No!" he gasped.

04 cracked a smile. "I didn't think so. Well, you still remember. It's all there. Master is just blocking it. And I bet if you Slee- I bet if you put *me* under, it would all still be there, too."

03 looked at him, and then turned to look at 02. He was frowning. "So they definitely did something to him." He furrowed his brow. "So what does this mean?" He lifted himself up onto his elbows.

04 took a deep breath. He still didn't really have any answers. "I...don't know. But I don't like it."

03 rolled his eyes elaborately. "Oh, *great*. So you melted my brain for nothing. Super."

04 stared at him, feeling his muzzle curl into a frown. "Not for *nothing*. At least now we know something is going on here."

03 narrowed his eyes. "Yeah, sure, that was worth putting me out. You had a bad feeling and now you still have a bad feeling." He swung his legs off the bed. "You know, this is why nobody likes you. You do nothing but cause trouble."

04 winced. That stung.

03 frowned down at him. "Maybe Master should wipe *you* next." He raised his lips, showing his teeth.

04 narrowed his eyes. "Kneel," he said, simply.

03 stared at him, his brow furrowed in confusion. And then he started moving, lifting himself off the bed, and his eyes instantly snapped open to circles.

"Wh-wh-wh-*what?!*" the big shepherd stammered. He took a few steps and lowered himself to his knees. Terrified, he knelt, staring up at 04.

Holy shit. It *worked*. 04 watched him with raised eyebrows. "Beg," the husky told him.

Eyes wide, the shepherd raised his hands into a begging pose, eyes wide, tail tucked between his legs. He arched his back, his muscular body in a perfect begging pose, his eyes wide and ears back, horrified.

"What is this?!" he gasped, his voice high and frightened. "What did you do to me?!"

04 stared at him, amazed. Fascinated, he crouched down facing the shepherd. Was he faking it? "Are you fucking with me?" he asked, suspiciously.

03 shivered. His big arms and chest flexed and he grit his teeth, fighting against unseen forces, trying to bring his arms down, and failing. He started panting. "What did you *do?!*" he demanded, starting to shake.

04 watched him, amazed. "I programmed you. I told you to do this if I told you to kneel," he said. He watched the frozen shepherd. "You really can't move?"

The other dog curled his lips up and snarled. His ears were up and he was mad now. It looked ridiculously out of place in the submissive begging pose. 03's back was arched with his ass out, his knees open, his balls swinging, his sheath hanging out.

04 stared at him. He looked down at 03's package. Sure enough, his sheath was plumped up.

The shepherd grit his teeth, growling, his entire body tensed as he fought to lower his arms. "L-l-let me go!" he snarled. "So help me, 04!" It was somewhere between a growl and a whimper.

The husky lowered himself to the floor, kneeling in front of 04. "You told me I could do this."

03 lifted his head, hissing, gritting his teeth. "*No I did not!*" he snarled.

04 watched him. "You told me it turns you on."

03 snapped his head down, eyes wide. He stared at 04 with something like terror.

Cautiously, he reached for 03's sheath.

"God dammit!" the shepherd whimpered.

He touched 03's package. The bigger dog flinched, and then whimpered.

03's sheath was hot to the touch and responded to 04's white paw immediately. The husky gently massaged, and 03's cock spilled into his hand immediately.

03 groaned. "04, please...*please...*" he whimpered. He begged 04 with his eyes.

His cock was fully hard now, and 04 lightly curled his fingers around, sliding gently up and down, lazily jacking the big shepherd off.

03 squeezed his eyes shut, struggling with his whole body and not moving an inch. He whined, plaintively, and then degraded into an actual whimper.

04 reached up and stroked his face. "Ssshhh, he said. "I know you love it."

Miserably, 03 half-opened his eyes.

"I could put you out again," he whispered to 03. "I could give you new commands. I could do anything I want to you."

In his hand, 03's cock hardened. The dog stared at him, inches away, his lips parted, his eyes half-closed, breathing hard.

04 leaned in, jacking the shepherd faster. "I could make you my slave. Would you like to be my butler, 03? Wear what I tell you? Serve *me* instead of Master?"

03 whined loudly, lifting his head. "Let me go!" he begged.

"Fine," 04 said. He pulled his hand away. "Maybe I'll play with your buddy instead."

03 snapped his eyes open. "Leave him alone!" he roared.

04 clumsily got to his feet. His knees hurt from all the kneeling. "Was he mad he didn't get to cum in the polar bear?" he asked, staggering to the bed. His legs were asleep.

"*Of course he was,*" 03 snarled, through his teeth, still in his submissive pose. "What do you think?!"

04 turned back to him. "Well! Let's make up for it!" he said. He turned to the massive 02 sprawled out on the bed. "02, are you listening?"

02's deep voice came immediately. "Yes, sir," he rumbled.

"02, when you wake up, you're going to be hornier than you've ever been. You're going to be so aroused you can't think. You're going to need to fuck the nearest thing. If you don't fuck a husky, you might die."

On the floor, frozen in a begging pose, 03's mouth dropped open.

"Do you understand me, 02?"

The big dog grunted. "Yes, sir. I might die."

04 grinned. "You're going to fuck a husky, and you're going to be like a robot. You're going to pump and pump and pump, like a robot." He thought for a moment. "You'll be a dogbot. Hump like an oil rig, long and slow and deep, until I tell you to stop." That was how 04 liked to be fucked, low and slow, until he came. He was going to get 02 off but he might as well make it fun for himself, too. "Do you understand?"

"I'll be dogbot. Fuck a husky," 02 said. The big dog was squirming. His big sheath opened up and his fat cock started to slide out.

04 stared. Oh. Right.

It only took him a second to find 02's lube in a drawer. He oiled 02's huge meatstick, using both hands on the dog's enormous knob. He liberally greased himself under his tail, washed his hands in the little sink, and turned around, bending over 02's desk.

"I'm gonna fuckin' kill you as soon as I can move," 03 snarled, hard and helpless on the other side of the floor.

04 glanced at him, and didn't respond. "02," he said, loudly. "Wake up."

On the bed, 02 snapped his eyes open. He sat up like Frankenstein's monster - stiff, eyes wide, and with a huge erection. He looked around, saw 03, barely registered his presence, and then lasered his eyes on 04's waiting asshole.

04 lifted his curly tail, grinning.

02 stared at him, stunned, alarmed. "I...I...I...I need to..." he stammered.

04 shook his muscular little butt. "It's okay, puppy. Come and get it."

02 moved like he was using his body for the first time. He staggered off the bed, his eyes locked on to 04's asshole.

04 took a deep breath.

02 put one big arm around 04's belly, holding him with startling strength, and one on his cock, guiding it in against the husky's vulnerable entrance.

04 felt 02's huge cock jam into his ass, wiggle for a moment, and then sink into him, splitting him wide open.

04 arched his back, hissing. "*Hnnngggghhh!*" he groaned. "Oh, God yes," he moaned. "*Fuck, I missed this,*" he snarled.

02 didn't even register the comment. He sank in to the hilt, paused a moment, and then started to draw out. He did it slow at first, establishing a rhythm. He was like a machine starting up.

04 arched his back, hard, leaning forward. He grit his teeth, hissing. 02 threatened to pull him back off his feet, and then sank back into the husky, shoving him forward again.

Sensing the husky's unsteadiness, 02 put his big hands on 04's hips and held him. He squeezed, actually digging his claws in, and now 04 really didn't even have to hold the desk or even hold himself in place, because 02 was bigger and stronger than 04 by orders of magnitude and the husky was not going *anywhere.*

"*Ah!*" 04 gasped, squirming. He resisted the urge to clench, bending over, panting. Drool dripped off his tongue as he panted, spotting 02's desktop with husky spit. 02 felt impossibly large inside him — taking 01 had been one thing, but the cat had just let 04 sink onto him and then played with him. 02 was fucking him.

"Ah! Ah! *Ah! Ah! Ah!*" 04 gasped, leaning forward to rest his elbows on the desk, as the massive king shepherd behind him just plowed him relentlessly.

04 settled in, letting his eyes drift shut, enjoying the heat and the fullness and the sounds. 02 was almost silent except for his heavy breathing. He really was a machine. He simply fucked and fucked and fucked, breathing heavily and drooling down 04's back, in and out, splitting the husky open like a pumping rig.

04's insides started to radiate pleasure, and he arched his back hard, curling his tail up as hard as he could, lifting himself up onto his toes to push back into the bigger dog. He could barely keep his eyes open. Pleasure radiated out from under his tail and filled every corner of his body. He wasn't hard, he never was when he was getting fucked, but he knew he could easily reach down and cum in a matter of a minute or so. It was good, it felt good.

He heard whimpering.

Ears perking, 04 snapped his head up. 02 did not stop fucking him and in fact did not even pause.

Baffled, 04 looked over his shoulder.

03 was still frozen in place, begging submissively, rock-hard, ears back. *He* was whimpering.

As 04 watched, the big shepherd grit his teeth, trying frantically to get out of his begging position. All he succeeded in doing was making himself shiver. He was still rock-hard, throbbing, his face flushed with arousal. A drop of pre ran down his iron-stiff cock, and the big dog shuddered from head to toe. He whimpered again.

04 sighed.

He *should* leave 03 in this position, and make him watch his best friend fuck 04's fluffy brains out. He'd been torturing 04 for months, and he obviously wasn't taking the husky's concerns seriously. He thought 04 was always causing trouble? Let him shiver on his knees for an hour or so and let him see what trouble *really* was. Maybe he would cum hands-free as he was trapped in a begging pose.

But then again, 03 was scared, and traumatized over what had happened to his best friend, and just trying to get by the same as 04 was, given the insane circumstances in which they lived.

So what should he do?

Sighing, 04 rolled his eyes.

"02, fuck me on all fours on the floor," he ordered.

The king shepherd didn't even respond, he just pulled, yanking 04 away from the desk, making him yelp loudly. 02 spun on his feet, taking 04 with him. The huge dog got onto all fours, pushing the husky with him, and by the time they were seated on their hands and knees he was fucking the smaller dog again.

04 got shoved forward by the inward thrust and yanked backward by the pullout, so 02 straightened up and dug his claws into the husky's hips again.

04 panted, spotting the floor with drool, trying to adjust.

Three feet away from them, 03 knelt, stunned. His wide eyes roved over both of the entangled dogs. His tongue lolled out. He looked like a mixture of aroused and scared.

04 looked at him, eyes half shut, tongue hanging out. 02 was back in a rhythm and it was turning his brain to happy jello again. "Hey," he mumbled to 03.

The shepherd swallowed, frowning. He looked miserable. "Please," he whimpered. "Let me out."

04 frowned. "Are you gonna be n-nice?" he gasped.

03 strained, gritting his teeth. He shivered again. His dick wiggled. He really needed release, too, 04 realized. "*Yes!*" he whimpered. His ears wouldn't rise from his head.

04 nodded, lazily, the big shepherd still vigorously fucking him. "Okay. If you come over here and use my mouth, I'll release you."

03 stared at him, his eyes widening. "Wh-what?"

04 raised his head and flashed his teeth. "Come over here and fuck my mouth!" He scowled. "I missed both of you." He looked away. "Get over here and muzzlefuck me!"

When he looked back, 03 was staring at him in stunned silence, his mouth open. He finally closed his mouth, and nodded. "Okay," he said.

04 narrowed his eyes. "You're released," he said.

03 collapsed like a puppet with cut strings, dropping immediately. He landed hard on his elbows, grunting loudly as he hit the floor of the trailer. He stayed there for a long moment, eyes wide, panting.

04 felt his ears fold back against his head. *This is where he snaps my neck*, he thought, watching the big shepherd warily.

02 reacted to none of this, continuing to vigorously fuck the husky's wet hole.

03 finally took a deep breath and let it out as a long, shuddery exhalation. He lifted himself shakily to his hands and knees, and then to his knees, crawling toward 04, eyes narrowed.

04 looked away. He cowered, his ears flat. He would have tucked his tail between his legs except he obviously couldn't with 02 back there.

"*You…little…bastard…*" 03 growled, advancing toward him.

04 licked his chops nervously. 03 was definitely going to be rough, assuming he even really did muzzlefuck 04 instead of just strangling him outright.

03 put his big mitt-like hands on 04's shoulders.

The husky flinched.

Now 02 *did* grunt, because 04 had clenched on his cock. He recovered a moment later.

03 did not grab 04's throat, or muzzle, or even his ears. To the husky's surprise, 03 reached under 04's chest and lifted him straight upward.

04 found himself lifted helplessly to his knees. He arched his back to accommodate the king shepherd still pounding his asshole.

03 was directly in front of him, and then crushed up *against* him. He reached around 04 to take 02's hands. "Here, buddy," he told him. "Hold him like this."

03 guided 02's huge arms to bearhug 04 from behind, holding him by the shoulders and chest. 02's massive arms enveloped 04, crushing him against his big belly, and the husky suddenly realized he couldn't possibly escape even if he wanted to, and then 02 started pumping again, and now it was *so* much worse. 02 was just shallowly humping now, barely sliding half of his length in and out, but it was so much harder because 04 couldn't move *at all*, and when 02 hilted he *really* hilted. His knot was starting to swell, and every time it passed into or out of 04's asshole it stretched him a little further.

04 squirmed helplessly, eyes wide, whimpering. He looked pleadingly up at 03.

The big shepherd smiled sadistically down at him. "You missed both of us, huh?" he said, low and dangerous. He leaned in, looming over 04, and reached for the husky's dick, flattening it against his body. "Did you miss this?"

He leaned down for a kiss and instantly shoved his huge flat tongue into 04's mouth, choking him. 04 writhed, helplessly caught in 02's grasp, and somehow the inescapable bearhug was made so much worse by the relentless invasion of his muzzle and his asshole simultaneously.

03 held him there a long time before he broke the kiss. As he pulled away a streamer of drool connected them. He reached up, now, forcing 04's muzzle open with his thumb.

04 struggled to yank his head away, but 03 was too strong and he couldn't get away.

He played with the husky's mouth, jamming his thumb in, and his cock, massaging him relentlessly at the same time. It was horribly overstimulating and shorting 04's brain out with pleasure.

"Did you miss *this?*" 03 growled.

04 whimpered. "Yetth!" he whined.

03 chuckled darkly. "I knew it. You *love* it, don't you? Helpless little puppy."

04 shivered. He'd wanted to suck 03 off. He'd wanted to bring them back together. Instead, 03 was torturing him with pleasure. He'd lost control, and he loved it.

"This is what you wanted, isn't it?" 03 teased him. He leaned in, looming, crushing him between 02 and 03. "You love this, you little slut. You're helpless to resist. You can't even argue with me. Look how much you love this."

"*Nnnhhhhhhhrowrooowrooooo!*" 04 whimpered. He *did* love it. He needed it so bad. He needed to cum. "*H-harderrr,*" he begged 03.

02 was the one to hear him, and thrust harder, lifting him up off of his knees. 04 gasped, mildly horrified to discover that he was being supported by 02's arms and his cock. His eyes went wide.

03 noticed, raised his eyebrows in surprise, and lowered his eyes, grinning sadistically. He was still inches away, still playing with 04's mostly-flaccid cock. His hands were huge and strong and unavoidable. 04 felt captured and exposed at the same time.

There was pleasure rising in his guts, pleasure he couldn't resist.

04 stared up at 03, eyes wide and desperate.

The big shepherd chuckled. "You can't handle much more, can you, little puppy? I can see it in your eyes." He leaned forward, nipping at the side of 04's neck, still playing relentlessly with his dick.

04 lifted his head, his eyes rolling back. His legs were starting to go numb. He squirmed, and 02 moaned behind him.

03 connected their muzzles again, shoving his tongue into 04's mouth, fighting with the husky's tongue.

"*Mmmmmmmmmm!*" 04 moaned, straining to talk around 03's muzzle. "*Tie me!*" he shouted.

Behind him, on the very next thrust, 02 popped into him.

The big dog's knot wasn't all the way inflated, but it was still a noticeable pop as it slid into 04, and it was too much for him. The husky shivered, arching his back, shaking violently, his ass and cock spasming as he came all over 03's hands. Neither of the shepherds let up, 02 still bucking as best he could tied inside the husky, and 03 shoving his tongue down 04's throat, still relentlessly massaging his spasming cock. "*Aaaah-aaahhh!*" 04 moaned. "*Cum!*" he squealed.

02's arms crushed him now — he had *barely* been holding 04 before, he realized, as the big dog almost squeezed the air out of his lungs — and bucked in one final time, and his breath turned to growling, panting breaths as his entire massive body tensed.

04 came for a long time, feeling the urge to buck in his hips, to hump, to smear 03's black paws with all of the seed in his body, but 03 kept up, pushing back against him, kissing him, crushing him between the two dogs' big bodies, so 04 couldn't even move, just grind. 04 whimpered and whined and shivered between them, and they both held him and squeezed him and kissed him.

The husky felt semen and anxiety pouring out of him, and he wasn't even sure when he was done. 03 broke the kiss and leaned in to nibble at his neck.

04 hung, helpless, panting.

02 took a long time to recover, too, perched on his knees, sweating and panting. He took a few deep breaths, letting them out as long sighs, and finally let out a long "hooooo-boy." He swallowed, leaned forward, and gently nuzzled 04's head and ears.

When he could finally breathe again, 04 cleared his throat. He took a deep breath, let it out, and took another. His horniness was finally sated.

"Lay me down," he said, raspily.

02 wasn't under his control anymore, but he complied regardless.

Putting his paws under him, feeling like his whole body was sore, 04 perched on all fours directly in front of 03's rigid, dripping cock.

The big dog seemed surprised. "You sure?" he asked, skeptically.

04 just stared up at him.

03 nodded. "Suit yourself!" he said. His tone was flippant but he looked relieved. He inched excitedly forward, poking his throbbing dick into 04's mouth, and immediately moaned in relief.

04 sucked diligently, closing his eyes, letting his conditioning take over. 03's cock was hot and familiar and reassuring in his mouth. The big shepherd grabbed his ears, straining to hold on with his messy hands, and 04 was rewarded with a steady stream of pre and then a delightfully satisfying rush of acrid cum on his tongue.

When the big dog had stopped grunting and shivering, they moved to the bed.

04 was still stuck to 02, who did his best to move the smaller dog without jostling him. When they got onto the bed, 02 cuddled up behind him, licking his ears and kissing his neck. He seemed pretty out of it, probably because 04 had *made* him fuck so hard for so long. As soon as they were laying down the dog seemed to get drowsy, and unsurprisingly, he was out before his knot had even deflated.

03 was…fine. He climbed in bed too, and he faced 04 because that was the only way he could face.

The husky stared at him. 03 looked back.

Finally, 04 frowned. "Do you really hate me?" he whimpered, softly.

03 blinked at him, shocked, and then his face slowly softened. "N…no, 04. I just…" He started over. "Things are just…weird right now. 02 really needs help and this is all…an adjustment. It's all I've been thinking about and…things got weird. I'm…I'm sorry. I don't hate you."

04 blinked at him, and then smiled. He started wagging, but then 02 grunted in his sleep, so he stopped.

03 watched the whole thing, and then rolled his eyes. He rolled his shoulders, getting comfortable.

04 looked him up and down. He deeply inhaled, taking in both of their scents. Comforting. Familiar.

03 stared at him from inches away. He was waiting for him to say something. Patiently. Calm. He knew something was on 04's mind. Again, it reminded 04 of the early days.

"Do you ever wonder…" he asked, his voice sounding foreign even to himself. "…about why we're here?" He swallowed. "About what Master is…doing to us? What the point of all this is?"

03 blinked at him. His golden eyes flicked away as he thought about it. "I mean…no, not really. I trust him."

04 frowned. That wasn't really conclusive. Master could have made 03 trust him. He probably did, in fact.

03 watched him. "You're still worried."

04 let out a long sigh. "They did something to 02," he said. "They…wiped him. His memories aren't just *repressed*, like ours. They…reset him, somehow. His memories are *gone*."

Behind him, 02 gently stirred. He rumbled, opening his huge mouth and yawning, smacking his lips directly into 04's ear, and then calmed down again, resting the weight of his huge head on 04's neck.

03's eyes left 04 to watch the other shepherd, and then flicked back down to the husky. "We got 02 *back*," he said. "The old 02."

04 stared. "We got *our* old 02 back. The *real* old 02 is gone forever." He swallowed, feeling himself start to shiver. "He's…he's dead. They killed him, 03," he said, tears forming in his eyes.

03 thought about that, frowning. "Well…if that was him coming through, then the *real* old 02 was an asshole." He reached up to stroke 04's face.

04 tried to come up with a rebuttal to that, but he couldn't, because 03 was right. He closed his mouth.

"It's okay, 04," 03 whispered to him. "*We're* okay. It's all gonna be okay."

Silently, 04 nodded. "I'm gonna make sure of that," he said, softly. "I'm gonna keep us safe. Me and you and 02 and 06." He took a breath and let it out as a shuddery sigh. "I'm gonna make sure we're all safe. Forever."

Quietly, 03 nodded. He didn't say anything in response. Just scooted a little closer, nose to nose with 04.

Behind the husky, 02 tightened his grasp, letting out a happy, satisfied rumble, and despite his anxiety, nestled in the warm pile of sweaty shepherds, 04 quickly fell asleep.

Root Cause

The next day was the worst day of 04's life, as far as he knew.

He woke up around 5 am, stuffed between 02 and 03, his entire body stiff. He carefully, and then haphazardly, extricated himself from the forest of shepherd limbs and bellies, crawled down off the dog-pile, picked up his pants and shirt, and staggered back across the connection hall to the husky trailer. It was silent and dark and the dead of night, the scant moonlight reflecting off the snow and eerily lighting the windows. The aurora borealis was in view, tinting the light that filtered in through the windows a gentle, hazy green.

He passed 06's room, not wanting to disturb him, and went right to his own room. He was pleasantly surprised to find 06 curled up in 04's bed.

The other husky barely stirred as 04 climbed into bed and cuddled up behind him. The dog radiated the scent of sweat, and cum, and jaguar. 04 took a deep breath, burying his nose in the other husky's ruff, and squeezed him tight. 06 barely stirred, except to let out a tired, affectionate grumble, and then went immediately back to sleep.

04 lay behind him, awake, thinking. Thinking about 03, who had been a cop in Tampa sometime around three and a half years ago, and himself, and the bear, and the mine, and 01, and Master, and what it all meant. He couldn't come up with anything, and to his surprise, listening to the soft, regular breathing of the other husky, feeling him warm in 04's arms, eventually he drifted off.

The morning was routine — 10 cooked a huge late breakfast for them, assisted by 11. It was pancakes with jarred strawberries and bacon and rehydrated eggs, and 04 felt like he was tasting food for the first time in weeks. Everyone came and went. He saw 02 and 03, together as always. 02 gave him a shy smile. 03 said nothing but put a comforting hand on 04's shoulder as he walked past. 04 was quiet but passed it off as a long, late night.

They didn't have the bulk of their tasks, but 04 still had to sweep the mess trailer, or by Monday the fur would be half a foot deep. 06 left him to go take a nap, and even 10 and 11 left the mess to go see 16 for a bit.

He was deep in thought, his back to the door, sweeping up a four-inch pile of dog fur, when the door opened behind him.

He heard someone start to say something, and then everything went black. And then he was out.

It took 04 a long time to wake up.

He was groggy. His thoughts were moving like cold grease, almost solid. His body wouldn't respond. He could tell he was lying on his back, but his arms wouldn't rise from his sides. His eyes wouldn't even open.

"04," said a small voice above him. "Come on, 04. Wake up."

The husky opened his eyes to slits, and saw a small lutrine face, inches away from him. He smelled him as soon as he saw him, and he could smell other things — cleaning solution and rubbing alcohol and hot equipment and otter.

04 snapped his eyes open.

Master stood over him, boring into him with his red eyes. 01 was behind him, towering over him in a black sweatshirt. 04 jerked violently in shock, his arms and chest spasming before he could even fully perceive what was around him, except his body didn't move. His wrists were restrained at his sides, surrounded by thick leather cuffs, held helplessly down to the table, and as he tried to free himself he realized his legs were shackled too. He was in the research trailer. He was on the gurney. He was *strapped down to the fucking gurney with Master and 01 standing over him.* His heart launched into his throat.

He looked up at Master, horrified. This wasn't happening. This couldn't be happening. *This couldn't be happening.*

The little otter opened his mouth. "04—" he started, gently.

His voice broke through 04's disbelief.

This *was* happening.

This was happening.

He was going to die.

Everything went red. 04 felt his body responding, yanking on the restraints, jerking, thrashing, flailing. He couldn't breathe. He was going to die and Master wouldn't even be the one to do it, because he was going to suffocate right here on the table.

Master said something, loudly, something 04 couldn't hear, because his brain was no longer processing sound. A thousand panicked thoughts were crashing through him every second.

> *they know what I did*
> *they're going to wipe me*
> *they're going to erase me*
> *I have to escape*
> *I'm going to die*
> *I can't breathe*
> *I can't breathe*
> *I can't breathe*

He wasn't getting away. He was starting to hurt himself. His arms and legs were ripping. His joints were going to tear before the leather did.

There was a sound, a long and terrified scream-howl, and 04 was stunned to realize that it was coming from himself.

01 surged toward him out of the background, and suddenly 04 felt himself crushed against the table, pushed down by something huge and black and warm and *immeasurably* stronger than him, and now his struggles didn't matter because he couldn't even move. It was on his chest and shoulders, pinning him to the gurney, and the warmth and strength started to leech through his terrified adrenaline rush, and he realized 01 was leaning on top of him, pinning him to the table with his full body weight.

He was crushed, held, pinned, and suddenly he could feel his body again. He took a long and ragged gasping breath.

01 leaned on him, hard, and 04 could finally resist the urge to tear at his restraints. He still couldn't breathe, and he gasped, panting, his tongue lolling out. His heart was racing, adrenaline burning through his veins, and his entire body would not

unclench. He squirmed against 01, tongue lolling out, and he could smell his own sweat and panic.

"—easy, easy, you're okay, easy, easy," 01 was mumbling, low and soft and comforting, and 04 could suddenly hear it.

He stared up at the cat: crazed, shaking, panting, gasping.

01 straightened up, his big hands on 04's chest, still holding him down. The black cat watched him, his yellow eyes wide and shocked.

04 sucked in a breath. "Please," he whimpered. His voice didn't sound like himself. "Please let me go," 04 whined. He could barely form the words. He just wanted to whine, to cry, to whimper.

"04, what's the m—"

"Please let me go! I'll be good. I promise. I won't be bad anymore." His heart hurt. His entire chest hurt. He was starting to cry. He cowered, his ears back, shaking, looking from the cat to the otter, and back. "I don't want to die."

01 stared at him, his brow furrowed, horrified, his feline features twisted into shock. "What?!" he gasped, stunned.

04 pushed up under him, trying to arch his back. Tears were streaming down his face. "Please! Please let me go!" he whimpered. His voice was shaking. It was getting hard to breathe again. "I won't tell anybody what I know. I won't use the triggers again. I promise." He was sobbing, now. It was getting hard to get words out. "I won't ask any more questions. I'll just be a good boy. I j-just wanna go back to my room. Please. *Please.*" He stared up at the jaguar, begging with his eyes, his breath hitching.

01 stared down at him, stunned.

Master peeked around the jaguar. He looked startled, eyes wide, disbelieving. "01, what is happening?" he asked. His voice was shaking.

The big cat frowned, staring at 04. "I don't know, sir," he said, his voice uncertain. "I'm going to put him out again."

04 felt his blood turn to ice.

I'm going to put him out.

He recoiled, his breath catching in his throat. 01 knew the trigger phrases, he realized, horrified.

He's gonna say it.

01 loomed over him. "04, *sleepy pu—*"

"NNOOOOAOWWROOOO!" 04 scream-howled. He arched his back, his entire body spasming.

01 jerked violently. He actually leapt off his feet, six inches or so off the ground.

"DON'T DO IT!" 04 screamed. He pulled on the restraints. He knew it was useless but his body wouldn't let him stop pulling. *"Please! Don't put me out don't put me out don't put me out!"* he howled. He squeezed his eyes shut, thrashing.

01 stared down at him, his eyes wide, his ears back. He looked terrified.

"Please please please!" 04 squeaked. He was shaking so hard that the restraints were starting to dig into his wrists again. His arms wouldn't unclench. "Don't do it. D-don't," he whimpered, desperately. He stared up at 01 plaintively.

01 watched him, and then turned down to look at Master.

Staring at the husky, Master swallowed. "Leave him," he said, softly. He frowned. He didn't look mad, or accusatory. He looked concerned, and shocked, like he couldn't believe what he was seeing. His eyes were wide.

04 snapped his head up to look at the jaguar. *"Why do you know that?!"* he scream-accused. "Why do you *know* that trigger phrase?!"

01 stared down at him. The jaguar's eyes went from wide to guilty, and suddenly he looked away.

04 stared up at him, and as he watched the big cat guiltily avoid eye contact, something horrible occurred to him, and then it all made sense.

He stared up at 01. "You don't…know…the trigger phrase," he said, slowly. "You…you *made* it."

01 wouldn't look at him.

04 sank back onto the gurney. The world felt very far away. His vision tracked back to the jaguar. "You're not a drone, are you," he heard himself ask.

The cat glanced at him, but only for a moment. He was grimacing.

"I'm sorry," he said, softly, finally.

So that was it. It had all been a lie. They weren't finally growing closer after all these years. 01 had been in on it from the start.

He really was alone.

Dazed, 04 felt himself go limp. He reflexively tried to put his arms around himself, so he could curl up in a dejected little ball, but he was still restrained.

Frustration and misery bubbled up inside him.

"ROWRROROOOUGHH!" he scream-howled, thrashing against his restraints, making the metal rattle violently against the sides of the gurney. Master and 01 both jumped, startled.

They stood in silence for a moment.

After a few moments, 01 glanced at Master, and looked back at the dejected husky. He set his jaw. "I'm going to let him out," he said.

Master's eyes widened. "Ooooone," he said, long and drawn out. "Are you sure that's a good idea?"

The big cat turned to glower down at him. "He's *upset*," he growled.

Master glanced up at the cat, and then looked back down at 04. "I don't want him to hurt himself," he said, his red eyes wide. He swallowed. "Or anyone else."

01 grunted. "Look at him. He's not even moving."

Master looked up at the cat one more time, and then back down at the husky. He let out a shaky breath. "Okay," he said. "Let him out."

01 nodded. He leaned over 04, taking his wrist, gently lifting his arm, and fumbled with the big buckle. He wouldn't look 04 in the eye. He unclasped the husky's arms, leaving 04 to rub his injured wrists, and then moved to his bare husky feet. He unclasped his ankles and returned to the side of the bed, where he slid one massive jaguar arm under his back. He was so big that 04 was almost in a sitting position by the time 01 got his arm under the husky's back. The jaguar lifted him carefully, tenderly, into a sitting position.

04 watched him.

"I'm sorry," 01 whispered. He didn't move away, just left his huge paws on 04's shoulders.

04 felt something inside him break, and lifted his paws to cover his face, as his chest clenched and something spilled out of him.

He cried for a long time, unable to stop or even help himself, tears running down his face and his hands, stinging his raw wrists, as he hitched and strained to breathe. 01 stood there the whole time, guarding him, one big hand on each of 04's shoulders. It still felt comforting, even though 01 was the reason he was crying, which really, truly, was absolutely the worst part of it all.

Finally, 04 felt he was empty. Empty of tears, empty of emotions. His energy was completely sapped. He just…ran out.

01 gently squeezed him and straightened up. Master appeared and handed 04 a pile of tissues. Feeling numb, 04 wiped his eyes and his nose, and set the wad of tissues on the gurney next to him.

With his exhaustion came clarity.

He looked at the two of them.

"Who are you?" he asked 01, softly.

The jaguar frowned. "I'm a neuroscientist," he said. He looked like he was intending to continue, but then he just…didn't.

04 nodded. "Okay," he said. He swallowed. "Don't put me out, please," he asked, flatly. His throat hurt and his voice was raspy. He felt like he was in someone else's body. "It's not helping."

01 shook his head. "I won't," he said.

Swallowing, 04 turned to Master. "And please stay out of my head," he asked, softly. His heart started pounding at the thought of asking something of Master, but he was desperate. He looked away, submissively, feeling his ears fold back. "For now. Please."

Master's eyebrows went up just a little, but it was only in surprise. He didn't look mad at all. "Okay," he said.

04 looked back and forth between them. "What's happening to me?" he asked, softly.

01 and Master looked at each other.

01 took a deep breath, and let it out as an uncertain sigh. He searched for his words for a long time. "We *think* you are remembering things. Even after we suppress them." He frowned. "Your memories are irregular. It's causing you…distress."

04 watched him, and slowly nodded. "Why me?" he asked.

01's face softened. "We don't know," he said, gently.

04 looked up at him, and then at Master. "Why did you have me tied up?" he asked, his voice shaking. He tried to keep the sound of betrayal out of his voice. It didn't work.

01 frowned. "I'm so sorry. I thought…I thought it would calm you." He let out a long sigh. "Sometimes it helps."

04 nodded. He swallowed, hard. He could think, now that he was out of the restraints. And breathe. He looked around, at the scary device that had been around 02's head, the one he thought they were going to use on him. "What does this machine do?" he asked.

01 and Master looked at each other. The otter cleared his throat. "You know I have…abilities."

04 nodded slowly. He swallowed. "You control minds."

Master took a long breath. He looked up, made eye contact. "My abilities are very strong but they're not…permanent. Eventually a subject will regress and start to remember the memories I've blocked."

04 felt his eyes widen. He should have wanted his memories back. Instead, the thought terrified him.

Master frowned. "The machine solves that problem. It's a targeted destruction of long-term memories. If the subject has nothing to regress to, he can't regress."

04 looked up at the big jaguar. "That's not what he's here for, then?" he said.

01 frowned.

Master glanced up at the jaguar, and then looked back down at 04. "No. 01 is here because fourteen confused dogs was a lot to handle, and deep hypnosis turned out to be the perfect tool for managing that. You're all blank slates — very receptive to hypnosis. His triggers keep you all calm. Complacent. Obedient."

04 felt the blood drain out of his face. He looked up at the big cat.

01 wouldn't look at him.

Swallowing, he looked back down at Master. "Why did you put 02 through the machine? Are you just…working through the drones?" He shivered. 03 would be next. And then him.

Master blinked, and then took a breath and let out a long sigh. "No," he said. "*That* was an *entirely* different problem." He looked up at 01.

The jaguar swallowed. "02 was experiencing… breakthroughs. He had a very… *strong* personality, and we were having difficulty controlling him." He frowned. "He didn't remember anything, but his past trauma and aggressions were coming through in his behavior here. It became…" He swallowed, hard. "…very bad."

04 glanced at Master. "So you did it for his *benefit?*" He narrowed his eyes.

The otter frowned. "Is that so hard to believe?"

04 stared back. "Have you done it to anyone else?"

Master maintained eye contact. "No," he said.

04 looked at him, and then up at 01. He swallowed. "Are you going to do it to me?" he asked, softly.

Master and 01 looked at each other.

"No," 01 said.

"Maybe," Master said.

04 turned to Master with horror. 01 swung his entire head around to glare murderously.

The otter took a shocked step back, raising his hands defensively. "Don't look at me like that!" He gestured at 04. "Look how miserable he is!" He turned to the husky. "Can you honestly tell me you wouldn't be happier starting over?" He frowned.

Involuntarily, 04 began shaking.

Master opened his mouth to say something else, but didn't say anything. "I'm sorry," he said, looking the terrified husky up and down. "Truly. This is uncharted territory." He took off his glasses and rubbed his eyes.

They were all silent for a moment.

01 stared at the husky. "04," he said, gently. "I need some information from you. Can you answer some questions for me?"

Silently, looking away, 04 nodded.

"How did you know the trigger phrase and the programming sequence?"

04 stared at the floor. "I don't know."

"Did you remember it?"

04's wrists were starting to sting painfully. He gently rubbed them, one at a time. His skin was raw and irritated under his matted-down fur. He'd probably pulled out half the fur on his wrists. "It just came to me," he answered, hollowly.

"Do you remember your name?"

"No," 04 answered.

"Do you remember anywhere you've lived before Alaska?"

"No," 04 said, staring out the window.

Suddenly, he felt it. A little itching at the back of his brain. Like something was trying to distract him.

Master was in his head. His heart launched into his throat.

He snapped his head to the otter, who was staring right at him. Horrified, he lurched away, slapping his hands over his ears. "*Get out!*" he screamed.

Both of them jumped. Master looked horrified and then guilty. "Oh God, I'm sorry" he squeaked. "Part of it is passive." The otter grimaced and swallowed hard. "I don't even think about it. It's just…an impulse. Like bouncing your leg or tapping your fingers." He frowned. "I'm so, so sorry. I was thinking about what you were feeling and it just happened."

04 stared at him, panting, and shivered.

"I just…see into brains sometimes," Master said. "I won't do it again."

04 frowned, and turned away. Shakily, he raised his eyes back up to 01. He swallowed, steeling himself.

"So now what?" the husky asked, softly.

Master and 01 looked slowly at each other, and then back to him.

"We don't know," Master said, softly.

01 frowned. "We were trying to determine what had changed your status. Which part of your programming is breaking down."

04 stared at them. It sounded like a lot of tinkering going on in his head. He lowered his head, his ears folding back. "Are you going to experiment on me?" he asked, softly.

Master grimaced. 01 furrowed his brow.

The otter swallowed, and let out a slow breath. "It's not...like that," he said, frowning.

04 stared at him in disbelief. "*How* is it not like that?" he asked, quietly.

The otter took a deep breath. "Look, this is not...we aren't doing...the point of this isn't..." He seemed frustrated. He took a deep breath and finally he spoke again. "There's no good way to describe what's going on here. Right now, let's concentrate on finding a solution."

01 sighed.

04 glanced up at him, and then turned back to stare dubiously at Master. He let out a long sigh. "A solution?"

Master raised an eyebrow. "Besides the obvious." His eyes flicked to the machine.

04 shivered. He swallowed. "Does your...control still work on me?" he asked Master.

The otter blinked his red eyes back at him. "Pardon?" he asked.

04 swallowed. "Can you still control my mind?" He looked away, his face feeling hot. He'd wanted to know just for the purpose of troubleshooting, but asking the question out loud was horrifying. And a little exciting.

Master stared at him, his little mouth hanging open. Finally he cocked his head, furrowing his brow. "Do you...want me to *try?*" he asked.

04 shivered. "Will you bring me back?"

Master stared at him. "Of course," he said, gently.

The husky watched him. He squeezed his hands into fists. "Okay," he said. "Then do it."

Master nodded.

Scared, excited, his heart pounding, 04 looked shyly at the small otter.

Master stared back at him, his red eyes focused and unblinking, and suddenly 04 felt the otter pouring into him. He gasped, jerking his head back, but Master was gushing into his brain like a tidal wave of scalding hot water, obliterating all of his thoughts and feelings and concerns and opinions, it was just Master, *he* was only Master, only Master's will. His body was gone and his brain was gone, and nothing mattered except the glowing red eyes in front of him and what Master wanted, and what Master would command him to do. His life and his existence and his God were Master.

The tidal wave subsided, and 04 found himself on his knees, on the floor, his muzzle pressed up against Master's crotch, clinging to the otter's short legs. He was rock-hard and he couldn't feel most of his body. He stared up at him, dazed, exhausted, and insanely, *he liked it.* The feeling of Master's hard cock against his muzzle, his musky otter scent filling 04's nostrils, was still bliss.

Master reached down and stroked his face. 04 shivered in pleasure.

"Well, I guess that isn't the problem," Master said, low and soft.

04 stared up at him. He still couldn't talk yet, and his whole body felt numb.

01 reached down, put his big hands under 04's armpits, and effortlessly lifted the husky off the floor. He hefted him like a cord of firewood, and set him down on the gurney.

04 blinked at him, and then frowned. "I hate it when you do that," he said, feeling his face heat up.

01 had the grace to look embarrassed. "Sorry," he said, softly.

Master pointed. "Don't be sorry. Now *you* try."

01 turned to him. "What?"

Master frowned. "We tried my abilities. Try using some triggers on him."

01 blinked at him and then turned back to 04, frowning.

The husky stiffened. He still felt betrayed by the lying jaguar. But Master did have a point.

Looking away, the dog sighed. "Please just do it," he said.

01 hesitated. "Are you sure?"

04 glanced at him. "Just do it!" he snapped.

The jaguar frowned. He looked down at 04, stooping down to his level.

04 looked away. His eyes suddenly felt wet, and he had to blink away tears. The big jaguar's attention felt like salt in a raw wound.

"04," 01 rumbled, softly. "Please look at me."

04 clenched his jaw. His heart was pounding. *I like you just fine*, 01 had told him. It had all been part of his lies. "I can't," he said, blinking again. This time the tears ran down his face.

01 let out a long sigh. "I understand," he said, softly. "It's okay, good puppy."

04 squeezed his eyes shut.

01's big hands reached up to stroke his face. "*Good, good puppy,*" he told him.

The words settled into 04. Something inside his brain shifted.

Startled, he opened his eyes.

The panther was stroking his face. His touch felt hot. Electric. 04 felt himself straighten up. He was starting to feel far away again. "Whh—" he mumbled, staring into the big cat's wide golden eyes.

"*Good, good puppy,*" 01 repeated, and now the words seemed to echo in 04's head.

He straightened up further, arching his back. He felt his muzzle open. His tongue lolled out. He was dizzy now, too, but it felt good. Energizing. His mind was at a standstill, his thoughts would not come, he could think of nothing but eagerness: *maybe he would say it again.*

01 squeezed the sides of his face, rubbing his muzzle. "*Good, good puppy,*" he said. "*Who's a good puppy?*"

04 felt his heart pounding. He held himself ramrod straight. His hands rose and curled at his chest, in a begging posture. He stared forward with unfocused eyes at the blurry black shape in front of him. "*I'm* a good puppy," he whined, shivering.

The cat in front of him was still talking, but he couldn't hear anything anymore. He didn't care what was happening. He just held still and stared straight ahead, drooling onto the floor, eyes wide and happy and unfocused.

Finally, something started to cut through the foggy haze surrounding him. "Come back to us, good boy. Breathe. Relax. Two. Getting closer. Starting to feel your body. Aaand....One."

04 opened his eyes, or at least tried to, except his eyes were already open. He blinked feverishly. For a moment he was confused, and then he remembered where he was and what was going on.

He looked around. He was kneeling on the gurney, hot, and rock-hard in his work pants. His shirt was pulled up around his chest and his bare belly was still tingling from the rubbing he had been getting. His stomach fur was all fluffed the wrong way. Startled, he looked at Master and 01.

04 felt himself flush. Folding his ears back, he scrambled back into a seated position, legs hanging over the gurney, tugging his shirt back down.

01 looked him over, frowning. "How was that?" he asked. "Effective?"

04 shot him a look. "Do you really have to ask?" he snapped.

01 stared at him, surprised, and then dipped his head, folding his ears back. He looked away, embarrassed.

04 felt a little bad. But what did he care? 01 didn't really care about him at all anyway.

Master snorted. "Great, so we're back at square one. My abilities aren't the problem, and your hypnosis isn't the problem." He raised an annoyed eyebrow.

04 looked back and forth between them.

That left only one solution.

He thought about 02 in the machine, and pictured himself wandering cluelessly around the facility. Opening doors he'd been through a thousand times, to see what was behind them. Introducing himself to his packmates, face vacantly happy and brainless. He started gently shivering. "You're going to wipe me, aren't you?"

01 stiffened. "I will not let that happen," he growled.

Master sighed. "Juan, maybe he's got a point," he said, his voice resigned. "It's very telling that 02 and 04 both escalated at the same time."

04 stared. He felt the blood slowly drain from his face.

Had…had he said J-

01 rose to his full height. "02 was a special case!" he snapped. "You know what was wrong with him. You know *what he'd done* before he got here!" He showed his huge feline teeth. "It's a miracle he lasted this long!"

04 stared, desperate to follow. Had he imagined it?

Master glared. "And we've ruled out your guitar theory."

"No we haven't!" 01 snapped. "Study after study has linked music to long-term memory recall!"

Master looked away. It was almost an eyeroll. "And that clearly was an *exacerbating factor* and not the root cause. Please, Juan, you of all people can't ignore—"

04 jerked violently in shock. All of the fur on his arms stood up.

He'd said it again.

Involuntarily, 04 let out a whimper.

They both fell silent and turned to him.

04 felt his heart pounding. His hackles stood up.

He swallowed. "Did…did you call him *Juan?*" he whispered.

They both stared at him. Their eyes widened. Master's mouth opened slightly. 01's ears folded back and his eyes snapped open. They both looked horrified.

04 cowered, his ears back.

They were both silent.

"You could hear that?" 01 asked, softly.

04 swallowed. "You have a name?" he asked, shakily.

Master looked from the husky to the jaguar, and back. "His programming is failing completely," he said, slowly, flatly.

04 dipped his head. Master was not happy. He felt himself beginning to shake.

01 swallowed. "You didn't hear *01*? You can hear him say *Juan*?" he asked, sharply.

04 just looked up at him, his ears back.

"We have to wipe him," Master said.

01 snapped his big head around. "*No!*" he roared. "I can fix this!"

Master flashed his scary little mustelid teeth. "Juan Carlos, do you not *remember* what he tried to do the last time he was lucid?" He was raising his voice. "To me? To us? The very *most recent time*?" He stabbed at 01 with a finger.

The jaguar's eyes were blazing. "So then what?! We just *erase his mind* without knowing why *any of this* happened? And then what! Another dog goes, we just wipe him too?" His voice was rising in pitch. "We can't do it! *I won't* do it! We need to know WHY!"

Master's face twisted into a growl. "He *cannot* be allowed to *return to lucidity* while you figure it out!" he snarled.

04 watched, his eyes widening. "A-a-...." He swallowed. He choked on the words. They both turned to him.

04 swallowed. "Are you afraid of me?" he asked.

Master and 01 looked at each other. Finally, Master sighed.

"I'm sorry, 04," he said. "You shouldn't have to see this." He let out a long sigh.

04 felt miserable. His guts were churning. 01's betrayal was bad enough. Now Master was so afraid of him he wanted him wiped. He put his face in his paws.

01 let out a strangled moan. "I'm so sorry. You're supposed to be happy," he said. "You were happy! You were all happy," he said, miserably.

Master stared for a moment, and then frowned. He looked up at 01. "When?" he asked.

01 stared for a moment. "What?" he asked.

Master looked at 04, and then back up at 01. "When was the last time he was happy?"

01 looked horrified, and then *devastated*. He opened his mouth, and then shut it. To 04's astonishment, the big cat started to shake.

Master frowned. "That wasn't a *dig*, you idiot. I mean *literally* — when was the last time he was happy?" He frowned. "That might give us a clue. And he might remember now that he's so lucid."

01 stared at him, took a slow breath, and let it out. Slowly, he turned to the husky. "04," he said. "You've been very afraid the last few weeks, haven't you?"

Guiltily, 04 nodded.

01 watched him. "Do you remember the last time…you felt safe?"

04 stared. He frowned, thinking about it. About the last time he truly felt contentment.

He smelled leather,
       and gasoline,
      and his best friend,
           and Master,
               close by,
                     his tail tapping 04's ankles.

He was excited for the drive, to see town, to get out of the facility, to see the ocean, to spend time with Master.

Hm.

"On the trip up to Prudhoe Bay. The first one," he said, softly.

01 watched him. "And when did you…lose that feeling?"

He thought about it.

    He

        heard

      the crunch of gravel,

     felt

the truck gently heave as it bounced in potholes, tugging the heavy trailer,

         smelled

the brush and the gravel and the rain and the minerals in the streams that came down off the mountains.

       Felt

the Suburban buck as they

           slowly

                 coasted

                     to a stop.

He saw 16's face as they pulled up next to him.

    Gray eyes,

        Pipe smoke and snow,

             … his hackles rose.

"The bear," he said. He looked up at Master. He swallowed. "I think…I think it all started then." He looked at Master. "Sitting behind you in the truck. That moment. I just knew something was wrong." He frowned. "I was terrified at that moment and it hasn't gone away since."

01 and Master looked at each other.

"So it *is* something external," 01 mused.

Master frowned. "It's 16. And we tried this already."

01 narrowed his eyes. "We don't know that. He just said that was the moment. What if he saw something else?"

Master thought about it, and then furrowed his brow. "I…suppose," he said. He seemed interested.

01 probed further. "Where were you when you saw that?"

The otter pondered. "The beginning of that old mine claim."

01's eyes widened excitedly. "What if he saw something else there?"

Master frowned. "What?"

01 leaned forward. "If he saw something that he would consider a credible survival risk, his subconscious could override all of his programming." He thought about it. "It could put his entire conditioning in jeopardy. A mind that wants to stay alive can override almost anything. *You'd* be able to put him under, but none of his programming would stick." He was excited now. "He'd be having breakthroughs all the time. Maybe even some memories resurfacing."

Master frowned, glancing down at 04, and back up. "I thought we dealt with this with all the security."

01 frowned. "Well, we thought we did."

Master stared at him. "Juan, what you're saying is…in *his opinion*," he pointed at 04, "*even after all we've done*…our lives are still in danger?"

01 stared at him.

They both turned to look at 04.

The husky swallowed.

At the head of the trailer, the door banged open, and they all jumped. The massive head and shoulders of a polar bear appeared, up at the ceiling, stooping to get in, as 16 surged into the room. It was straight out of a monster movie.

04 was looking right at the door when it happened and he could not keep the scream from his lips.

16 either didn't notice or didn't care. He went right up to 01 and Master, stooping as the trailer only had eight foot ceilings. "Sirs!" he said. "I need to talk to you!" he said. Someone's coming. From the mine. On foot."

They all stared.

04 felt his blood run cold.

"On *foot?*" Master said, incredulously. "We're fifteen miles from the mine."

16 nodded, stooping in the trailer. "Yes, sir," he said. He stoop-walked across the research trailer to a large flatscreen monitor. 04's eyes widened as he realized that 16 had a handgun tucked into his waistband at the small of his back. "Please come here, sir," he said.

Master glanced at 04, frowning. "I'm so sorry. We'll work this out. I promise." The otter quickly shuffled after 16.

04 couldn't see what 16 was doing, but he saw the monitor boot up and then the feeds of several security cameras flipping through, one after another. Finally, the feed settled on the end of their access road, approaching the facility.

04 and 01 looked at each other. 01 looked nervous. His tail swished behind him anxiously.

Frowning, 04 slid off the gurney and padded after Master and 16. His bare feet were cold on the trailer floor. 01 followed after him. 04 could hear the jaguar's feet thumping lightly along behind him.

As he got to the computer, he saw the feed of their access road. A bright green rectangle kept jumping around the same figure in the distance, tracking the figure's movement. In the corner, SENSOR 9 and SENSOR 10 were blinking in red. He got a closer look.

There was a young woman walking toward the facility.

04 stared, his jaws dropping open. He couldn't tell her species, only that she wasn't wearing enough clothing. The air temperature could not have been above freezing and the girl only wore a jacket, with a shawl wrapped around her head and shoulders. It wasn't anything thick enough to combat the frigid arctic wind. She was holding her arms around her shoulders and walking forward into the wind.

"How far out?" Master asked.

16 looked down at him. "A little under five miles. She just tripped the motion sensors."

Master turned to him. "She walked *ten miles* already?"

Frowning severely, 16 nodded.

On the monitor, three more boxes started flashing red. SENSOR 01 SENSOR 02 SENSOR 03. After a moment SENSOR 28 SENSOR 29 started flashing too.

04 felt his heart start pounding.

"That's nowhere near her," 16 grunted. He grabbed for the computer mouse and feverishly clicked. The feeds flipped through. Finally, the monitor settled on Camera One. 04 recognized the turnoff to the Dalton Highway.

There was a pickup truck rapidly approaching the turnoff. It was coming from the mine, headed toward the highway.

04 felt his heart start pounding. *Coming from the mine.*

As they watched, the truck skidded to a rapid stop. The feed wasn't great and the truck was too far away, but 04 recognized the make and model. It was a beat-up old crew cab Dodge Ram. But something looked off about it.

The scale was wrong. It was too tall.

As the driver's door swung open, he realized why.

This was not a Ram, the standard-size pickup which would have accommodated 04 or Master. It was a *Ram XL*, which was built for folks 01 and 16's size.

They really did get another polar bear, 04 thought, his head spinning.

He was wrong, as it turned out. As the door rocked open and a huge booted foot swung out, 04 saw a big muzzle, and broad shoulders under a tactical jacket, and pointed ears, and a huge, thick tail.

His hackles rose and he felt the blood drain from his face.

Wolves.

His back to the camera, the massive wolf stared into the distance, looking around. As they watched, he retrieved a pair of binoculars from the truck. Effortlessly, he leapt up into the bed. The truck bucked gently under his weight.

Scanning the horizon, the wolf's tail swished angrily behind him. Standing in the bed of the truck, he towered over the cab. He must have been at least eight feet tall. Maybe nine.

Swallowing, 04 thought of the other feed. *They're looking for the girl*, he thought. *They're looking for the girl and they went the wrong way.*

Soon they would realize their mistake, and head the other way up the old mining road.

Right to them.

No one else got out of the truck, but of course they didn't need to for 04 to know they were there.

Where there was one wolf, there were always more.

They were all silent, and then Master turned to look up at 16. "What is going on?" he asked, quietly.

16 turned to frown at him. "I don't know, sir," he said. He changed the feed back to the girl. Silently, steadily, the figure in the distance marched toward them.

They all watched.

04 swallowed.

"It's happening," he heard himself say.

STOLEN

The five of them stared at the monitor and watched the young woman walk down the gravel road to their facility.

After that, everything happened very fast.

"Go get her," Master said.

16 snapped his head around. It wasn't easy for the polar bear, since he was stooping in the research trailer, but he managed. "Sir?!" he gasped. "That's an incredible security risk."

Master looked up at him. "It's 15° out there. It's a miracle she made it this far. Go get her. Bring a radio and take 02 or 03." The otter frowned.

16 frowned. "Sir, this may be a trap."

Something buzzed in 04's brain. "It's not a trap," the husky said. "She escaped."

They all turned to look at him.

01 was the first one to speak. The big jaguar leaned down to eye level. "Fourrrr," the cat said. "How do you know that?"

The husky just shook his head. "I…I don't know," he said, softly. His muzzle tried to twist into a miserable frown, but he didn't want to cry in front of 01 again, so he just clenched his teeth, holding his breath.

Master turned to look back at the polar bear. The small otter spoke again, his voice low and flat. "Get her. Now."

16 frowned, but he also nodded. "Right away sir. I'll bring her back to the cabin." Grimacing, he turned and shuffled quickly out the door.

The rest of them turned to look back at the monitor. The hulking unknown wolf was climbing back into the pickup truck. 04 had thought he was gray, but now he realized the wolf was white. A huge white wolf.

01 swallowed, staring at the same monitor. "Are they going to intercept 16?" he asked. "They're clearly looking for her. There's not a lot of options on this road."

"It's twenty miles from the main road back to the mine," Master said. "We're fifteen miles in the other direction. If she just tripped the sensors, she's only five miles out. They should be back with plenty of time." He spoke with authority, but he was frowning.

01 nodded. "Okay. And that gives us…an hour before they show up here looking for her?" His brow was furrowed, and he kept clenching his huge jaws. He looked like his entire upper body was tensed.

04 listened to him.

He's wrong, a voice whispered in his head. *They won't come here. Not right away, anyway.* That was wrong. And he knew why.

The husky swallowed, hard. "After dark," he whispered. He shivered, and cleared his throat, so he could speak louder. "Th-they'll wait until dark."

The otter and the jaguar turned to look at him. They stared at him for a moment. 04 felt himself wither under their gazes.

"Why?" Master said, finally.

04 swallowed. He felt so *off.* Everything was wrong. Information was bubbling up into his head but he didn't know any of it, until it was just *there.* "They think… they think they have the advantage," he said. "They've been casing us, but they didn't find the motion sensors, or they wouldn't keep tripping them. So, they think we're clueless. They'll probably try to surprise us after… after dark." It just poured out of him. It was like another person *was* speaking through his mouth.

And wasn't that true? His repressed past self was trying to un-repress himself. Someone was speaking through 04's mouth. He felt a smile split his face and he had to bite back a hysterical laugh, even as he blinked back tears.

Master and 01 stared at him, eyes wide, and exchanged a glance.

04 swallowed. He felt sick, in the pit of his stomach. "It's getting worse," he whimpered. "Whatever's happening to me." He felt himself shaking, and looked up. "But it doesn't matter. Because those wolves are coming. What time is sunset tonight?"

Master and 01 exchanged a glance again. 01 went to a nearby computer screen. He clicked for a few moments. "Sunset today is at 6:09 pm," he said, low and concerned.

04 padded over and leaned over his shoulder. "And right now it's…4:30."

They all exchanged a glance.

"We need to get ready," 04 said, reaching up to wipe at his eyes.

A radio crackled. "16 TO BASE, DO YOU COPY, OVER," crackled 16's deep voice. They all jumped.

It took Master a moment to find it. There was a shortwave radio plugged into a charging station on Master's main desk in the research trailer. 04 stared. That was new.

Master picked up the handheld. "This is base, go ahead, over," he said.

"Sir, does anybody—" 16 was interrupted.

There was a young woman's voice, high and frantic. She was speaking some kind of foreign language, eastern European. Polish? No, it was-

"Sir, does anyone at the facility speak *Russian?*" 16 crackled over the radio.

Master looked up at 01. Frowning, he let out a reluctant sigh.

The jaguar straightened, his eyes widening. "Sir, you can't! Language processing is one of the most complex mental processes—"

Master frowned so severely that 01 just stopped talking. He keyed the radio button. "Yes, someone does. Meet in the mess," he said.

"Copy, sir. 16—"

The bear was interrupted by the girl again. This time, she was speaking English, albeit broken and heavily accented.

"*Stolen! We are stolen!*" she cried. "*You must help!*"

04 knew that already - did he?! - but it made the fur on his arms stand on end regardless.

There was a moment of radio silence. "16 out," came the final succinct reply.

They looked at each other.

01 composed himself and swallowed. "Sir, if you make him do that, you could trigger additional memories. He wasn't that far behind 04," the jaguar said, breathing hard. 04 wondered who the hell the cat was talking about.

Master raised an eyebrow. "I don't think we have a choice," he said. "She might know what's really going on at the mine."

04 swallowed. "Doesn't 16 know?" he asked, softly.

They both turned to look at him, and he had to fight the urge to cower.

01 glanced at Master.

The otter gestured hurriedly. "Tell him!" he said.

The jaguar frowned. "No. He remembers very little, even under hypnosis. He'd only been at the mine a few days when Master took him, and only talked to the owners over the phone. He only ever went to his own trailer. He knew virtually nothing, and I got the feeling he hadn't cared to find out."

Master frowned. "All the more reason we need 07 to talk to the girl."

04 blinked. 07? 07 could speak Russian?

01 turned back to the otter. "Sir, you might set him off too, then. This... sir, you could make this whole thing collapse."

The small otter stared up at him. After a moment, he smiled humorlessly, and let out a long, weary sigh. "Juan Carlos," he said, gently, a smile on his face. "Can't you feel it? Deep down in your heart? It's already coming down."

01 just stared at him, his mouth opening slightly. He looked like he didn't even know how to react to that.

Master turned down to 04. "04. I realize this is a struggle for you. Are you... fit for duty?"

04 straightened up. He felt like he was going crazy, but he also knew deep down that the mine situation might end all of them, right now, tonight. He might lose his mind, but at least he would still be alive. "I'll fight to my last breath, sir," he said.

Master stared at him, blinking, and let out a soft chuckle. "I *sincerely* hope it doesn't come to that." He chuckled. "Find 07 and 10 and report to the mess. Don't bring the malamutes. Hurry."

04 nodded. He felt energized and stable. Insanely, now that the thing he'd been worried about — whatever that was — was actually *happening*, he almost felt...relieved?

"Right away, sir," he said. "Are my boots in my cabin?"

Master blinked at him, and then turned. "No, they're right here." He moved toward the gurney but 01 beat him. The big cat reached for his boots and held them out for 04, watching him very carefully.

"Give me those," 04 snapped. He snatched his boots out of 01's hands and bent to put them on.

01 winced, and then nodded.

04 had his boots on in a few moments. "See you in the mess," he said, and then bolted for the door.

07 had been working out in the gym trailer with the malamutes, in his workout shorts and a sleeveless t-shirt. The husky was surprised and confused but once he saw 04 sign the word *Emergency*, he followed without question. 14 and 15 watched him go, wide-eyed and concerned.

Chef shepherd 10 had been in 16's cabin, worrying. They'd been together when the alarms had gone off and 16 had rushed off, and he was already on high alert. 04 noticed he had a sidearm in a hip holster. 10 followed without question, too. The slim husky 11 was also in the cabin and insisted on coming with, and 04 didn't feel like he had time to argue so he didn't protest. Master and 01 were already in the mess.

Master turned to 10 and 11 as soon as the shepherd and the husky cleared the fire door into the mess. "10. We need coffee and soup. Hot but not too hot. 11, find a blanket and one of the electric heaters."

They both stared at him, eyes wide. It wasn't disobedience, just shock.

Master's face tightened into a frown. "We're about to have a guest. She just walked most of the way from the mine. She's not dressed for it. Hurry, please," he said, sharply.

10 and 11 nodded, glanced at each other, and scurried off — 10 to the kitchen side of the double-wide mess trailer, and 11 to the storage room in the back of the trailer.

The motion sensors went off. They all flinched.

04 turned to the bank of monitors up on the trailer wall. There were four television-sized monitors, all of them currently showing feeds from cameras on top of the trailers. Three of them showed nothing. The fourth showed a large white crew cab dual-rear-tire pickup heading down their access road. 04 had a moment of panic, thinking it was the wolves, before he noticed 16 behind the wheel. He'd expected to see the Suburban, but of course 16 wouldn't have fit in that. This was a vehicle he'd never seen before.

The radio crackled. "Back," 16 said, simply.

Master had carried his handheld from the research trailer. "Come right to the loading dock in the mess," he said.

"Roger," 16 crackled.

His brow furrowing, 04 stared. "Did… did we get a new truck?" he asked Master and 01.

The small otter nodded.

Feeling numb, 04 stared, and then finally closed his mouth. He furrowed his brow, looking back and forth between the two of them. Buying a new truck would have been a big deal. And 04 just simply…hadn't noticed. "What the fuck did you *do* to me?" he asked, softly.

11 was coming out of the storage locker when 04 said it. He froze, eyes wide. In utter disbelief, he looked back and forth between 04 and the first and second in command.

They didn't have time to answer. There was a loud diesel rumble and crunching of snow at the rear of the trailer.

Master was the first to head to the rear. His tail waving agitatedly behind him, the small otter threw open the big lever that unlocked the loading dock, bent down, and yanked as hard as he could at the base of the door. The crusted snow held for a moment, and then released with a sharp crack.

The mess trailer was a doublewide with two eight-foot wide doors at the back, running floor to ceiling. Master opened the one on the dining side, and as he yanked with all his strength and the panel door thunder-clunked open, the cold roared into the trailer. 04 felt it on his legs and then his entire body, and then the trailer heater kicked on immediately, blowing hot air from the top down. And then he saw what was on the other side and forgot all of it.

In addition to a massive F-450 that 04 could not remember ever seeing before, 16 and 02 stood in the snow. The nine-foot-plus polar bear and seven-foot German shepherd stood protectively on either side of a figure who could not have been more than four feet tall. She was an ermine, a weasel or a marten — marten, probably, judging by her chocolate-brown fur — and she didn't look older than her mid-twenties. Just a young woman. She was wearing black cotton pants and street shoes that just looked like gym shoes to 04. She was draped in 02's massive puffer jacket, which went down to her knees, under which she was wearing only a tobacco-colored thick knit jacket. What 04 had assumed was a shawl was actually a ratty-looking knit blanket wrapped around her head and shoulders. The girl did not have any gloves. She was shivering and she looked at all of them in the trailer with wide, concerned, deep brown eyes.

"C'mon, up you go," 02 said. He reached down for the girl's shoulders.

She flinched and whirled to stare at him, frightened. 02 jumped. The big dog stared back down, startled.

They stared at each other.

"Hey!" 04 said. They both looked at him. He looked down at the girl. "Lift!" He mimed raising something up with his hands. "He," he pointed to 02, "will lift you!" he pointed at the girl. He mimed lifting again.

The girl frowned, glanced back at 02, and then looked up at 04.

Swallowing, 02 tried again. This time the girl let him put his big hands under her arms, and smoothly lifted her up into the trailer.

She took a few hesitant steps into the trailer.

Master pulled out a chair for the girl, and as 02 and 16 climbed into the trailer and pulled the door back down, 11 handed her a huge blanket. She shrugged out of 02's coat and wrapped herself in the blanket, still shivering, and staggering to the chair. 11 ran off for the portable heater and 10 appeared with coffee and a bowl of chicken soup, both of which put off plumes of steam like tiny locomotives in the freezing trailer while the air heated back up.

The girl eyed the soup and coffee as 10 slid them gently across the table to her and lunged for the soup first, drinking it directly out of the bowl. She snatched the coffee next, downing it in one long series of pulls.

She looked up. "*Yeshche?*" she asked. The meaning was unmistakable.

10 nodded and swiftly loped off with the bowl and the mug.

The girl looked around at them again. She looked at all of them, with that severe stare only small mustelids could muster — 01, and 04, and Master, and 11, and finally 07.

Her eyes settled on him.

She narrowed her eyes and said something.

It sounded to 04 like "*a ti govarrish po-ruushki?*" Ruuski. That meant Russian. She was asking if he spoke Russian.

They all turned to 07.

07 was the smallest of the huskies, two inches shorter than 04, and his face was mostly black, including his eye mask, so when his eyes widened into circles and all the blood drained out of his face, they could really see it.

His ears folding back, he started to back away, horrified.

04 frowned. What the hell?

Master frowned. "07, would you be so kind?" he said.

07 looked at the otter, and then back to the girl. He raised his hands. They were shaking. "No," he signed. He kept doing it over and over again. "*No, no, no, no, no.*"

04 watched in disbelief. 07 was terrified. His tail tucked between his legs and his ears wouldn't rise up. He was hunching over in fear. 04 stepped in front of him.

"Hey, it's ok!" he signed. "*Please only translate. Don't be scared.*"

07 turned to him and signed furiously.

"*No, please no, please no, I don't want to do it.*" His hands were moving so fast that 04 could barely keep up. "*I don't want to speak, I can't go back, I'm scared, PLEASE!*" The sign for "*please*" was a flat hand over the chest in a circle, and 07 did the gesture so hard it tugged his shirt up, exposing his belly.

04 stared at him. He was shocked.

07 begged him with his eyes.

The husky thought frantically. 07 *could* speak, right? Of course. He just *didn't* because he was always with 14 and 15, and one of the malamutes was deaf. Right? That's all it was. *Right?*

Master let out a long sigh. "I was afraid of this. 01, would you mind *persuading* 07 to—"

They were going to *make* him. 01 was going to use a trigger phrase on poor helpless 07.

04 whirled. "No!" he snapped, glaring at Master and 01.

The otter stared back at him, red eyes wide. Next to him, 01's eyebrows rose in disbelief.

04 narrowed his eyes. "I'll do it." He turned back to the other husky.

07 stared at him, silently, blue eyes wide and panicked.

04 reached up and put his hands on the smaller husky's shoulders. "07," he said, softly, slowly. "Listen to me."

07's brow furrowed, as he watched 04 speak to him without signing. His face twisted into a miserable frown.

04 continued gently holding the other husky. "Listen to me. Nobody is going to hurt you. I *won't let* anybody hurt you. Okay?"

07 stared at him, and swallowed. He raised his hands. "*Who is she?*" he signed with shaking paws. "*Did she come for me?*"

04 looked down at his hands, and then up into his eyes. "*No. She escaped. She came from the mine. We need to know what's really going on there.*" He swallowed. "*We need to talk to her.*"

07 stared at him, and then looked over 04's shoulder at the girl. He returned his gaze to the other husky, and swallowed.

"*I will be safe. You promise?*" he signed. His hands were shaking so badly that 04 almost couldn't make the words out. He was blinking back tears.

04 frowned. He thought of the terror that had possessed him on the gurney just a few minutes ago. What had happened to 07? What had happened to *any* of them?

He felt a steely pang of resolve in his guts. He lifted his own hands.

"*I will die before I let anything happen to you,*" he signed to 07. "*To any of you.*"

The other husky stared at him, frowned, took a breath, let it out as a long shaky sigh, and nodded.

He slipped past 04, took a deep breath, and cleared his throat. He walked up to the girl. He glanced back at 04, nervously, and then turned back to her.

"*Privet. Kak vas zovut?*" he said to her. His voice was high and gentle. It didn't sound familiar at all.

04 watched in silence and eventually decided that he'd never *actually* heard 07's voice before.

The girl lit up. She started talking in Russian, and didn't stop for a long time. 04 heard what he thought was a place name, *Srednekolymsk*, and then possibly *America*. He also heard the name *Irina*.

07 watched with progressively greater shock. Stunned, he turned to the rest of them and raised his hands.

"*She says she was kidnapped.*"

"What?!" Master said.

07 wasn't done. "*Men took them. They said they were taking them to America, but they won't let them leave the camp. There is not enough food. They are becoming sick. She escaped.* "

"Santo Cristo," 01 said. "How many are they holding?"

07 turned to him. "*Twelve.*"

Something bubbled up in 04's brain. "Ask her if they took their passports," he said. His voice sounded far away.

07 stared at him, and then turned back to the girl. "*Oni zabrali vashi pasporta?*" 04 still couldn't quite get used to the idea of sound coming out of 07's mouth.

The girl lit up again. Her answer started with "*Da*," and went on for a long time.

07 listened with wide eyes, and translated. He turned back to the group. "*Yes, the men say that if they are caught without passports they will be sent to prison.*"

04 swallowed. Something bubbled up in his brain. "Ask her if her husband is dead," he said, flatly.

They all turned to look at him.

Did he really just ask that? He needed to know that. *Why* did he need to know that? He felt drunk. His eyes lost focus for a moment. He blinked.

07's mouth slightly opened. He looked stunned. "*What?*" he signed, slowly.

04 scowled. He felt himself swaying on his feet. "Just ask her, please," he said. He felt the impulse to snarl. But he would never snarl at another husky.

07 blinked at him, and then turned back to the girl. He swallowed and asked her a short question in Russian.

The girl frowned, and then grimaced. She answered for a long time again.

07 nodded, frowning sympathetically, and turned back to the rest of them. "*She is not married. But her mother is in the group, and her father is dead. That's why they're going to America.*" He frowned at 04. "*How did you know that?*"

04 felt himself starting to get dizzy. "That's who they prey on," he said. Was his voice slurring? "Women who are vulnerable because of a death in the family." He was having a hard time keeping his eyes all the way open. "They...they lose their income and that's how they get them." The room felt too bright. Something was happening to him. "How many wolves are there?"

07 stared at him a moment, and then he realized what 04 had asked. His white eyebrows rose in fear. He stared at 04, stunned into silence, and then slowly turned back to the girl. Irina, that's what she said her name was, right? 04 turned back to Irina, watching dully.

07 asked a slow, nervous question.

Irina frowned with absolute dreadful severity.

"*Tri,*" she said.

07 stared at her in horror, and then turned slowly back to the group.

He held up three fingers.

04 stared at that, and it was actually enough to shock him out of his stupor.

Jesus Christ. Three wolves.

They would be between 01 and 16's size, eight to nine feet. Three of them. They could probably fight four dogs apiece without even breaking a sweat. Wolves were big and mean and at that size they would have a hard time even taking them down with some of their firearms.

They all exchanged concerned glances.

10 appeared with a full bowl and mug. 11 was right behind him with a plate with toasted bread and a glass of water. They silently put the things in front of her.

Irina said something to 10, nodding. He nodded back. She looked up at 07 and asked him something very pointed.

07 stared at her. He swallowed, and his answer was somewhat stilted.

Nodding, she looked around, looked down at the food in front of her. Silently, she began eating again, this time using a spoon.

07 swallowed. "*She's asking what we're going to do.*"

02 suddenly cleared his throat. "What *are* we going to do?"

01 looked down at Irina and then to Master. "We need to contact the authorities."

The otter looked up at him and let out a long sigh. He was frowning. "We're six hours from the nearest help. Those wolves are going to be here in…" He checked his watch. "90 minutes."

16 grunted. "If they come here, it will be the last thing they do. And then we can rescue the women."

01 frowned. The big cat looked at the girl. "Is this…trafficking?"

The word made 04's ears perk. Something twinged in his brain.

Master let out another shaky sigh. "It sure sounds like it."

"It is," 04 heard himself say.

Everyone turned to look at him.

It was happening again.

He straightened up. "Th… they're taking them straight south. They'll force them into domestic work or entertainment, maybe worse." His head was starting to pound. It was making him dizzy and nauseated. He felt his eyes half-close but he couldn't stop talking. He could see the route in his head, highlighted in red. "They'll probably end up in Vegas, maybe Reno. Could…could head to Los Angel-."

His headache flared and everything got dark for a second.

When his vision came back, he was on the floor.

Everyone was standing over him. 01 was cradling him in his big arms, a terrified look on the big cat's face.

His brain was static. He couldn't move. His whole body was weak. He tried to say something, and the only thing that came out was a long, protracted groan. "*Hhhhhhhhhhhhhhhuhhmmmgggghhh,*" 04 heard come out of his own mouth. The husky's legs wouldn't work and he couldn't lift his arms. He felt heavy and broken.

01 leaned over him. He stared into his eyes. "Take a deep breath for me, puppy."

Staring up at him, into his beautiful eyes, 04 inhaled. It was ingrained in him at this point. It was practically a reflex. 01 told him to inhale, 04 heard and obeyed. He stared up at the jaguar, his lungs filling with air. Already, he felt better.

01 maintained his gaze. "Hold it."

04 held his lungs, full, waiting.

"And let it out."

04 exhaled, long and relaxed. He felt his eyes half-close. It felt good.

"Again, puppy. Inhale. Breathe in my voice."

Inhale.

"Hold it…"

Hold it.

"Breathe out the confusion."

04 exhaled, long and slow, and felt his disorientation and nausea slowly flow out of his body.

"Gooooooodddd," 01 rumbled, gently rocking him. 04 could smell him now, warm and comforting. "Again."

04 stared up at him, staring into his yellow eyes, and inhaled, and held it, and let it out. He stared up at the beautiful jaguar, lying limp in his arms, just absorbing his warmth and slowly breathing.

01 watched him. Slowly, he stroked 04's fuzzy face.

Everything felt calm and right again. 04 stared up at the jaguar.

Slowly, relaxed, the husky swallowed. "I'm still mad at you," he rumbled.

01 nodded. "I know," he said, very softly.

Blinking, 04 looked up at the rest of them. He abruptly became aware of talking. Loud talking.

"We are *not doing it!*" Master was shouting.

16 was leaning toward him, curling his upper lip up in a snarl, stooping over to make eye contact with the short otter. Next to him, 02's eyes were wide and shocked. "You know it's the only way! The nearest help is hours away, even by helicopter, and we are *not* equipped for a *firefight!* Do you think 08 and 13 can treat *gunshot wounds?!*"

Master leaned forward. "I don't care! We're not going to go in and *slaughter them!*"

16 grit his teeth. "You're putting our lives *and* their lives at risk!" He pointed toward Irina, whose eyes widened.

Master stared at both of them. He grit his teeth, furrowing his brow. The small otter looked furious. But he stopped arguing.

04 glanced up at 01, eyes wide, concerned.

The jaguar frowned down at him. "It's okay, 04," he said, gently.

04 frowned. It wasn't okay, though. Something was nagging at him, and it was very much *not* okay.

"We can't kill them," 04 said. He tried to think of why but couldn't come up with anything. "Something…something *worse* will happen."

The jaguar blinked down at him. "Wh…what?" he asked softly.

04's thoughts were racing. There was something else at play here. Something worse. "Th…there's something else. It's not just us. Or even them." He looked at Irina.

His headache was coming back. He thought, hard, searching his mind. His vision was starting to get fuzzy. "I'm...I'm trying to remember..." His balance suddenly went off, and he felt like the room was tilting. "I'm trying..." he whimpered.

The jaguar frowned.

Master appeared standing over them. "Juan," he said, softly. "It's time."

The jaguar blinked at him, in confusion, and then suddenly gasped in recognition. He furrowed his brow, tightening his grip around 04, protectively. He squeezed him so hard, almost reflexively. He probably wasn't even aware he was doing it. "No," he growled. "*Absolutely not!*" He looked like he was going to start snarling.

04 looked at 01, startled, and then over to Master.

"Time for wh-what?" he asked, quietly.

01 gathered the husky up, squeezing him, staring daggers into Master. "You *cannot*. We have never *done* that before," he snarled. "It's been *three years*. He has formed countless *neural pathways*, physical pathways, since then. I'm not going to let you short out his brain!"

Oh.

Three years.

04 stared.

He understood.

04 thought about it.

This was it. This was his chance to fix it. He could fix all of it.

The husky swallowed.

"Juan Carlos," he said, softly.

Eyes widening, 01 looked down at him.

04 swallowed. "You have to let him do it."

The jaguar stared at him, eyes wide and disbelieving, his mouth hanging open. It took him a moment to get his bearings. "N-no!" he finally snapped. "*¡Absolutamente no!*"

04 frowned. "You know you have to," he said, flatly. "You have to let him restore my memories."

01 snarled, showing his teeth. His canines were the size of 04's fingers. It was terrifying. "*I won't do it!*" he snarled. "We don't know what it will do to you!" He snapped his head upward. "Let me work on 16! He might have more useful memories! He might have seen what we're up against!"

16's eyebrows rose in surprise.

Master frowned. "You know why that won't work. We don't need their memories. We need 04's decision making. He obviously knows what he's doing. But he can't do it unless he can access his memories himself."

01 looked down at the dog, and then up at the otter. His face contorted into a miserable frown. "You can't. It's too risky. W-w-we've never done this before at all!" His voice was getting higher.

Master frowned. "Juan...you know we need an expert here. 04 will know exactly what to do in this situation."

01 glared at him, squeezing 04 tight. He held him as if he was afraid Master and 16 were going to drag him off.

04 swallowed. "Please," he said.

The jaguar looked down at him.

04 looked up at him. "Please. It'll be okay," he said. "I know it will. Let me help. That's all I've wanted to do these last few weeks. Help and keep us safe."

01 frowned, swallowing. "04," he said, tenderly, cradling his face with his huge hand. "You can't. It's not safe. I promised to keep you safe and I'm not going to let you do this."

04 stared. 01 wasn't going to relent.

He stared up at the jaguar.

He felt a pit of nausea form in his stomach for what he was about to do.

Narrowing his eyes, 04 contorted his face into a contemptuous sneer. "Yeah?" he growled. "Did you *promise* to keep me safe?"

Startled, 01's eyes widened.

04 flashed his teeth. "And what *exactly* have you done to keep me safe? *Juan?*" he growled.

01 stared at him, his mouth dropping open. His ears gently folded back at his head. He stared down at 04, cowering involuntarily, staring at him in shock and horror. He looked like the blood was draining out of his face. "I...I...I..." he said, softly.

04 wriggled out of his grasp, and 01 just let him. He lifted himself up onto his arms, staring the big cat down. "Shall I inventory all the ways you failed? A promise only means something if you can *do* the thing you promise," he spat. "So get the fuck out of the way and let *me* try to keep us safe, and pray to God I do a better job than you did."

01 stared at him, eyes perfectly circular, ears back, his pupils dilated. The jaguar didn't move. He didn't speak. He didn't even breathe. He just stared. Devastated.

04 ignored the wave of guilt and nausea that suffused him. He didn't mean it. He really didn't. But he needed to say it to get 01 out of the way if he was going to save their lives.

04 staggered to his feet. He swayed for a moment, and then he steadied. He turned to Master. "Let's go. Where are we doing this?"

The otter stared back at him, stunned, mouth open, eyes wide. After a moment he looked down at 01, and then back up to 04. He swallowed. "Research trailer," he managed to squeak out.

04 nodded, turned, ignored the feeling of the floor tilting underneath him, and turned to the mess door. He took hold of the big metal crash bar that opened the fire doors, steadied himself on the cold metal, and tried to push. He broke a sweat trying to push it open on unsteady paws, but after a moment he got it. He stepped out into the connection hallway, relieved it was a few degrees cooler.

He glanced back behind him to see if Master was following, and guiltily, looked back at 01. The jaguar was still kneeling, reeling, disbelieving, immobile, shattered.

04 fought a frown and turned down the hallway.

I cannot believe I'm doing this, 04 thought, as he climbed back on to the gurney in the research trailer. This was the last place on earth he'd ever wanted to be, and here he was willingly crawling up onto the 02-scale bed. "Is this going to hurt?"

Master frowned. "I…don't think so," he said. "We've…*I've* never done this before. Not after this long."

04 settled his fluffy butt into place. "Well, I guess I'm going to find out."

They stared at each other.

Master frowned. "You don't have to do this," he said. The otter looked distressed.

04 watched him. "You know I do," he said, softly.

Master nodded. He nodded a few long moments, gritting his teeth, grimacing, and finally blinking back tears. "04…for what it's worth…I never meant for any of this to happen. I never meant to put you through this. And…I want to thank you for what you're doing."

04 watched him. Had he ever seen Master emotional before?

Wow, he thought. *He really does give a shit about us.*

The dog cracked a smile. "Of course, Master. Just doing my duty," he said, smiling.

The otter nodded, took a deep breath, let out a long sigh, and swallowed. "Okay," he said. "Are you ready?"

04 thought about it. He was about to get his memories back. He was about to see the life that had been stolen away from him.

"No," he answered, honestly.

Master chuckled. "Me either," he admitted. He forced a smile.

04 swallowed. "If I die, tell 01 I didn't mean it. I just said that so he would let me go." He clenched his teeth. He was trying not to cry. "Tell him I love him and I'm sorry. And tell 06 and all the dogs that I love them, too, and I did it for all of us."

Master watched him for a moment, and then nodded slowly. "You're a good dog, 04," he said, softly.

It should have meant nothing, given the circumstances. It should not have made 04 feel better, given the circumstances. And yet, it did.

He cracked a little smile. "Thank you, Master."

The otter took a deep breath. "Okay, puppy. Let's go. Lean back and just look into my eyes."

Swallowing, 04 nodded, and looked into the otter's unblinking red eyes.

Abrupt, as it always was, a wave of pure, hot power crashed over him. He gasped.

It was hot.

And humid.

And wet.

I smell salt, he thought, for half a second, and then he was gone.

Sunrise

1250 DAYS AGO…

Andrew Dunn lay back on his towel in the sand, arms up, forearms under his head, legs crossed. The morning sun warmed his lithe muscular body, clad in only a sheath-clinging red speedo and a pair of mirrored sunglasses, which let him surreptitiously watch any of the bikini beach babes that checked out his body as they walked past. Which was a lot of them. Andrew knew he was gorgeous, with his perfect body and his lustrous inky black and glowing white fur, and it wasn't like there were many Siberian huskies running around Tampa, Florida.

It was mid-May, and 75°, even at 7:00 in the morning, which was more than warm enough for Dunn to bask in the light of the just-risen sun. He relished the cool salty breeze as it rushed in from the ocean, rustling his fur and keeping him from heating up too much.

Next to him his phone buzzed.

"Rawroooooooooo," he groaned. He'd *just* lain down. It was 7 am on a Wednesday. Who the hell was calling? Lifting his sunglasses, he rolled onto his side and rummaged for his phone.

There was one message. It was from the junior intelligence analyst. It was so like him, showing up at work at 7 on the dot. Dunn intended to roll in at least an hour later.

He looked at the message.

> *Good morning Agent Dunn, sorry to disturb you, that cop called at 3 am. He sounded pissed.*

Dunn blinked at the message. Staring at it, he felt a grin spread across his face.

So, the cop was pissed, huh?

"Good," he said, out loud.

Chuckling, tucking his phone back into his gym bag, Dunn rolled back over.

Well.

Today was going to be a *very* good day.

Dunn rolled into the field office parking lot at his customary 8:07 am. He was an early riser, but in the first few days of his career a more seasoned agent had told him he should always be fifteen minutes *early*, and as a result he made it a stubborn point to always be at least five minutes late.

He left his red Jeep unlocked, as he always did. After all, who was going to steal a car from the parking lot of an FBI field office?

The junior intelligence analyst was waiting for him as soon as he cleared security. He was a Canadian lynx, fresh out of Quantico, and he had been assigned to Dunn perhaps as part of a personal attack.

"Hello, Agent Dunn," the kid said, gray eyes wide and eager.

Dunn frowned at the lynx. He lifted his sunglasses up onto his forehead, swinging his messenger bag around behind him, resting against his hip holster. "Jesus, Carmine," he said. "I don't even have my coffee yet." They swift-walked down the hall.

The lynx smiled shyly at him. "I got it for you, actually. It's on your desk."

Dunn raised a skeptical eyebrow. "Venti white chocolate soy m—"

"...soy mocha latte, extra sugar," Carmine said, beaming. "*Iced.* Just the way you like it!"

Dunn stopped in his tracks. "Iced?!" he snapped.

Carmine stared at him. "That was a joke. I know you ha—"

"I hate cold things!" the husky snapped at him.

The lynx half-closed his eyes. "Yes. I know you hate cold things; I was there when you yelled at the lobby barista. It's one thousand degrees."

Dunn started walking again, stuffing his hands into the pockets of his suit pants. "It's not really customary for a junior analyst to be *cute*, Carmine," he half-growled.

The lynx beamed innocently. "Can't help it, Agent Dunn!" he said. "Anyway, the other thing on your desk is that file you asked for."

Dunn's white eyebrows leapt up. "What?!" he asked. "Why didn't you lead with that?"

They came to the lobby stairs. Dunn took them two at a time, and Carmine hopped up the stairs effortlessly alongside him. The lynx never had any trouble keeping up with the husky. Dunn wasn't sure he quite liked that.

The lynx shrugged. "You always say 'coffee first,' Agent Dunn." He smiled. "Anyway, let me know if you have any questions. I think you'll like what I came up with."

Dunn nodded at the lynx, and turned into his office.

Sipping his scalding-hot coffee, Dunn flipped through the manila folder that Carmine had left on his desk.

It was good work. Dunn hated to admit it, but Carmine always did good work. The husky flipped through various ledgers, records of financial statements, phone records, a series of receipts for large purchases, and bank statements obtained under one very over-broad court order, issued by a friendly judge, which Chase and Bank of America had been all too happy to accept.

He flipped back to the opening page. The otter didn't look like much. He definitely didn't look like he should be able to wield massive influence. And yet a matter of weeks after rolling into Florida, he'd managed to amass considerable fortune. He'd gone from a credit score of 580 to owning a fifty four-foot yacht in the Westshore Marina. *Something* was going on.

Dunn reviewed the whole file and nothing leapt out at him. The otter didn't seem to be involved in drugs, or gambling, or trafficking, yet he was reaping rewards most-often associated with a life of crime. That meant he had something far more valuable: influence.

The otter's "gifts" were coming from a wide range of people: socialites, celebrities, CEO's, CFO's, even a known high-profile local organized crime kingpin.

Dunn stared at the otter's face.

He didn't look very impressive. He kind of looked like an idiot, actually.

He should be easy to catch. He had no priors, no arrests, and though he had considerable funds in the bank, he didn't seem to be very formidable.

Check out the last few pages! Carmine had written.

Dunn flipped to the back of the report.

It looked like much of the same — financial records — but now they were in Spanish. There were a few transactions from Sao Paulo, Brazil, and one in Bogota, Columbia. And then, a completely unfamiliar type of writing, that Dunn eventually recognized as Indonesian.

He frowned. He'd seen this before. The otter was getting ready to move. He'd sensed that parties, parties like Dunn, had taken an interest in him, and he was getting ready to bail. He just had to decide where.

Scratching his fuzzy chin, Dunn sat back in his chair.

And then he thought of the cop.

He smiled.

How fortuitous, the husky thought.

"*Venti white chocolate soy mocha latte, extra sugar!* ICED!" screamed the barista, eighteen inches from him.

Dunn felt his left eye twitch and a growl rising in his throat. "*That's supposed to be—*" he started.

The barista saw him and visibly recoiled. "Oh Christ, it's *you*," the man said. "I'll remake it. Just don't throw it this time," he said, wincing.

Dunn grunted. He resisted the urge to raise his upper lip and show his teeth.

He glanced behind him to see if the cops showed up. Two big German shepherds, one in a navy blue Tampa Police Department uniform and one in a shirt and tie, were just entering the building, with bright yellow temporary entry passes stuck to their shirts.

Dunn tried to keep the grin off his face. "Bring it to my table," he said to the barista.

"Asshole," the kid muttered, which normally would have set him off, except this was about to be too good.

"Officer Kamienski! Officer Brady!" he said, walking up to the two big dogs.

They were both taller than him. Kamienski, in the shirt and tie, was about six inches taller than Dunn. He had a mostly-black face and an extremely sour frown. He was a long-hair shepherd, his luxurious face fur combed into a neat, handsome beard.

Brady, in the uniform, was even bigger and even madder. He was the standard black and tan, probably pushing seven feet, definitely a king shepherd. He had big shoulders and a big gut and a big mean frown on his face. He was heavy all over, with a concerning amount of muscle on him.

The bigger cop dog opened his mouth to talk, but the smaller one put his hand up in front of him, shooting him a glare. The big king shep snapped his mouth shut and glared at the smaller shepherd. Dunn got a feeling this happened a lot.

The longhair dog turned to the husky. "Dunn, I presume," he said. He bore into Dunn with piercing yellow eyes.

"You presume correctly!" Dunn said, unable to keep the smile off his face. "Have a seat! Can I get you anything?"

Neither of the dogs responded. They just both walked to a table and sat down. It was the furthest table from anyone else, Dunn noted.

He smiled, taking a seat, poking his curly tail through the chair behind him as he wagged congenially. Great. So they knew why they were here.

Smiling, he looked the two shepherds over. "You know, you guys don't *have* to be cops just because you're both German shepherds."

Kamienski rolled his eyes. Brady just glared at him, golden eyes locked and intense. Kamienski was tall and trim, fit and muscular, but Brady was the one that Dunn wouldn't want to fight — he had a gut on him, but he was thick all over, built like a brick shithouse. If Brady came after you, you would *feel* it.

Kamienski sighed. "That's amazing," he said flatly. "We've never heard that before. What can we help you with, Agent Dunn?"

The husky beamed at him. "*Special* Agent Dunn," he corrected. "So are you two like partners? I wasn't expecting two of you to show up." He looked at Brady. "Only him."

Brady stared him down and Dunn saw his left eye twitch. The big king shepherd held perfectly still. Staring.

Dunn knew that look. Brady was getting ready to attack. The husky suppressed a smile.

Kamienski blinked at him, his golden eyes confused in his mostly-black face. "We...we were. I was recently promoted to detective."

Dunn turned to him. "That's great!" he said. "Congratulations!"

Kamienski forced a smile. "Thank you, *Special* Agent," he said. He stared. "Why are we here?"

Dunn raised an eyebrow. "Well. This might be relevant to your new role." He slid a manilla file folder across the table to them.

Warily, his ears ratcheting just a hair backwards, Kamienski opened the folder. He and Brady peered inside.

There was only one item inside the folder: an 8½ by 11-inch printout, on standard office paper, of a clip from a security camera. It was a night scene, high up, from a camera that was probably too high to see from the street. It showed a dark parking lot, the rear entrances of a strip mall, four dumpsters, half a dozen bushes, and Officer Brady, looking surreptitiously over his shoulder, as he dragged a limp humanoid figure by its ankles, trailing its arms, the figure's head bent at a terrifying and unnatural angle, toward the open rear door of a Ford Expedition patrol SUV.

It was a still from a video he had been sent anonymously. It would have been easy to figure out whose camera the video came from, considering the position, except Dunn knew who this victim was: one of the powerful Florida drug cartels was missing a favorite son, and the corpse Brady was dragging in this video matched the description. The owner of the camera had sent the video to the FBI for the same reason that Dunn was now using it to blackmail Brady: if this video ever made it out, Brady would not be prosecuted. He wouldn't be alive long enough. A few days would go by and he would just…disappear.

It was a little bit of a risk putting this out in front of Kamienski, since Dunn didn't know if the other shepherd knew. But based on a detailed search into Brady's past, specifically a few witnesses to his conduct who changed their stories or disappeared, this wasn't the first "problem" he had solved in this matter. And if he'd gotten away with it this long, he probably had help.

Dunn smiled at them as he waited for the picture to sink in.

Kamienski's eyes widened. Brady stood up so fast his chair crashed over behind him, the hard plastic banging on the stone floor behind him. His eyes locked onto Dunn, wide, murderous. He was showing his teeth, and leaning forward, and his whole body was tense.

Smiling up at the dog, Dunn reached for his hip holster.

Brady stared, frozen, murderous.

The smaller shepherd snapped his head up. "*LET. ME. HANDLE. THIS*," he growled. It was loud enough to be audible at other tables, but people were already looking.

Brady didn't respond. He didn't even move. He just glared at Dunn.

The husky grinned incorrigibly up at him. "You should do it," he said, softly.

Kamienski frowned. "Stop it," he said, sharply.

Dunn didn't take his eyes off the bigger dog. "Go ahead, Brady. Attack me, an armed FBI agent, in the lobby of my field office. I am *begging* you. I can't wait to see what happens."

Brady burned holes into him with his eyes, breathing hard, his eyes still wide and murderous. Finally, he tore his gaze away, and looked to the other dog.

Kamienski frowned up at him. "Sit down," he said.

Silently, Brady turned, his massive body moving like a crane, and robotically picked up his chair. Without a word, he sat down next to the detective, glaring at Dunn the whole time.

Kamienski looked at him, and then back to Dunn. "What do you *want?*" he asked.

Dunn recoiled in mock horror, putting his paw over his mouth. "What do I want?" he repeated. "What makes you think I *want* something, Kamienski?" he asked.

Kamienski rolled his eyes again. "Please, Dunn, spare me the cute act," he said. "I'm not going to fucking date you. We all know exactly what this is. What do you want in exchange for...overlooking this?"

Dunn flashed his teeth in a big smile. "Well, you're right. I need you to help me find someone." He cocked his head. "This one is off the books. I might have my own use for him."

Kamienski sneered. "Why the fuck are you telling me?"

Dunn beamed. "Because if you fuck me over you won't even last long enough to go to trial." He smiled, wagging.

Kamienski stared at him. Brady just glowered.

If he could get away with snapping my neck, he would do it right here, Dunn thought.

He could barely keep the grin off his face.

Kamienski let out a snort. "Who's the mark?"

Dunn turned to his side and stuck his hands into his briefcase.

Kamienski tensed as soon as Dunn reached for his briefcase, but Brady outright flinched. The big dog leaned forward, putting his hand on his own hip holster.

Dunn glared at him, pulling another file folder out of his briefcase. "Easy, bro," he said. "You'll have a lot harder time covering *me* up." He frowned as he slid the manilla folder across to Kamienski.

The big shepherd flipped the folder open and looked at the first page. It was an edited version of the file Carmine had dug up on the otter. The dog frowned. "This guy? Seriously?" he asked.

Dunn raised an eyebrow. "He knows I'm on to him. And he's getting help. Be fast and be quiet. I don't want to spook him. If you fuckers are good at anything, it's

navigating the gross parts of this city. And I already know you can be discreet." He smirked. "Find him for me, or find yourself on the news."

Kamienski nodded. He frowned. "Fine. We'll find him." He took a deep breath. "You're a real piece of shit, Special Agent Dunn."

That made Dunn smile. "Same to you, Detective Kamienski." He turned to the other dog.

Brady leaned in and finally spoke. He kept his voice low.

"*I'm gonna fucking skin you alive,*" he hissed.

Kamienski turned to him. "*Brady!*" he snapped. "*Stop it!*"

Dunn smiled at him. "Officer Brady, I only have to send this video to *one person* and your life is over." He pursed his lips. "You're lucky the concerned landowner sent this video to me instead of the cartel, or you would already be in six weighted garbage bags at the bottom of Hillsborough Bay."

Brady was undeterred. He leaned forward even further. "You better watch your back, you prissy little shit," he growled.

Dunn grinned at him. "Always do, Officer!" he said, brightly.

Kamienski lifted himself to his feet and pulled Brady up after him. He had to physically pull on Brady's arm to get the dog to give up his murderous death glare at Dunn. They headed for the lobby doors, and just before they went through, Brady turned to throw one more homicidal glare at Dunn.

And then they were gone.

Dunn was still working when he got a text from Kamienski.

His second cellphone chimed, which was a delisted number that he only gave to a few people. He checked it.

Found the otter. Need to meet.

Frowning, Dunn checked the time on the phone. 1:15 am.

He tapped out a reply.

Now??

The answer came in a few seconds.

Yes. He's getting ready to move. Tonight. Bring your files.

Dunn grimaced. "Shit," he hissed.

Where?

Again, an instant reply.

Old Tampa Bay Center.

Dunn frowned.

The old mall? By the stadium?

He checked his watch. That was only a few miles away. This time of night, he could be there in 10 minutes.

Yes. Hurry.

Dunn scrambled to his feet, snatching up his car keys and the otter file.

Be there in ten,

he tapped back.

I'll be waiting,

Kamienski sent back.

Fast-walking down to his Jeep, Dunn shrugged out of his suit jacket and took off his tie.

He peeked at the shirt underneath. It was a Nike athletic shirt that fit his lithe chest snugly. That would do. He had his button-down unbuttoned by the time he got to the car, and whipped it off before he climbed in. As a general rule, whenever Dunn was doing something shady, he tried to look as little like an FBI agent as possible, and the first step of that was losing the shirt and tie. He was still wearing his suit pants and dress shoes, but if he was found by some security guard he wouldn't be immediately copped for an agent.

It was colder now, and windy. The ocean breeze had turned cool.

Firing up his Jeep, Dunn turned off the radio — pop music had begun blasting as soon as the engine started — and drove swiftly out of the parking lot.

The night was dead. Dunn didn't see another car. There were barely even any lights on downtown, just the assorted bright signs on skyscrapers in the skyline downtown and the glowing blue triangular top of the SunTrust Centre.

It was all surface streets to the old mall. It was so close he wouldn't even be taking any highways.

As he drove, he thought about Kamienski and Brady. They had come through with the otter, or at least Kamienski had, but he was already having second thoughts about their business relationship. Dunn kept a lot of his blackmail victims around to abuse them again and again, in case they could be useful later, but Brady had felt really unstable, and of course he was probably a multiple murderer. That part didn't bother

Dunn one bit, but he might prove to be a liability later. Dunn decided he would probably leak the video once he got *his hands on the otter*.

The thought made him smile. His hands on the otter. This was going to be good. The otter looked like he would be a pushover. Dunn was confident he only needed a couple minutes alone in a remote place with the otter and the little lutrine would be terrified of him. Once the otter was under his control, Dunn could lean on him for tips on the otter's wealthy benefactors — whatever the otter was using to blackmail them. He could open and initiate case after case. He'd be a director in five years. And *then* let his asshole father and stepmother push him on his life choices.

Blue eyes up and alert, Dunn pulled into what remained of the Tampa Bay Center mall.

Tampa Bay Center had opened sometime in the '70s and closed sometime in the early 2000s. Dunn didn't know the specifics, and he didn't particularly care. Why did a shopping mall wither and die, even in the heart of a bustling city, even across from a major stadium? That was a mystery lost to time and Dunn's indifference. All he knew were the facts: Tampa Bay Center had closed two decades ago, it had been demolished shortly thereafter, and the only thing remotely of note anywhere on the grounds now was a big new Buccaneers training facility.

Bizarrely, the rest of the dead mall was still clearly recognizable, but only as a perverse version of its former self. The mall itself was gone, razed to its concrete foundation, partially obscured by grass in places but still plainly visible in its original strange shape. In defiance of all logic, the parking lot remained, two decades later, still forming the identifiable outline of the missing mall. The lot was sometimes used for stadium overflow parking, so it was still maintained, but nothing had been rebuilt in the outline of the huge demolished building. It was a mall parking lot for no mall, a physical artifact without a purpose, the hollow ghost of its former life. And it was where Dunn was headed.

It was a unique place for a nighttime meeting, but Dunn wasn't surprised. It was remote and abandoned but still in the center of town, widely-visible but unoccupied. A gunshot would be heard, and cops would be called, but they were unlikely to be disturbed. It was a reasonable place for Kamienski to suggest. Dunn had met informants there before.

It didn't take him long to spot Kamienski. There was one cutout in the massive parking lot, a small greenbelt dotted with mature trees, and next to that was a large SUV. It was a black Cadillac Escalade XL, which seemed a little pricey on a detective's salary, not to mention ostentatious, but it was the only car in a parking lot with a thousand spaces, so Dunn figured that was Kamienski.

Pulling up a few spaces away, Dunn surveyed the situation. The big shepherd was behind the wheel. He turned to Dunn as he pulled up.

Cautiously, Dunn put the Jeep in park, but didn't turn it off. He opened the Jeep's thin side door.

Kamienski got out, too. His golden eyes were a little wide in his black face.

Good. It was only him.

Dunn stared at him. "What have you got?" he asked. He didn't have time for pleasantries.

The shepherd detective stared at him. He was wearing the same button-down shirt but missing his tie. "Agent Dunn?" he asked, hesitantly.

Dunn blinked at him. He frowned, more severely. What the hell? It was dark out, but it wasn't *that* dark. "Yeah, it's me," he said. "What have you got?" he asked again. He glanced into Kamienski's car. It looked empty. Where *was* Brady? "Did you find the otter?"

Kamienski stared at him for a moment, and then took a deep breath. "Yeah. We found him."

Dunn's heart began pounding. His goal was so close. But unfortunately it depended on two crooked cops. Speaking of whom...."Where's your friend?" he asked, sharply. He walked up to the shepherd.

Kamienski stared back at him. He looked hesitant. The shepherd detective had been calm and self-assured earlier, but now he was tense and unsure. "My friend?" he asked, furrowing his brow.

Dunn rolled his eyes. "Don't play dumb, please. Your big asshole friend. Brady."

Kamienski blinked, and then nodded. "Oh," he said. He took a deep breath. "He's with the otter."

Dunn stared at him. "Keeping tabs on him?"

Kamienski blinked, and then nodded. "Yeah. Keeping tabs on him."

Dunn frowned. "Where's the otter?" he asked.

Kamienski stared at him for a second, and then turned toward the skyline.

The husky furrowed his brow.

The shepherd pointed.

Dunn frowned.

There was something wrong with Kamienski's ears.

The husky stared. He couldn't tell what was wrong, but Kamienski's ear fluff looked wrong.

Then Kamienski said "There," and Dunn was distracted. He followed the shepherd's finger.

The detective was pointing at the skyline. To Dunn's surprise, Kamienski pointed at the tall, triangular-topped Element tower, in the heart of downtown.

Dunn felt his jaw drop. "Are you kidding? He's *in the center of downtown?*"

Kamienski turned back to him. He nodded, deadly serious.

"How did you find him?" Dunn asked.

The shepherd shrugged. "Asked around. Finally hit on a doorman. I've talked to him before, so he told me what he knew."

Dunn shook his head. "Jesus. I knew the otter wasn't being subtle, but I expected him to be more careful than this." He frowned. "What did you say about him leaving?"

Kamienski frowned. "I think he's getting ready to move. I saw a lot of boxes. Looked like packing crates."

Dunn frowned. "Packing crates? For what?"

The shepherd shook his head. "I only saw the crates."

Dunn nodded thoughtfully. Shit. If the otter was getting ready to move, that didn't leave the husky much time. He would have to freeze his assets as soon as the banks opened in the morning. And he would have to make contact tonight.

"Did you know he has an accomplice?" Kamienski asked, suddenly.

Dunn blinked at him. "What?" he snapped.

Kamienski nodded slowly. "Yeah. Do you know anything about him? Might have been a big cat. Do you have any information on that?"

Dunn stared at him. He tried to swallow his astonishment. The otter had an accomplice?! "I don't have any intel on that so far," he said, as relaxed as possible.

Kamienski nodded. "And where do you think he's going?"

Dunn took a second to process that, and then frowned. "Why the fuck would I tell *you* that?"

Kamienski blinked, and then swallowed. His face was calm. No, he was trying to keep his face calm. He frowned. "I saw a lot *tonight*. But none of it made sense. Do you know of anywhere he might be going? If you tell me, I can maybe confirm or deny."

Dunn frowned. "I'm not telling you anything."

Kamienski's ears tilted forward and he showed his teeth. "Dunn, he's leaving *tonight*," he snapped. "Tell me what you know, and I'll tell you which of the places he's going. Then you can show up there and wait for him."

Dunn narrowed his eyes. "Absolutely not. Take me to him. Now."

The shepherd's eyes widened, and Dunn watched his jaw slowly open. He saw all the shepherd's bottom teeth, as Kamienski stared at him dumbly. "Wh...what?" he whispered.

Dunn frowned. "Take me to him," he repeated, louder.

Kamienski stared, his eyes widening. "Wh-what? No!" he snapped. He swallowed. "He...he knows you're looking for him! You're gonna spook him! He'll bail and you'll never find him again."

Dunn leaned forward, flashing his teeth. Kamienski was six inches taller than him but Dunn knew from experience he could out-crazy most men. "The fuck I won't!" he snarled. "Take me to him *tonight*. I'm going to make contact and then he's not fucking going anywhere."

Kamienski's eyes were perfectly circular now. "What?! No! *Why!*" he demanded.

Dunn was mad now. He let his rage show on his face as he leaned forward. "Because I'm going to *use him*, Kamienski," he snarled. "I'm going to threaten his miserable shit-weasel ass, and I'm going to get all of his contacts, and I'm going to *take* whatever dirt he has on them and then whatever fucking influence he has will be *mine!*" he snapped. "And *you're* gonna let me, unless you want me to send that fucking video to the cartel myself, and then *maybe* you'll be lucky enough to be with your big friend when the cartel catches him, and cuts him into thirty little pieces!" he roared.

Kamienski was scared now. He cowered, his ears folding back. "Wh-what?!" he cried. "No! *You have to go!*" he whimpered. "Leave me to it! I'll handle it! J-just tell me where you think he has resources and I'll tell you where he's going!"

Dunn had had enough. He snapped his arms out and grabbed Kamienski by the shirt.

"*Ah!*" the shepherd barked, flinching in fear.

"*Kamienski!*" Dunn snarled, standing on his toes to get right into the shepherd's face. "It's you or the fuckin' otter tonight! So pick, *right now*, you black and tan asshole!"

Kamienski watched him, golden eyes wide and terrified, ears back, panting in fear, and then a miserable, *sad*, regretful grimace split his black face. He looked like he was about to start crying.

"I'm sorry," the shepherd whispered, and Dunn's breath caught in his throat.

"Wh—" Dunn started, but that's all the sound he got out.

Kamienski's arms shot up. One of them grabbed Dunn's scruff, tightening viciously, pulling his head painfully backward, wrenching his jaw open.

The other shot up and tightened around Dunn's throat.

Kamienski lifted him off his feet, by his neck.

"*Hrchkk!*" Dunn gasped, as his air was cut off.

Kamienski squeezed his throat, *hard*, hard enough to cut off not only the husky's air supply, but the blood flow to his brain. He tried to gasp, his adrenaline kicking in, flailing and spasming in Kamienski's grasp. Panic leapt up into his brain as the blood and the oxygen stopped, and the husky's entire body stiffened. He saw stars, immediately, and his back arched as his lungs tried to fill with air and couldn't.

"Don't resist him!" Kamienski told him. He looked miserable. He begged Dunn with his eyes. "If you resist, he'll have to hurt you!" he hissed. His eyes were wide and pleading.

Dunn's blood ran ice cold. He finally realized what was wrong with Kamienski's ears.

Blood. He'd been bleeding from his ears. From both of them.

The otter had gotten to him.

In the moment before he passed out, Dunn kneel-flinched his powerful leg up, and kneed the shepherd right in the genitals.

"*Awrrk!*" Kamienski screamed, crumpling to his knees and collapsing to a heap, dropping Dunn in the process.

Dunn went down hard in the parking lot, slamming onto his side. "*Aaahrgh!*" he gasped as all the wind left him. But he couldn't recover. He had to get away. He didn't even go for his gun. He had to get out.

Dunn went into husky flight mode, scrabbling on his feet, scuffing his dress shoes, scrambling into an all-fours half-run, and then propelling himself onto his feet by sheer inertia. He launched himself in the direction of the Jeep, lit and running, just fifteen feet away. He saw the next steps in his mind: wrench the door open, throw himself in, throw it in gear, stand on the accelerator, peel out across the hollow shell parking lot, speed toward the exit, speed onto a main street, speed away, get away, speed away, get away, speed away.

He sprinted ten feet before Brady hit him.

The king shepherd was bigger than Kamienski, much bigger, and he hit Dunn at a full run, from a direction the husky hadn't even been looking. He hit him, and scooped him up, scooped him *right off his feet*, and let their inertia carry them in the direction they had been going, right into the side of the Jeep.

The impact was worse than hitting the ground. The impact was worse than a car accident. Brady hitting him hurt, but Brady smashing him into the side of the Jeep was an impact he felt in his bones.

"*Awrghk!*" was the only sound Dunn managed to make, more of a squeak than a scream, as 400 pounds of German shepherd crushed him, and all of the air left his body, and he *felt* the Jeep's sheet metal give under the crushing force presented by his body, and he *felt* his collarbone snap in his shoulder, and he hit his head and his nervous system shorted out and for a few moments he didn't feel anything at all.

Gasping, gagging, his whole body screaming, Dunn would have collapsed onto the asphalt a second time, except the huge German shepherd was holding him now, squeezing him tightly. He writhed, reeling, struggling to stay conscious, gasping for air.

"What do I do with him?!" Brady was gasping. "*Sir, help!*" he whimpered. "*What do I do?*"

"Hold him there," said a voice Dunn didn't recognize, and it made his blood run cold.

Reeling, his tongue hanging out, Dunn struggled to turn his head and focus.

Someone was coming.

Kamienski was still there, and Brady was holding him, and someone else was coming.

It was the otter.

Dunn let out a whimper.

The otter stared at him, stared into his eyes, and then,

and

then

,

something happened

, the otter stared at him, and Dunn noticed he had red eyes, and then

something

happened

.

Dunn *felt something*, felt a scratching in his mind, felt like he was trying to remember something, only *he* wasn't trying to remember something, something else, *someone else* was in his head, HIS HEAD, trying to remember something, and Dunn figured it all out. Eyes widening, trapped in the big shepherd's grasp, Special Agent Andrew Dunn figured it all out.

The otter was in his head when that thought made its way through, and he smiled. He saw it, he *felt* when the husky figured it out, and *he smiled*.

The otter wasn't blackmailing anyone. He didn't have any influence. He didn't know any deep dark secrets.

He was taking control of them.

Dunn felt all of his fur stand on end.

"*Please…*" he started, and that was the last coherent, untainted vocalization the husky would ever make.

The otter stared at him, getting closer, and suddenly that was all Dunn could see, the otter's eyes, hazy, like he was viewing them through intense heat, and then the otter *poured* into him, gushed into his mind, like molten metal gushing through Dunn's eyes, melting the soft flesh as it tore into his brain cavity, and he screamed. He screamed and fell, and felt like he kept falling, because he couldn't feel his body hit the ground.

> *It hurt,*
> *it was hot,*
> *it kept coming,*
> *it was the otter,*
> *pouring into him,*
> *crashing over him like a wave,*
> *taller than him,*
> *lifting him up and sweeping him away,*
> *pouring over him like water,*
> *like lava,*
> *like hot boiling earth.*

Dunn screamed. He couldn't help but scream. It burned. He was dying. His body stopped responding. His brain was on fire.

The otter had reached him now, crouched down, climbed on top of him, and Dunn realized he was on the ground on his back, and on some level he could feel the mustelid's weight on him. He hardly weighed anything, he was short and insignificant. Dunn barely felt him. He put his hands on his ears, screaming, writhing, arching his back, as the otter straddled him and then lay on him.

"**STOP FIGHTING ME,**" the otter said, and Dunn couldn't tell if it was out loud or just in his head.

He was being crushed, buried. He was disappearing.

The otter was on top of him, now. Dunn could smell him. No, the otter's smell *consumed* him. It was burning into his brain.

The otter reached down and grabbed Dunn's face, encircled the husky's muzzle and eyes with his webbed paws.

"**YOU WANT ME,**" he ordered, and it was true.

Dunn writhed, struggling to maintain control. He couldn't feel his body. He could only feel the otter on top of him. He suddenly felt thick otter fur in his fingers, felt the otter's lithe, muscular body in his arms, and he realized he was encircling the otter in his arms, his hands under the otter's shirt, squeezing him. He was holding him. He crushed the otter against his own body. *He needed him.* He needed the otter inside him. He needed the otter to absorb and destroy him.

"*Rawroooo!*" Dunn scream-howled. "Get out of my head! PLEASE! I have a family!" he howled. "Please please please please PLEASE!"

The otter didn't outwardly respond, but Dunn knew he wouldn't be relenting.

He was being buried, scalding hot soil raining down on top of him, covering him, sealing him away.

The otter kept pouring into his mind, coming and coming, and Dunn felt himself burning away, glowing and melting and evaporating. He was a lesser metal in the gold of the otter's desire. His body would stay but *he* would be gone. "*Please!*" he scream-groaned.

"I'm sorry," the otter said to him, out loud, and Dunn finally got his eyes to focus, and looked at him.

He looked at him.

The otter didn't look like much, older than Dunn, small, muscular, a little chubby. Soft features. Red eyes.

Red, sorry, eyes.

Dunn stared into his eyes, and grimaced, because he knew this was the end.

The otter gushed into him, and the husky felt his body respond. It destroyed him. His nervous system was on fire. It was like cocaine and ecstasy at the same time. He was dying of pleasure.

He was burning.

He felt himself bucking and gasping and realized he was cumming, he was rock-hard and cumming as he ground against the otter, sucking in as much air as his lungs would hold, filing his nose with the otter's scent, imprinting onto what was left of his mind,

and with that last white-hot burst of pleasure
 the very last bit of him buckled,
  and then he was gone.

Silently, he wakes up.

His head is pounding. His body is limp. He doesn't feel the urge to sit up, or to speak, or even to open his eyes.

He doesn't have a reason to do any of that.

He doesn't have a reason to do anything at all.

He is nothing.

He has reason to do nothing.

He is empty.

The ground is hard and cold, and he can taste blood in his mouth, but it doesn't matter. Nothing matters. Truly, genuinely, he is a hollow man.

He can't move.

Or, he won't?

Either way, he doesn't.

After a little while, or maybe a long time, he becomes aware of voices. He hears them, but he doesn't try to track them, or understand them, because none of it matters to him. After another little while, hands appear under him, and lift him up, and carry him somewhere. He still doesn't open his eyes.

The hands put him somewhere soft, and then he feels movement. Gentle rocking, speeding up, slowing down.

It goes on for a long, long time, and then it stops.

There's more talking.

He hears a few words that make it into his brain. The words are close, and he feels a tiny flicker of recognition at the gentle timbre of the man's voice. He knows him, maybe? He doesn't know anyone or anything, actually, but that voice felt a little familiar.

"*Juan Carlos, I need you!*" is what the voice says.

He still has not opened his eyes, but he's listening, now.

There are footsteps, hard and heavy, running up to him. There is a gasp. "*Dios mio, que has hecho?!*" says a deep voice, directly next to him.

There are arms on him again. This time they're insistent.

A big hand pries one of his eyes open.

Silently, he observes.

It's a large black cat, holding him now. Eyes wide, mouth open. "Can you hear me?" he asks, hesitantly.

He *can* hear, but he doesn't have any reason to move, or respond, so he just stares.

The cat turns, away from him. "*What's the matter with you?*" he screams. It's loud, directly next to him. "What have you done?!"

Someone else appears in his line of vision. "Things got a little…intense."

There was that voice again.

He looks. One of his ears flicks. He feels it as if it belongs to someone else.

It's an otter now. He does not know him after all. He watches.

The black cat looks down at him, frowning.

He looks back up at the cat, one eye open, one eye closed, limp in the cat's arms.

The cat inhales deeply, and then exhales, and raises a big cat hand. He holds up his index finger in front of his face.

"Follow my finger," he rumbles, low and deep. He moves his finger to one side, and then back across his face to the other.

He watches, simply because it is an object moving in his field of vision. Back, and then forth, and then back again.

"Good," the cat tells him. "Good husky. That's a good husky for me."

The husky stares. He opens his other eye now, watching the cat's finger go slowly back and forth.

"That's *very* good," the cat says. "Now breathe in for me." The cat takes a deep breath, still watching the husky, his chest expanding.

As the cat inhales, the husky does, too, filling his lungs with air. He's still watching the cat's finger pass in front of his face, both eyes open wide now.

"Hold it."

Back.

He holds the breath.

Forth.

"Good. Now exhale."

Back.

He lets out a long, slow breath, feeling lighter as he does it.

Forth.

The husky stares, feeling his vision start to go fuzzy, and he observes that something is happening to him. The cat keeps talking, but the words get fuzzy. They go right into him. Become a part of him.

"Relax. Good. Good boy. As you watch, you'll feel sensation coming back into your body. First in your toes…"

The husky feels his toes tingle. Reflexively, he wiggles them. He is wearing shoes, which he feels against his toes.

"And then moving up your legs…"

The husky abruptly feels the ground underneath his legs and butt. He shifts, still staring obediently up at the cat. His legs feel stiff.

"And then up your chest, down into your arms…"

The husky takes a deep breath, curling his hands into fists. His hands feel useless and numb, like he hasn't ever moved them before.

"And finally up *into your head*."

Suddenly, the husky's eyes feel dry. He blinks them a few times, still watching the cat.

The cat mutters a few more gentle things to him, things he didn't really process. Suddenly he realizes he's been breathing too shallowly. He's barely been breathing at all.

He sucks in a breath, inhaling sharply, gasping, and sits up. "*Ahhhhh!*" he gasps. He's lightheaded immediately.

"There you go. Easy. *Calmateeee*," the cat whispered to him. He is a big cat, enormously tall and thin, black from head to toe. A jaguar. He rubs the husky's back with one massive hand, and the husky's skin tingles under his fur. His shoulder hurts, a dull, throbbing pain.

The husky blinks up at the cat, looking around. There are three other people in the room, two dogs and an otter. The otter is exuding something, a kind of electric charge. One of the dogs looks injured. The husky doesn't know who any of them are. He doesn't know who *he* is, either.

He stares. There is a pang of fear deep in his chest. Who is he? "I—" He tries to talk but he can barely get words out. He clears his throat and falls silent. He feels himself starting to shake.

The cat frowns concernedly down at him. "Shhh, it's okay, puppy," he whispers. "Don't worry. I'll keep you safe." He has a thick accent and he speaks with gravitas and calm. The words pour into the husky's ears.

Swallowing, the husky watches him. The cat is authoritative and strong. He'll help. Clearing his throat, shivering gently, the husky nods.

The cat turns to the otter. *"What have you done?"* he growls, making his chest shake.

The otter frowns severely at him. "Stop that. You know exactly what I did."

The cat narrows his eyes. He looks mad. The husky is glad the cat isn't mad at him. *"You* said you were going to get rid of him. You said you could trick him about our escape, and make him go away! And instead you capture him and *look what you've done to him!"*

The otter frowns. He looks like he's going to argue, and then slowly, he lowers his eyes and sighs. "We tried, Juan," he says. "He wouldn't take no for an answer. He's a fucking FBI agent, for Christ's sake."

The cat looks down at the husky. "He *was,"* he says, softly.

The husky stares back up at him, eyes wide. He has no idea what's going on. He's beginning to get frightened.

One of the dogs clears his throat. His face is mostly black. "It's my fault, sirs," he whimpers, miserably. "I'm sorry! I failed you!"

The otter lets out a breath. "No, you didn't, sweetie. It was a risky plan. You did amazingly. Come here. Both of you."

The two big dogs approach the otter, one of them limping painfully, and bend down. He pets both of them, telling them what good dogs they are. They begin wagging and panting.

The husky feels his heart start pounding.

He watches, the otter reaching up to rub both of the dogs' heads. They squirm in pleasure, shivering with happiness, even the injured one.

The husky feels something.

Longing?

The cat looks down at him, and it catches his eyes. He looks up.

The jaguar looks down at him, his eyes full of sadness. They're the saddest eyes the husky has ever seen in his whole life, as far as he knows.

"I am sorry," the cat whispers to him, his voice quiet, shaking, barely audible. "I am so, so sorry."

The husky doesn't understand what the cat is sorry for. So he just doesn't reply.

The cat reaches up and gently strokes his head, staring down at him, still staring at him with those sad, sad eyes.

The husky has no idea why this is happening, but it feels nice, so he just lays there and lets the big cat pet him.

Finally, the cat lets out a long, defeated sigh. He takes a deep breath, and turns his head.

"At least, did you get the files?" the cat grumbles.

The otter stops petting the two big dogs, gives each of them a kiss on his forehead, and turns. "Yes, just a second," he says.

The little otter turns and walks away, to a car, and for the first time the husky realizes they are in a garage. There are two big vehicles in there with them. The otter walks to a damaged red one, wrenches the door open with some effort, hops up into it, and rummages around for a few minutes. He comes back out with his hands full of papers.

He is frowning.

For some reason, this makes the husky's ears fold back against his head.

"What's the matter?" the cat asks.

The otter is frowning. "There is…a lot here."

The cat blinks at him. "How much?"

The small mustelid grits his teeth. "Everything. My assets. Cash movements. *Benefactors.*"

The cat stares at him, frowning. "*Benefactors*, eh?"

The otter looks up, lowering the papers, blinking.

The cat frowns. "So they know what you can do," he says, tonelessly.

The otter watches him for a moment, and then looks down at the dog in the jaguar's arms.

The husky widens his eyes. He stares, his heart pounding.

The otter looks back up at the cat. "They have…an idea," he says, slowly.

They were silent for a few long moments. The husky looks back and forth between the two of them. The other two dogs just watch, too. The dogs are all respectfully silent.

The cat inhales, and then lets out another long, sad sigh.

"This is going to keep happening, isn't it," he says, flatly.

The otter, lost in thought, breaks, and looks up at him. He stares, and then silently, he nods. After a moment, he closes his eyes.

"It's out now. They know. This is what we were afraid of. They're putting together what you can do. They're going to keep coming. And coming. And coming."

Silently, still not opening his eyes, the otter continues to nod.

The cat takes a shallow breath. He looks up.

"This is…basically the end for us," he says, somberly.

The otter opens his eyes. He just looks at the jaguar, and sighs. They stare at one another. Silently, he nods.

"Yeah," the otter says. "It is."

They're silent for a moment.

They are miserable. Broken. Despondent.

Silently, the husky puts a hand gently on the cat's forearm.

The jaguar turns his head, surprised, and looks down. He observes the husky, first with confusion, and then with horror, and then with revulsion. *Revulsion.*

"Do not comfort *me*," the big cat growls, and for the first time the husky feels fear, absolute terror in the pit of his stomach. "We are the reason you are here. We deserve to *suffer*."

Wide-eyed, the husky takes his hand back. He curls his hands into fists at his sides, swallowing.

The jaguar looks immediately regretful, and then lets out a long, frustrated sigh. "It will be better this way," he tells the husky. The jaguar looks up. "Where will we go?" he asks.

The otter snaps out of his thoughts and looks up. He flips back through the papers. After a few moments, he looks up at the cat, grimacing. "They found Bali," he says, softly, grimly.

The cat blinks at him, his mouth open in surprise, staring. "Did they," he asks, flatly.

The otter holds up a piece of paper. "Yes." He keeps flipping.

The cat lets out a long sigh. "And Morelia?"

The otter is still flipping. "And Morelia."

The jaguar grimaces. "And Bogota?"

The otter looks up, frowning. "I'm sorry," he says.

The jaguar closes his eyes and turns his head away. The husky wants to touch his arm comfortingly, but he's scared now.

After a long moment, the cat opens his eyes. "What is left? What do you have left in your little otter bank account that we can spirit away to with no notice?"

The otter blinks, and swallows, and lets out a long, exhausted sigh. "There's one last option. It's in…*Alaska*."

The cat is shocked. "*Alaska?*" he repeats.

The otter nods. "It's north of Fairbanks. Unpopulated territory. It's a few hundred miles inside the Arctic circle. Old research station."

The cat opens his eyes. He stares for a few long moments, and then takes a shallow breath.

"I suppose we will be going north," he says.

The otter nods. "I suppose we will."

The cat blinks, rapidly, clenching his jaw, and then looks down at the husky.

The husky's mouth dries up as soon as the cat looks down at him.

"Can you stand?" the jaguar asks him, emotionlessly.

The husky swallows. "Y-y-y-yes, I think so," he says.

The cat nods. "I will help you." He puts his arms under the husky's shoulders and carefully lifts him to his feet.

The husky is shaky on his feet, but he doesn't want to fall in front of the cat.

"Very good," the cat tells him, and the husky nods.

The jaguar turns back to the otter. "We're going to have to give them names, you know," he said.

The otter blinks. "Really?" He looks at the husky, and then at the other two dogs, his red eyes wide. "Why? Can't we just use their real names?"

The cat glowers at him. "I do not think that would be wise. Names have intensive memory recall. You should give them new names. Try not to give them anything unique, either. I don't want to taint them with a sense of self." He looks at the dogs, and when his eyes settle on the husky, it makes his heart pound. "I may be a forced fugitive, but I'm still a researcher, and I don't want you *fucking up* my subjects." He bites the words off.

The otter looks at them. He has gentle eyes, and he smiles. It makes the husky's heart pound again, but this time out of happiness.

"Well then, I'll just give them numbers," the otter says. "In the order we…acquired them." He points at the tallest dog and stares at him for a moment. The dog stares back, his eyes widening. "You'll be 02." He moves to the next biggest one. "You'll be 03."

And then he turns to the husky, and his eyes seem to luminesce for a moment, and the husky feels his brain soften. His eyes start to unfocus. "And you will be 04," says the otter, and just like that 04 knows it to be true with every fiber of his being.

04 takes a deep breath, swaying, blinking, feeling foggy and dizzy. After a moment, he shakes his head, and he feels better. He makes eye contact with the other two dogs, 02 and 03, and he knows they felt it as strongly as he did. They're all wagging. It's hard not to.

The cat frowns. "I do not understand. Who's 01?"

The otter gives him an evil little smile.

The cat blinks, and then glares. "*Bastardo*," he mutters.

The otter beams. "Now now, then, 01, you don't want to taint the research subjects, do you?"

The jaguar narrows his eyes. "No, I suppose I don't. *Sir*." He looks up at the dogs. "You may call me 01." He rises to his full height, reaching almost the ceiling of the garage, and 04 feels a sharp chill dance down his spine.

02 clears his throat. "S-sir," he says, to the otter. "Wh...what's..." It takes him a few moments to work up the nerve to ask the question he wanted. "What is your name, sir?" he finally asks.

The otter beams, and it makes 04's heart dance in his chest. "Thank you for asking, 02! Boys, you may call me...*Master*."

04 stares worshipfully. He feels his tail begin wagging. *Master*.

"Thank you, Master," he says, softly, trying it out, and then Master turns to smile at him, and it makes him so happy he almost feels dizzy.

Master turns to 01 and takes a deep breath. "Well...are we ready?" he asks.

01 looks at the dogs, and lets out a long sigh. "No. But we should be going."

Master nods. "Right."

They leave the red car behind and walk to the black car. 04 trails hesitantly behind.

02 and 03 move instinctively to the back seat. They both turn to 04.

"You gotta sit in the middle," 02 tells him. "You're the smallest."

04 stares up at the two big dogs, realizes he has to sit between them, and feels his ears tilt back. His tail tucks up between his legs, and he puts his arms around his stomach, despite how much it makes his shoulder hurt.

02 smiles at him. "It's okay," the big dog says. "We'll keep you safe."

03 nods eagerly. "You don't have to be scared or mad any more. You're part of our pack now."

They both lean in and lick his face, and it's impossible for 04 not to feel elated at the sensations.

With 02's help, the husky clambers up into the tall SUV.

In the driver's seat, the enormous jaguar turns around. "Seat belts on, please," he rumbles, severely.

04 can't get his seatbelt on but 03 helps him with it.

Master turns, dwarfed in the massive passenger seat. "All right, boys, are you ready for a road trip?" he asks, smiling.

"Yes, Master," all the dogs answer, vacant smiles on their faces.

Beaming, wagging, 04 wasn't sure he knew what a road trip was, but he was ready to take one with Master. 04 was ready to follow Master to the end of the earth.

And he would.

Sunset

When 04 woke up he was on the floor of the research trailer.

It was cold. He smelled antiseptic, and metal, and rubber, and blood, and otter, and cat.

He remembered the facility, and Master, and the trips to Prudhoe Bay, and the shepherds and the malamutes, and the experiments, and the cabin, and the melt tank, and cuddling up behind 06, pressed up against him, feeling his warmth, gently nuzzling his fluffy neck fur, swimming in his scent, saying nothing, watching the soft, gentle green of the northern lights through the tiny window in his room.

He also remembered Tampa Bay, and his office, and the smell of the lobby Starbucks at 7:00 am, and the palm trees, and the leather of his Jeep, and the violent thunderstorms that rolled through Florida every afternoon at 4:00 pm, and laying in the warm sand, smelling the morning air and the salt and water and minerals in the air as it blew in off the ocean, rustling his fur as he listened to the gentle rhythm of the waves.

04 opened his eyes. Agent Dunn looked around.

01 was holding him. He was looking down at the husky, brow furrowed, eyes wet, biting back a frown. He had been crying.

04 looked up at him.

The jaguar swallowed. "04?" he whispered, hesitantly. He bit his lip as he waited for a response.

The husky stared at him, and felt something building inside of him, something born of his old life as Agent Dunn, something he had spent the last few weeks fighting. It roared forth from his core, like a volcano erupting, and this time he didn't try to fight it. This time he channeled it.

"*RAWROOROOROOROOOROO!*" he barked, lunging for 01's face.

01 was very fast or very startled, 04 couldn't tell which, but the big cat flinched, and he did it with his entire body. 01 launched away from him, dumping 04 onto the

linoleum floor and skidding backward, crashing into a counter so hard that his body pushed it backwards, notepads and medical equipment crashing down on him.

04 felt his teeth snap together. He lifted himself onto all fours, his hackles raising. He looked around.

01 was here, obviously, his back to the counter opposite the gurney, staring at him with horror. So was 02, his eyes wide, ears back, frozen in place. 02 was so shocked he was holding his breath. 04 let his eyes linger on the king shepherd. He'd put on a lot of muscle in the time since he had been Officer Brady. As 04 stared at him, the big dog withered under his gaze.

04 narrowed his eyes, and then turned back to 01. He showed his teeth.

"Where is he?" he growled.

01 swallowed. "Where is w-who?" he asked.

He had an accent, 04 realized. 01 had an accent, and 04 was hearing it for the first time. South American.

"You know who," 04 snarled. "That god damn otter!"

02's eyes somehow widened further. His mouth dropped open. He looked like he was going to faint.

The door to the research trailer opened.

04 snapped his head around. He stood up. He was shaky, but he wasn't going to fall.

Master was standing in the doorway.

They made eye contact, and 04 knew the otter could tell he was different.

"*You,*" the husky growled.

01 staggered to his feet. "04, please, stay calm," he begged. He definitely had an accent. Columbian, probably. "Your brain is under so much stress right now, please, I do not want you to get—"

"SHUT UP!" 04 roared. 01 fell silent immediately, golden eyes wide.

They all stared at him.

Master frowned. He looked older than 04 remembered. His enormous otter whiskers drooped, and there were lines around his eyes. He swallowed.

04 stared at him. He didn't feel any of the reverence he had felt for Master. He didn't luminesce the way he usually did. Instead of exultation, the husky felt only revulsion.

"That's it?" the husky said, his voice dripping with contempt.

Master's brow furrowed. "Wh-what?" he asked, hesitantly.

04 took a step towards him. "That's *all this is?*" He gestured at the research trailer around him. "All of this is because you're hiding?"

Master blinked, and then frowned.

04 took another step towards him. "You're not even researching anything here, are you?" he snapped. He looked at 01 too.

01 lowered his eyes.

"ARE YOU?!" 04 screamed. His voice echoed off the hard surfaces in the trailer.

Both of them were silent.

04's heart was pounding. His head was throbbing. "This isn't a fucking *research station*! This is your fucking *winter hideout* because you used your stupid gift *for money* and you got *fucking caught*! And the only reason you have us here is to maintain this fucking place in this *GOD DAMN SNOWY HELLSCAPE!*"

He looked at both of them. 01 wouldn't even look at him. The big jaguar's shoulders sagged. Master was looking at him, but wasn't saying anything. The otter was just taking it, staring back with that sad pathetic little frown.

"*ANSWER ME!*" 04 roared.

01 flinched. Master swallowed.

"You're right," the otter said.

04 felt his entire body shaking. "So that's it? That's all?"

The otter frowned. He took a deep breath. "That's all," he said. Somber. Resigned.

04 nodded. His thoughts were racing. All this time. He'd been wrestling with the purpose of this place all this time, and that was it. Nothing more.

"I should have put a fucking bullet in you," he snarled.

01's eyes widened. 02 lifted his hands to cover his muzzle.

Master just frowned.

"You stole our lives," 04 growled, "and you spawned this *horrible place*, and you *KEPT US HERE*," he screamed. "And you *FUCKING! KILLED A MAN!*" He pointed violently toward 02, who actually recoiled in surprise and horror. "*So you could HIDE!*" He was shrieking now, his voice high and shrill. "*JUST BECAUSE YOU STOLE SOME FUCKING MONEY! AND SOME CARS! AND A CONDO! IN FUCKING FLORIDA!*"

His voice echoed back to him. No one else spoke. Or moved. Or even breathed.

04 stood there, staring at Master, glaring daggers into him. He was panting.

Master stared, and then frowned, and then nodded.

04's rage started to subside, and sadness took its place. He felt his face twist into a grimace, and he bit back a sob that was threatening to roll out. "Was it worth it?" he demanded. His voice broke as he said it.

Master stared at him, watching him with those evil red eyes.

04 stared back. He was still panting. It was a struggle to hold himself up.

The otter took a deep breath, and let it out as a long sigh. When he spoke it was calm, and collected, and gentle. "04," he said, softly, tenderly. "What do you think would happen if they found me?"

04 narrowed his eyes. What the hell was this? "If *who* found you?" he demanded.

Master shrugged. "Anyone," he said. He was speaking in a normal, conversational tone, and he stepped closer to 04 as he did it. "The police, say. Or maybe your FBI. The United States government."

04 frowned.

"What would happen if *they* got a hold of me, *and they knew what I could do?*"

The husky swallowed.

Master narrowed his red eyes. "What if *any government on earth* got a hold of me, with my abilities, and they knew what they had?"

04 stared at him.

He had wanted to use Master for his own purposes. To accomplish his goals. He wasn't going to let him rot in prison. Oh no, and waste that potential? He hadn't even thought twice about it. He was going to use Master for his own purposes.

And he hadn't even known what Master was *really* capable of.

What if he had known? What would he have done *then?*

And what would that look like in the hands of the United States military? Or *any* military? Or any dictator across the world? What would Dunn have done if he'd known about Master's unlimited power? What would he have wanted? What would that look like *on a global scale?* He'd stolen cars and condos — what if he'd been turned against prime ministers, presidents, generals?

What would that look like?

04 felt the blood drain out of his face. The balance of power would be annihilated. There would be no stopping any entity with Master at their disposal. No one would even know what was happening until the world was completely in the hands of whoever had located and understood Master first. He would be a more dangerous weapon than the fucking nukes.

He stared at the otter.

Master watched the thought travel through his head.

Feeling dizzy, 04 leaned back against the vinyl of the gurney.

Master stared at him. "What would happen, 04?" he asked, his voice gentle and tender.

The husky swallowed.

"The end of the world," he heard himself say.

Master nodded.

04 looked at 01. The jaguar met his eyes. The big cat's eyes were soft and sympathetic.

He turned back to the otter. "So what?" he asked. "If you're such a threat, why didn't you just put a bullet in your head?" he asked. He clenched his jaw to bite back the sob that was threatening to escape.

Again, 02's eyes widened even further and he looked like he was going to faint. The big dog's ears were cemented to his head. He was holding perfectly still except for a gentle tremor.

Master frowned sourly, and then looked at 01. "Do you want to tell him, Juan Carlos?"

04 felt his arm fur rise, as he turned to look at the jaguar.

The jaguar looked at Master, and then, with a sigh, opened his mouth. "We…do not know if he is the only one."

We do not know. If he is the only one.

04 felt dizzy again. He snapped his gaze back to Master. "*What?!*" he roared. 02 flinched at the noise.

Master frowned. "We haven't been able to figure out why I'm like this," he said. He glanced at 01. "I contacted Juan Carlos a few months before you found me. I asked him to study me to determine how I could do…this. We were unable to determine what made it possible."

04 pivoted.

01 frowned. "I could not determine the root cause for Master's abilities. We don't know if it's environmental, or genetic. We don't know if there are…others like him."

04 snapped his head back.

Master frowned. "So we *do* study. We monitor the effects on you dogs. And we see if there's any way to resist it. And we watch the world for signs of…what I do. Because I don't think anybody else on earth knows what to look for."

The husky watched him. "Is there?"

Master blinked. "Is there what?"

04 narrowed his eyes. "Is there any way to resist you?"

The otter frowned. "No. Not so far," he said, slowly.

04 nodded, slowly. He looked down.

Jesus.

He was feeling empty again, even though now he was overflowing.

There was a knock at the door. They all turned.

It was a small, slim husky, who crept silently into the room. 11. It was the husky they called 11. He glanced at 04, his ears flat against his head, and 04 realized he had definitely been listening outside the door. Or maybe 04 had just been audible in the entire facility.

"S-s-sorry to interrupt," the little dog said. "But 16 asked me to tell you the time. It's 5:15." He swallowed.

04 stared at him, wondering why the fuck the dog had walked all the way over here just to tell them the time.

And then he remembered the wolves.

All of *that* information poured back into his head. It felt like it had been a month ago.

"Oh, shit," he muttered. He looked back up at Master. "Fuck. Take me to the girl who escaped," he said.

Master glanced at 01, and then nodded.

They turned and left.

04 stepped back into the mess trailer.

He'd only been gone a half hour. It felt like a hundred years.

As 04 cleared the fire door from the connection hallway, he looked around the room.

It looked familiar, but as a place he had once known. Like going back to Quantico, or his childhood home. It seemed like a place he had known, once, long ago.

The girl was seated at the table, with two of the dogs. The bear was behind them. They all looked up at him.

04 looked at the girl with the trained eye of an expert. She was a pine marten, and judging by her face and hair, late teens or early twenties. Her hair was short and tied back. She was wearing a t-shirt, under the blanket, something cheap and basic.

The marten was probably from one of the northern villages on the Russian continent, more than likely one towards the east. There were a number of fairly large cities, by north Russian standards, to the south of the Eastern Siberian sea, mostly along the Kolyma and Omolon Rivers. There were smaller towns and settlements all over the Russian far east, and close to the river they were easily accessible to the Eastern Siberian Sea. From there it was a quick trip to the Chukchi Sea and then onward into North American waters, either south through the Bering Strait to the continental US or Canada, or east around Point Barrow if you wanted to smuggle your trafficking victims through a tiny town of 2,000 people and a few thousand oil workers, none of whom would be particularly motivated to ask you a lot of questions.

He made eye contact with the girl. She looked straight back at him, brown eyes searching. She stared at him for a moment, and then looked at the dogs at the table with her.

04 followed her gaze.

They didn't look familiar.

One of them was the chef, 04 remembered that. He was a big shepherd, not as big as Kamienski, but big. He was thick and muscular, with a pot belly and a square, slightly-round muzzle. He had a crew cut, and wide golden eyes, and a broad burn scar across the base of his muzzle, just at the bridge of his nose. He looked ex-military. Marine, maybe? No: Army. He was seated at the table with the girl, eyebrows up, staring at him.

The other one was a husky, smaller than 04, with a black eye mask. His nose had been broken, 04 noted. Not recently. A long time ago. His muzzle was a little out of shape. He was seated next to the girl, and he looked up at 04 with wide, concerned eyes.

He knows, 04 thought. He knew 04 wasn't 04 anymore.

The smaller husky lifted his hands and signed something. It was obviously sign language.

04 couldn't remember what it meant.

Horrified, he stared. The small husky stared back, his mouth opening, and then his face fell. He looked so scared.

04 stared in horror. He barely knew them. He could remember their numbers, 07 and 10, but he didn't *know* them. They were as foreign to him as Irina. There was a polar bear here, too, and 04 felt nothing. What if he felt like this for all the dogs? What about 06? Would he feel nothing when he saw him, too?

04 whirled. Where was the cat?! *There.* He spotted 01, just inside the mess doorway, and lunged toward him.

The jaguar's eyes shot up as the husky approached him.

"*YOU!*" 04 demanded. He stalked up to him.

01 stared at him. "Wh-what?!" he asked, cautiously.

04 grabbed the jaguar's wrist and continued past him, crashing into the bar to open the fire door to the connection hallway. He leaned forward, pulling with all of his husky strength, and almost yanked 01 off his feet as he continued out into the hallway.

When they were in the hall, 04 pushed the door closed and turned to look at him. He advanced on him, and 01 backed away.

"You! Fix me!" 04 growled.

The jaguar blinked down at him. "F-fix you?" he asked, incredulously.

04 scowled at him, glaring almost straight up. "*FIX ME!*" he snarled. "They mean nothing to me! WHY DO THEY MEAN NOTHING TO ME, JUAN?" he demanded. He was probably audible inside the mess but he didn't care.

The jaguar stared at him, wide-eyed. He grimaced. "I told you not to do it!" he mewled, miserably.

"You know I had to!" 04 yelled at him. He reached up and punched the jaguar in the chest, making a loud thump and making 01 jerk. "You! Fix! Me!" he yelled, punching the jaguar in the chest on each word, making his fist and his entire arm vibrate. "RIGHT! NOW! BRING HIM BACK! BRING 04 BACK! I DON'T WANT TO BE DUNN ANYMORE!"

Moving fast, too fast to avoid, 01 snapped his huge hands up and grabbed both sides of 04's head. He bent down to face him.

The husky flinched, yelping, but 01 was too strong and he was too shocked to evade. "Wh-wh-!" he started, gasping. Yowling, he reached up and grabbed at 01's wrists. It was like tugging at tree branches.

"SSH!" 01 growl-hissed, sharply, inches from his face. 04 flinched in shock.

01 stared at him, golden eyes boring into him half a foot away at most. His yellow eyes were wide, and staring right into 04's eyes. He was inescapable.

"Wh-wh-wh—" 04 stammered, his heart pounding.

"Look at me," 01 said, low and growly and dangerous. It thundered over him. "Look into my eyes."

04 stared into the jaguar's eyes, completely helpless. He couldn't move. He couldn't even breathe.

01 stared back at him, eyes wide, probing, unblinking, looking into his very soul, and 04 felt the golden yellow seep into him, overtake him, suffuse his very mind, and his eyes started to unfocus. He had one last lucid thought — *oh, thank God, it still works* — and then his thoughts started to slow down.

01 was beautiful. He really was. Eyes of gold in a sea of black. 04 stared, as best he could with his unfocused eyes, feeling the tension drain out of his hands, as he lowered his arms to his side, and let them dangle.

The husky swayed, steadied by the jaguar's big, strong, warm hands around his head.

"Look into my eyes, and give yourself to me," 01 rumbled, from inches away, and 04 felt himself floating away in his eyes.

Staring, his mouth hanging open, 04 gave himself to the jaguar.

"04," the jaguar said. "Dunn. Listen to me."

The husky felt his heart start pounding, even though he couldn't open his eyes. He was listening. *All* of him was listening. 04, Dunn, all of him was completely captivated by the jaguar before him.

"Listen to me. You are a good husky. You are *one* husky." 01 moved his enormous hand and began stroking 04's face and ears. It felt heavenly. "04 is inside you. Dunn is inside you. You have access to everything you are. You only have to remember…and decide."

Stroke.

Stroke.

Stroke.

"Say it back to me."

04 stared at him, his mouth feeling heavy. "Rem'mber…and decide…" he mumbled back.

01 grunted. "*Very good boy. Again.*"

04 swayed on his feet. "Remember, and decide," he rumbled. It felt good to say. It was a nice thought.

01 moved his hands and stroked both sides of 04's jaw with his big, thick thumbs. "Very good. Again."

04 arched his back, letting his tongue loll out. His whole body felt pleasure. "Remember…and decide…" he whimpered, squirming in pleasure.

01 squeezed his face. "*Very, very good.* Now I'm going to count you up, from one to three. And when you wake up you can exhibit whatever facet of your mind you

want to. It's all there at your disposal. One. Feeling yourself floating gently toward consciousness."

04 stared vacantly forward, feeling his tongue loll out.

"Two. Feeling your body. Feeling the air around you."

He could tell friends were nearby. The hallway was cold. There was food and someone he didn't know in the vicinity.

"Three. Wake." 01 removed his hands.

04 snapped his eyes fully open.

The jaguar was standing over him, frowning, searching him.

04 looked up at the giant cat looming over him, and silently felt his ears tilt back and his tail tuck in between his legs. He felt submissive and nervous.

So…normal.

Swallowing, he looked up at the big cat.

"Thank you," he whispered.

01 stared at him, and nodded somberly. "Of course," he said.

04 had a lot more to say to him. But of course they didn't have time.

The husky turned, feeling a little dazed, and opened the door to the mess. He went through, letting out a shaky breath. 01 trailed in behind him.

The husky surveyed all of them. 16 was here, watching him with concern from his post in the corner. 10 and 11 and 07 were here, too, and 02 had come from the research trailer.

07 looked up at 04. He stared, his eyes boring into him.

04 gave him a shaky smile.

07 watched him, peering, his brow furrowing, and glanced at 11. "*He's back*", he signed. He scrambled out of his seat and stepped up to 04. 11 did, too.

They both swept him up in a hug, one from each side, and 04 felt a wave of relief crash over him like a warm ocean wave.

Their scents enveloped him, and both the dogs pushed their muzzles in and nuzzled him, and 07 licked his face and 11 let out a little whimper, and he let himself be held up by their soft, strong, fuzzy bodies, and let out a long, tense, relaxing sigh.

He hadn't realized how much he'd been missing them. He needed to see 06 as soon as he possibly could, but he basked in the glow of the members of his pack he was fortunate enough to have with him.

"Jesus Christ, you scared the shit out of me," 11 whispered in his ear, squeezing him. "I could hear you screaming." His voice was shaking. "Whatever it is, we're here for you. We've got you." He was whimpering.

04 squeezed them both back, one hand around each of their waists.

07 nipped at his muzzle. "You…you are all right?" he asked, hesitantly. He said it out loud. He had a thick Russian accent. Very thick.

04 turned to look at him, eyes wide. It was definitely the first time 07 had ever said anything out loud to him, in English, at least. He swallowed and lifted his hands. "*Yes. I'm sorry I scared you.*"

07 looked concerned, and then let out a long, relieved sigh. He lifted his hands. "*Don't worry,*" he signed. He leaned in again to press his forehead against the side of 04's head.

04 basked in his warmth and scent. He lowered his hands and squeezed both of the other huskies again. He felt good and right to be back with his pack.

07 muzzle-bonked him, and 04 again noticed that 07's muzzle had an ever-so-slight ridge in it. His muzzle had noticeably been broken. 04 had definitely never seen it before. He frowned. Had Master and 01 been hiding the factors that set the dogs apart? He wondered, did 07 even know it?

07 and 11 both pulled their heads back, staring lovingly at him, and 04 pushed the thought away, letting out a shaky sigh.

He managed a weak smile and wriggled out of their grasps. He lifted his hands again, looking at 07. "*Can you still translate for me?*"

07 blinked at him, and then nodded.

They all turned to look at the girl seated at the table.

She looked skeptically up at him.

04 took a deep breath, and composed himself.

He smiled at the marten, not too big, not showing too much teeth. Gentle. Reassuring. It was his "Victim Interview" smile. He slowly took a seat at the table across from her.

"Hello," he said, signing as he went so 07 could follow and translate. "My name is Andrew." He had to spell it out in ASL for 07's benefit. "I'm so sorry for what you've been through."

07's eyes widened a little at the name, but he started speaking Russian, and 04 definitely heard him repeat the name.

Irina listened to the other husky, and then started speaking.

07 signed as she went. "*Hello. My name is Irina.*" Again, he had to spell out the name.

04 nodded. "Can we get you anything? Do you need to use a restroom?"

07 translated. Irina listened, facing 04. She replied.

"No," 07 signed. "*Thank you. The dog took me.*" 07 looked a little miffed at the last sentence, but translated nonetheless.

04 nodded. "Thank you. Irina, I need to ask you a few questions. We're expecting the wolves to come looking for you."

07 translated. Irina immediately frowned, and nodded. "Yes," she said, directly to 04. She switched to Russian and 07 translated.

"They will be after me. They have my mother."

04 watched her. She was upset but determined. "Where are you from?"

She told him, through 07. She was from a small town called Srednekolymsk on the river Kolyma. Her father had died along with their source of income. They gave the last of their savings to a group of men who promised they would take them to America to work in Las Vegas. She, with her mother and ten other women, all small mustelids, had spent two days in the cargo hold of a small ship. They'd been picked up after dark by a different group of men, all wolves, in Prudhoe Bay and bussed south in a van. The men were holding them at the old mine until "things calmed down" and they could continue south. There wasn't any food, the old mine trailer was not heated, and some of the women were sick and that was when Irina had decided to escape.

She told the story impassively, like it had happened to someone else.

04 nodded. "Thank you so much, Irina. You are very brave. We will take care of you while you're here. The wolves will not be getting you back."

Irina stared at him. The marten looked between him and 07, and then asked a very long, very pointed question to 04.

He looked to 07.

The smaller husky swallowed. "*Are you going to help us?*" he signed. "*You need to help them.*"

04 nodded. "Yes. We will hide you and then we're going to arrest the wolves. You'll be back with your mother tonight." He offered her a smile and hoped he wasn't lying.

She stared skeptically at him, then back at 07, then back at him.

"Promise?" she said, in English, narrowing her eyes.

04 blinked at her, and then nodded, solemnly. "Yes. I promise," he said.

Nodding, satisfied, Irina leaned back in her chair.

Taking a deep breath, 04 rose from his seat. He walked over to the kitchen side of the mess, stepped up to the big stainless steel prep counter in the center, waving the others to follow him.

Master and 01 followed immediately. 07 stayed at the table with Irina. 11 and 02 trailed after 04. 16 hunched down and crossed to that side of the room. He barely fit in the space, his huge shoulders barely clearing the gap between cabinets as he wedged into the room. He actually squatted down, sitting on his ass, which was probably more comfortable than stooping.

04 checked his watch. It was 5:35. Sundown was in a little over half an hour.

He looked up.

One otter, one jaguar, two huskies, two German shepherds, and a polar bear all stared back at him.

They all looked to him for guidance.

I guess I made Director after all, he thought.

He cleared his throat. "Well, it's definitely trafficking," he said. "Obviously. And we're too far away to call in FBI reinforcements."

Master grimaced. "How many do you think there are? Is this some huge operation?" He wrung his hands together.

04 laughed. "No. Not at all. It's a tiny operation. It's probably just the assholes in that truck."

They all stared at him.

"How do you know that?" 01 asked, frowning.

04 sighed and crossed his arms. "Because they're *idiots*. They're operating from American soil, which is just…incredibly risky and pointless. And they set up shop fifteen miles from a research facility. The entire north slope of Alaska, and they set up *between us and the highway*. They're total morons. It has to be a tiny operation." He frowned.

Master and 01 exchanged a look.

"And this is bad?" 01 said.

04 took a deep breath. "Yes. It's very concerning. If they're stupid, they'll be a lot more dangerous. They don't have anybody backing them up. They're going to be very skittish and take a lot of risks. It's just them versus us, and they know it."

16 cleared his throat, but it was more of a growl. "All the more reason to descend upon them and wipe them out."

04 felt his fur bristle. He turned. "16, those women came here in the hull of a fishing boat."

16 glared at him. The polar bear looked terrifying. "So what?"

04 narrowed his eyes. "So, the next group is probably already on the way."

The bear stared at him.

04 frowned. "That's how these operations work. They establish a route, they're very intensely active for a few weeks, and then they bail. They're never in the same place for long and so they don't get caught." He shrugged. "There's probably a second group in Russia right now and they probably already sent another group over."

The bear was thinking now. His eyes drifted off of 04. He was thinking, and frowning.

04 watched him. "And if this group was hiding in the hull of a boat...and didn't get let out until they were picked up..."

16 looked up. "What happens if nobody picks up the next group," he said flatly.

Next to him, 11 shivered. "*Jesus*," the little dog said.

04 nodded. "Yeah. So one of them needs to be alive to tell us where the next group will be or it gets... bad." He swallowed, looking toward Irina. "And I would *like* to capture most of these assholes so we can grill them for info and try to track down some of their prior victims. Who knows how long they've been at this?"

Master looked at 16, and then down to 04.

"So what do we do?" the small otter asked.

04 turned to him. "So...I'm guessing you can't mind-control more than one person."

02 reacted the most strongly to this, his eyes widening. 10 and 11 started to look uncomfortable, like 04 was broaching some taboo. He supposed he was.

The otter frowned. "No. Not at a time," he said. He glanced up at 01.

04 nodded. "Mm. Does it work nonverbally?"

Master nodded. "Yes."

04 raised an eyebrow. "Are you sure?" He frowned. "How do you know?"

Master frowned. He raised his hands. "*How do you THINK I know?*" he signed. The sign for "*think*" was pointing at his own head, and he did it extra hard, bouncing his index finger off his forehead.

Oh. Right. Either 14 or 15 was deaf. And it worked just fine on both of them.

04 nodded. "Okay. So..." He looked up at 01. "Will this work via translation? What if the wolves only speak Russian and 07 has to translate?"

01 frowned. "It's not language-based. He can...synthesize brainwaves. In other men's brains." The big jaguar shifted uncomfortably, eyeing the other dogs, who all looked vaguely wide-eyed. "He can look at men and force a brainwave pattern on them. It makes them extremely...suggestible."

04 nodded. "I see." He thought of the horrible pain he'd felt as Master brute-forced his brain to bend to his whim. "I...notice your technique has...improved."

Master stared at him for a moment, and then visibly grimaced.

04 stared at him for a moment, and then looked back up at 01. "And what about the memory block?"

11's blue eyes widened a little more. He looked so upset that they were discussing this. Silently, 10 reached up and put a comforting hand on the slim husky's shoulder.

01 thought about 04's question, and then let out a shaky sigh. "I…do not know." He frowned. "It shouldn't work. It is…very frustrating."

04 stared at him, and let out a long breath. "Got it."

Okay. He was starting to get an idea. But he needed a backup.

He turned to 16. The enormous polar bear was watching the entire exchange, frowning.

04 glanced at Irina, and then back at 16. "How many dogs do you have *proficient* with firearms?" He frowned. "Not familiar. Proficient."

16's eyebrows rose, and then he grinned. "Thank you for finally asking. About half the team. You, 03, 05. 07 is okay. 10, 12 and 13, and 14 and 15."

04 thought of the long rifle cases. "Any snipers?"

16 nodded. "14 and 15 are accurate to 500 meters."

04 raised his eyebrows. "Really? This soon?"

16 nodded his gigantic head. "They're deaf so the noise from the rifles doesn't bother them at all. They got good fast." He raised an eyebrow. "I think they made it a competition."

04 frowned. *They* were deaf? Huh. He'd thought only one of the malamutes was. He just couldn't remember which.

But that was strange, right? Why couldn't he remember which?

Pushing the thought from his mind, he looked back up at 16. "Do you have night scopes?"

16 frowned severely. "The sun doesn't rise here for an entire month. *Of course* I have night scopes."

04 smiled at him. "Good man." He turned to 01. "Your projector. From the cabin."

01's eyes widened a little. "Yes?"

04 watched him. "Could you push a live feed to that? From one of the security cameras?"

The jaguar blinked at him. "I…suppose," he said. He furrowing his brow. "Yes, I'm quite sure."

04 nodded. "Thank you." The husky turned back to Master. "Okay. I have a plan...but I don't know if you're going to like it." He checked his watch. It was 5:41. They had 25 minutes. He looked up. "And we need to get all the dogs together. Now. Like...right now."

Sixty seconds later, most of the dogs were in the cabin.

04 wanted to greet them, all of them, but he couldn't. He didn't have time.

"How many earpieces do we have?" he grunted, pawing through a box. He was standing up at the corner of the cabin, next to the table where he had sat shirtless in 02's lap and made out with 03, jerking off both dogs through their sweatpants, a thousand years ago.

16 frowned. "I told you, enough. Everyone will get one."

04 nodded. "And who do you have to be ears for the malamutes? Might want to send huskies since they'll be outside."

16 narrowed his eyes. "Yes, I thought of that. 06 and 11. Neither of them learned to shoot and that leaves us with 12 onsite and 13 closer in case there are...injuries."

04 frowned at the last part. "Speaking of 06, where is he?" He turned around. The cabin was full of dogs but he didn't see his best friend.

The enormous polar bear grunted. "Give him a second. I sent 11 to get everyone. The quarters were probably his last stop."

Looking toward the door, 04 nodded.

"Hey, are you...okay?" the big bear rumbled.

04 turned back to face him. "Do you have time to fix me if I say no?"

16 stared impassively at him, blinking his calm gray eyes, and slowly checked his watch. "No," he said, definitively.

04 raised his white eyebrows. "I guess it doesn't matter then."

16 nodded. "I'm sorry."

The husky was about to answer when he heard a gruff voice behind him.

"I *knew* this would be your fault," came a growl that made his fur stand up. "What kind of trouble are you causing now?"

Hackles rising, his mouth opening to let his tongue spill out, 04 slowly turned and found himself face to face with Detective Kamienski.

03 had lost the little bit of pudge he'd had back in Florida, and he was more trim in the face, though his long coat still lent him a bearded look. He'd put on quite a bit of muscle but he still had the same expression: barely-concealed annoyance.

04 stared at him, mouth open. He felt his eyes widen and suddenly he couldn't talk.

03 sensed the husky's anxiousness immediately. His golden eyes slowly widened. "What's the matter with you?" he asked. "You look like you've seen a ghost."

04 was in the process of stammering out a reply when 02 appeared.

The bigger king shepherd gently guided 03 away. "He'll explain in a second," he said, looking back at 04. "Things are…complicated."

04 snapped his jaw shut. Jesus Christ.

11 appeared at his side. "Everyone's here, sir!" he barked.

04 nodded. *Did he just call me sir?* "Thank you. Where's 06?"

"04!" came a voice above the din.

04 snapped his head around. His heart was pounding. He needed 06 so bad. Hopefully they had time for a —

The other dog came into view and all the thoughts fell out of 04's head.

06 rushed up to him. "Are you okay?! I've been looking everywhere for you! I couldn't find you and then 16 locked us down and—"

04 didn't hear any of it.

06 had a massive wound across his face, starting on the left side of his muzzle, traveling back and up through his eye, and gouging the entire left side of his head, where he was also missing his ear. He was *missing his fucking ear*. His left eye was white, and 04 realized there was no way he wasn't blind in that eye. His best friend stood before him, horribly mangled.

04 stood frozen, horrified, his blood running cold. He had a moment of absolute panic where he thought the wound was new, was fresh, he was about to scream that 06 needed a doctor, but then in a heartbeat he realized the wounds were old. Scarred. 06 had been horribly mangled but it had happened a while ago.

He couldn't speak. 06 had been like this. *He had always been like this.* 04 was just seeing him for the first time.

06 stood before him, startled, and then slowly his remaining ear flattened against his head. He stared at 04 with an expression of growing dread, his brow furrowed on the right side, but not on the left where his nerve endings were probably destroyed. He swallowed. "What's the matter? Wh-wh-why are you looking at me like that?" he whispered, his voice shaking.

He doesn't know.

04 stared at him. He couldn't talk. He couldn't even breathe.

06 watched him, one blue eye and one white eye, both perfectly circular. Gently, terrified and silent, he began shivering.

My perfect beautiful boy.

04 swallowed the lump in his throat. "I...I have my memories back." He blinked back tears. Who had done this to his perfect boy? How had this happened?

06's one eyebrow went up. "Wh-...what?" he asked, softly. His mouth opened a little in shock. "From...from forever?"

It was all hitting 04 now. 06 had been horribly mangled and 04 hadn't even known. Someone had tried to kill his best friend. His light. He tasted copper in his mouth.

06's expression softened and he tilted his head sympathetically. "Oh, buddy..." he said, gently. He put his arms out. "C'mere."

He thinks I need comfort. He has one eye and a ragged stump for an ear and he wants to comfort me.

04 really didn't think he had time, but he needed to hold 06 in his arms, or he wasn't going to be able to go on. He leaned forward into the hug, put his arms around his best friend, tightening his grip and squeezing him as hard as he dared.

"It's okay, buddy, I got you. I'm here for you," said the mangled husky in his arms, and then 04 buried his face in 06's shoulder and deeply inhaled his scent, and now 06 *was* comforting him, 06 was what he needed, 06 was the one he was fighting to protect, and his warmth and scent and soft, gentle, comforting muttering filled 04 with resolve. He pushed his head up against 06's strong neck as the other husky squeezed him, and he shivered, letting his tears fall down his face, because 06 was going to be strong for him.

"I love you so much," he whispered into 06's neck fluff.

"I love you too," 06 mumbled back to him, giving him a big squeeze. "I have you. It's all going to be okay now."

04 took a deep breath, allowed himself ten more seconds in 06's scent and warmth, and reluctantly broke the embrace, holding 06 at arm's length.

The other husky stared back at him, frowning in concern. The edges of his muzzle scar were jagged and white, deep and brutal.

"It's all going to be okay," 04 whispered. "I'll die before I let anything happen to you," he growled.

06 swallowed, and nodded, and then leaned forward and kissed his nose. "Okay," he said. "But don't die."

It caught 04 off-guard, and he couldn't stop the laugh that escaped his muzzle.

06 smiled back at him.

"You're perfect," 04 told him, and he meant it.

06's smile turned into a big grin. "I know," he said.

04 nodded, leaned in to muzzle-bump his best friend one more time, and then stood up.

"All right, dogs!" he said. "Listen up. Here's the plan!"

To be continued in "Drone Convergence"...

About The Author

Bill Siracusa, Author.

Bill Siracusa, also known as "UnstableBill", has been a furry and writer since the period before time began (the 90's).

Bill got his start writing fanfiction for furry Keenspot comics and is proof that, with enough time and dedication, any hobby can become a dangerous, all-consuming hyperfixation. Bill is delighted to bring the Drone Collection to FurPlanet and prove to the world once and for all that all narratives are improved by adding a harem of hypnotized huskies. Bill lives in Chicago with his hyena husband and their cats and can be found on socials at @unstablebill.

04 will return in Drone 2: Convergence

About The Editors

Ajax B. Coriander, Copy Editor and Layout Designer.

Ajax is an editor, writer, and is the daily operations manger for FurPlante. He lives in Dallas with his publishers/boyfriends/domestic wolves and is under the ever present danger of being crushed to death under 500 pounds of Kyell Gold books during 30% of his working hours.

He can be found at https://bears.town/@Saintajax33 on Mastodon and he can be found other places through:

https://allmylinks.com/saintajax33

Or

http://www.ajaxwriter.com/

Theresa Hahn, Main Contributing Editor.

Theresa has been assiduously avoiding social media since 2007 – she still prefers a good old-fashioned phone call to catch up with friends. She has known Bill since the late 90's, and sat next to him in one infamous college English class.

Theresa lives in Chicagoland, where she is still waiting to be adopted by her next cat – she just needs to find one that's calm enough not to worry about being crushed by the 3,000 books lining the walls of her apartment.

About the Artist

Snarky Sardine, Cover and Interior Illustration artist.

Lives in New Zealand and Drone is his publishing debut. When he's not drawing harem huskies for Bill, his true passion is marine life and how to make them hot gay fishmen to post online. Snarky can be found on Bluesky at @snarkysardine and Furaffinity at www.furaffinity.net/user/snarkysardine/